# BOMBAY FEVER

**Sidin Vadukut** is an editor, columnist and foreign correspondent with *Mint*. His previous books include the best-selling *Dork* trilogy—office-culture humour novels; *The Sceptical Patriot*—a collection of essays on Indian history; and *The Corpse That Spoke*—the true story of a British-Indian family that vanished under mysterious circumstances.

Sidin is currently completing a Master's in Historical Research at Birkbeck College, University of London. In October 2017, he will start a doctoral research programme on charity in the medieval economy. He previously graduated from the National Institute of Technology, Trichy, and the Indian Institute of Management, Ahmedabad.

Sidin lives in London with his wife and daughter. He supports Arsenal Football Club. #COYG

# BOMBAY FEVER

## Sidin Vadukut

**SIMON &
SCHUSTER**

London · New York · Sydney · Toronto · New Delhi

A CBS COMPANY

*To K and S: The guys in marketing have assured me that this will make millions*

*To everybody else: This is a work of fiction—outrage accordingly*

'How many valiant men, how many fair ladies, how many sprightly youths [. . .] breakfasted in the morning with their kinsfolk, comrades and friends and that same night supped with their ancestors in the other world!'

– Giovanni Boccaccio,
*The Decameron*

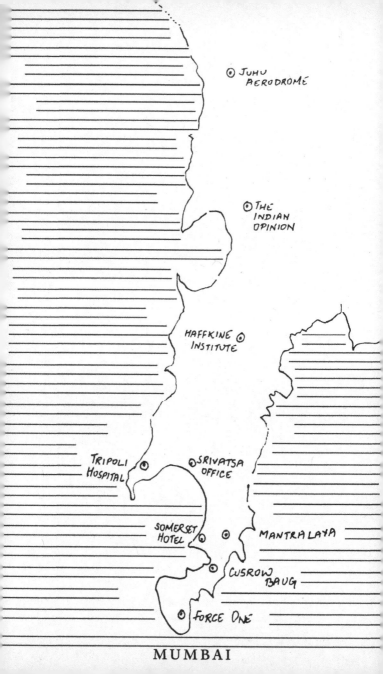

MUMBAI

# 1

**86 days before the outbreak**

Everything has a beginning. And Bombay Fever began in Geneva, Switzerland.

Hormazd Patel, a twenty-seven-year-old man who lived in Mumbai with his mother, looked glumly at the table in front of him. On it, arranged from left to right in order of increasing price, was an array of Swiss wrist watches. They were beautiful, all made from a variety of expensive metals and precious stones. The ones to the left were simple and elegant and cost no more than five or six thousand euros each. The one to the far right was a chunky, limited edition, double tourbillon watch that cost nearly a million euros.

'And there you have it,' said the man sitting across the table from Hormazd. The man wore a fashionable, tight-fitting suit and spoke with a thick French accent. 'These are the key novelties for this year. From the elegant to the luxurious.'

'So what do you think?' he asked Hormazd after a pause. 'Is it exciting for the Indian market?'

'These are the best watches I've seen at the fair this year!' said Hormazd.

It was a good lie, well told. This was Hormazd's seventh trip to the SIHH watch and jewellery trade show in Switzerland. In these seven years, he had sat through hundreds of such product presentations. And after each one, without exception, company representatives expected him to convey enthusiasm. It was how the industry worked. And Hormazd played by the rules.

'I must tell you, Raymond,' Hormazd said, 'each year I think your company has achieved the ultimate. And each year you outdo yourself. These watches are simply magnificent. Kudos, Raymond. Bravo.'

Raymond Dufour beamed and turned around on his swivel chair. On a shelf behind him was a glass bowl filled to the brim with pen drives emblazoned with his company's logo.

Hormazd took a deep breath, looked down at his shoes, and rolled his eyes.

Raymond swivelled back on his chair, reached across the table, and handed the pen drive. Hormazd promptly slipped it into the pocket of his blazer. 'So, what would Mr Editor like to ask me?' This was Raymond's polite way of saying that the product presentation was over. It was now time for the interview.

Hormazd took a moment to clear his mind. *Just one more. Just get this over with and you're done for the trip. May as well do it properly.*

Hormazd opened his notebook and made sure his iPad was still recording audio.

'Tell me Raymond,' Hormazd started, 'why did you choose to go with a double tourbillon this year?'

Raymond leaned back in his chair, paused for a moment to summon a well-rehearsed answer from memory, and then began to speak.

'Each year we want to push the limits . . .'

Twelve minutes later, both men got up from their chairs. The watches were whisked away from the table by a security guard wearing an earpiece, who quickly and discreetly counted the number of items on the tray. Nothing was missing.

Raymond escorted Hormazd out of the meeting room and into the lobby of the brand's booth. There were very few people around, and the silence was somewhat unusual. Most of the other booths in the large hall in Geneva's Palexpo Convention Centre were empty.

'Please wait a moment. I have a gift for you,' said Raymond. The Frenchman sounded winded, his façade slowly cracking, the exhaustion beginning to show.

'Did you have a good fair? Good response from the retailers?' Hormazd asked with the breezy tone he saved for casual, 'off the record' chats.

Raymond paused for a second and wiped the sweat from his forehead with this hand. The meeting room had been extremely warm.

'Not bad,' he said after a pause. 'The response has met our expectations.'

'Good to hear,' Hormazd replied.

*I knew it! Those watches were terrible. And Raymond knows it too. They are going to have a very, very bad year.*

A few minutes later the security guard returned with a large cloth bag. Raymond handed it to Hormazd. 'I hope you write good things about our watches, yes? Email me if you need anything, okay, Hormazd?'

Both men firmly shook hands.

Hormazd walked out of the booth, down one of the broad avenues that ran the length of the exhibition hall, and then up a flight of stairs to the media centre.

The media centre was empty except for a small group of Indian journalists chatting around a coffee machine. Hormazd walked up to them. They all shook hands, patted each other on the back, and then congratulated one another on the conclusion of yet another trade fair.

'When are you returning to India?' *The Times of India* features editor asked Hormazd.

'Tomorrow evening . . .'

'Any plans for first half tomorrow? Some of us were thinking of going down to Lausanne for a few hours.'

'You guys go. I'm just going to chill at the hotel.

Tired, yaar. Don't want to run around too much tomorrow.' Hormazd spoke as he watched the machine spit out a cup of acrid coffee.

'Boss, you can chill on the flight back home. Come with us, no? You never come with us anywhere.'

This was true. Hormazd was pleasant and sociable enough during the trade fair. And he dutifully attended the numerous media dinners that took place each night. But that was all. He spent the rest of his time during these trips eating by himself in the hotel coffee shop, no matter how bad the food was, or lying in bed listening to audiobooks. As exhausted as he was, Hormazd couldn't wait to return to the hotel, drop into bed, slip on his headphones, and get back to an Inspector Maigret novel by George Simenon.

'Look, Hormazd, you can listen to that audiobook of yours throughout the journey to Lausanne and back. Nobody is going to disturb you. Besides, it will add atmosphere to your book. It will feel more . . . mysterious.'

Everybody laughed and so did Hormazd. He thought for a moment and then agreed.

'Fine, fine. I'll come. But please make sure we are back in Geneva in time for the flight. I do not want to be running to the airport.'

It was at that moment that Hormazd sealed the fate of thousands of lives. Including his own. He was about to cause terrors beyond his worst nightmares.

# 2

## 86 days before the outbreak

An hour or so after the Indian journalists left the media centre, Kanimozhi Balasingham walked in pushing a heavy trolley stacked with cleaning products. Kanimozhi was short, lean and muscular. She looked more like an athlete than a cleaning lady.

In her native Sri Lanka, Kanimozhi, as a child, had been a successful athlete—a good sprinter and an even better long-distance runner. But it was the long jump at which she excelled. Had she persisted with it, Kanimozhi may well have represented Sri Lanka at the Asian Games or perhaps even the Olympics. But when she was around eleven years old, her parents had fled the Sri Lankan civil war and sought asylum in Switzerland.

Now, Kanimozhi was a Swiss citizen, and spoke both French and German fluently. But what she gained in languages and safety, she lost in the form of athletic talent. She jumped a few times at school in Geneva. It never worked out. She couldn't quite match her exploits in Jaffna.

Kanimozhi looked around the media centre. *Not*

*bad. Shouldn't take more than an hour to tidy up. Maybe an hour-and-a-half.*

She parked her trolley near a bank of telephones and began to work through a checklist. First, any garbage lying on the floor. Then, tables and chairs. Finally, the coffee machine and the snack bar.

Around sixty-five minutes later, as Kanimozhi wiped down a leather sofa, she drifted away into thought. *The trade fair has been hard work. But the money has been good. What next? I have to find something to do after class. When is that auto fair due to happen? I wonder if they need cleaners . . .*

At that precise moment, Kanimozhi noticed an iPad on the table next to the coffee machine. She stood up straight and looked around. The hall was empty. She walked over to the table, picked the tablet up, slipped it into a pocket in her overalls, and carried on with her work.

Half an hour later, she returned the trolley to the janitorial office. Kanimozhi then changed into a T-shirt, jeans and an old, frayed down jacket. She picked up her wages and walked to the tram stop outside the exhibition centre. She took Tram No. 13 from Palexpo to a café by Lake Geneva. She walked in, ordered a cup of tea, and sat at a table by the window overlooking the road outside.

She coughed a few times as she opened the iPad's Photos app and swiped through the images.

*Handsome fellow. Indian by the looks of it. Not a Tamil. No. Not a Tamil.*

She coughed again. And cleared her throat. She thought about her cough, and then decided that it must be because of the sudden change in her surroundings.

Kanimozhi had just returned from Sri Lanka after a month-long trip to visit her grandparents. If it were up to her she would have never come back. She loved her relatives and adored the weather and the food back home. But her father wouldn't let her stay. As far as he was concerned, for the Balasinghams, Switzerland was the future. Sri Lanka was past.

It was a nice iPad mini. The latest model. And Kanimozhi knew plenty of shops in Geneva that would take it off her, no questions asked. She could use the cash. For the last few months, ever since she had booked her flight tickets to Sri Lanka, she had saved all her pocket money and wages from her various part-time jobs. Kanimozhi then spent all of it installing two air conditioners in her grandparents' home. The old man and woman had been a little bewildered when the delivery men came with the Samsung units. But a few hours later, they were pleased with the outcome.

'Now you can tell everybody that your granddaughter has brought a little Geneva into your home,' Kanimozhi told them proudly.

If the ACs had come at a high price, this iPad would go some way towards making up for the expense.

Kanimozhi thought about it for a while. Then she seemed to hesitate.

No.

She opened the Gmail app, searched for 'hotel booking', and quickly found Hormazd's reservation. She picked up her mobile phone, coughed twice, and then punched in the hotel's phone number.

### 86 days before the outbreak

'You have a bad cough,' said Hormazd as Kanimozhi clutched her cup of tea.

She coughed deeply and nodded. 'I don't know why. Suddenly from this evening I've been coughing badly.'

Hormazd sipped on his coffee.

Kanimozhi had called the hotel an hour-and-a-half ago. The receptionist had tried putting the call through repeatedly. Each time, nobody picked up.

Hormazd had been in bed with his headphones on and hadn't heard the phone ring. Finally, when Kanimozhi persisted with her calls, the hotel sent somebody upstairs with a cordless phone.

At first, Hormazd had been surprised—he hadn't noticed the missing iPad till Kanimozhi's call came through. He asked her to wait at the café and then called for a taxi.

'Are you sure a cup of tea is enough? Can I buy you dinner or at least give you some money?'

Kanimozhi shook her head vigorously. 'Please sir. No. I just wanted to help.'

'I cannot thank you enough.'

Hormazd told her that his iPad was the centre of his life. It had all his photos, notes, emails and recordings from the fair.

'So, do you go back to India tomorrow?'

'Yes, in the evening. But first we are going to Lausanne. For a trip. It's going to be a waste of time. But my colleagues have forced me to go.'

'Lausanne is very nice. How are you going?'

'I think we're hiring cars.'

'Oh, in that case . . .' Kanimozhi was about to say something, then changed her mind. Instead she asked, 'Are you Hindu?'

'No. Parsi. But what were you going to say?'

Kanimozhi suddenly exploded into a fit of coughing. She covered her mouth with a paper napkin.

'Sorry. Wow. I need to go see a doctor. So, I was going to say . . . there is a Murugan temple just outside Lausanne. It is very new and very nice. If you have time you should go there.'

Kanimozhi told Hormazd that the temple had been funded by Sri Lankan refugees, and the idol had been flown in from Chennai. Hormazd promised to tell his friends about it. After thanking her again profusely, he got up, walked out of the café, and jogged to a cab across the road.

Kanimozhi watched him go.

*Nice man. Wonder if he will go to the . . . maybe . . . maybe I will go tomorrow. Why not? I can ask Murugan to reward me for returning the iPad . . .*

# 3

85 days before the outbreak

The next morning, the group of Indian journalists stopped at the temple on their way to Lausanne. Hormazd had insisted. Later, investigators would wonder why a Parsi boy with no apparent interest in any religion, not even his own, decided to visit a Murugan temple in Switzerland. Why didn't he just drive by?

'Hormazd, this place is amazing,' said one the journalists, as the group stood in the courtyard of the Lausanne Murugan temple.

Hormazd agreed. It was an impressive place of worship. Mostly because it was so new. *This looks like someone took Babulnath, dry-cleaned it, and shipped it to Lausanne.* He was happy he had taken Kanimozhi's recommendation seriously.

The group took lots of pictures. Some prayed. Some bought souvenirs from a little gift shop. Then, around forty minutes later, they all decided to carry on to Lausanne. Hormazd was the last to walk out of the compound, when he heard a cough behind him.

He turned around and immediately recognised

Kanimozhi standing in the courtyard. She was wearing the same frayed jacket. As she coughed, she leaned against an ornate lamp post for support.

'Hormazd, *chalo yaar* . . .'

*Wow. That cough has really . . .*

Kanimozhi let go of the lamp post and fell to the ground. There was a crack as her left cheek hit the stone pavement. Hormazd ran towards her. He knelt by her side, lifted her up by the shoulders and placed her head on his lap. Her face was mottled with blue and grey spots. There was a deep purple bruise on her cheek.

'Oh my god, are you all right . . .?'

Suddenly, Kanimozhi went quiet. Her eyes bulged, her mouth opened in a silent scream, and her back arched.

'SOMEBODY CALL AN AMBULANCE . . .'

A man ran towards the gift shop.

Kanimozhi snapped her head back. Hormazd heard a rasping sound.

And then something happened that, in the months to come, would happen over and over again. And each time it happened it would shock those who witnessed it. Even medical practitioners and public health workers, who in their careers had seen some of the worst outbreaks of disease in the world, would watch in awe and disgust. Nothing had prepared them for this. Eventually, someone came up with a name for this final stage in the life of the patient: 'meltdown'.

No one would ever forget the first time they witnessed a body in 'meltdown'.

There, in the courtyard of the Lausanne Murugan temple, Kanimozhi was in the throes of 'meltdown'. Jets of dark, thick blood erupted simultaneously from her mouth, ears, nose and rectum. They exploded on to Hormazd, drenching his clothes and pooling around on the stone pavement. Within moments, it began to turn into a dark sludge that stank.

Hormazd began to scream.

By the time the ambulance crew arrived, seventeen minutes later, Hormazd and the Indian group were nowhere to be found. They had bundled themselves into their cars and had sped back to Geneva.

In time to come . . .

The Swiss police were initially keen to track down these tourists. Most of all, they were eager to find the man who appeared on CCTV cameras, trying to help the dying woman. What happened to him? Had he fallen ill? Did he know her?

But, as days passed, the police began to lose interest. The autopsy on the woman had been inconclusive. She had died from some form of haemorrhagic fever. One policeman suggested that perhaps Kanimozhi had been poisoned. Maybe she had been involved with some unsettled vendetta from the Sri Lankan civil war. Tests for most known poisons returned negative.

When, after a month, no one else in Lausanne showed similar symptoms, the police closed the case and handed the frozen body back to the Balasinghams. Local authorities in Lausanne concluded that perhaps she had caught something during her trip to Sri Lanka.

By then, the microscopic bug that had destroyed Kanimozhi Balasingham had travelled halfway across the world. It had taken the long route from Jaffna to Mumbai. And now it found itself in an exceedingly friendly environment.

It could get down to doing what it did best—kill.

# 4

**Justice Kashyap Commission of Inquiry**

*Reference: PS 4/PI 17/Maha/Session 4*
*File type: Raw transcript of interview, audio recording*
*Location: Provisional Lok Sabha Complex, Port Blair*
*Security clearance level: 2*
*Note: This recording features two voices*

Justice Kashyap [JK]: Start recording. Two members. PLSC. 23 February. Can you please state your name and occupation?

Aayush Vajpeyi [AV]: Aayush Vajpeyi. Special assistant to the Indian high commissioner to New Zealand.

JK: Thank you for coming all the way to Port Blair. Can you state your Aadhar number please? For the record?

AV: 14L1437.

JK: At the time of the incident that this commission is currently investigating what was your occupation?

AV: At the time of the outbreak, I was posted in Mumbai as a social medical officer.

JK: What do you mean by social medical officer? An SMO?

AV: Sir . . . everybody knows this . . .

JK: Mr Vajpeyi, some of the questions put to you by the commission will be of an obvious nature. Many of these things have been covered by the media and in other official reports. But I would still like you to answer them. It is in the interest of the nation to have all possible details on record.

AV: Of course. I understand perfectly, sir.

JK: Very good. So please explain what the responsibilities of an SMO were at the time of your posting in Mumbai.

AV: The SMO was a new designation, created three years ago, within the public health system. As a part of a new national plan to combat drug-resistant diseases . . .

JK: This is the Srivatsa programme?

AV: Yes, sir.

JK: How did the SMO fit into Srivatsa?

AV: Ummm . . . I think I should first explain Srivatsa . . .

JK: Please go ahead. We have plenty of time.

AV: I will not get into the absolute details here. Unless you want me to . . . okay. Around the year

2010, researchers began to find strains of well-known diseases in India that were not responding to the usual antibiotics used to treat them. TB patients . . . tuberculosis patients . . . for instance . . . were simply not responding to TB medicines. And even if they were, doctors were being forced to administer higher concentrations of these drugs . . .

JK: Were the diseases themselves changing? Becoming stronger?

AV: Yes. But not exactly. Let me explain it like this. Assume, sir, that you are suffering from a disease. Say TB. You have a hundred cells of TB inside you. Let's say that 75 per cent of these are killed by normal doses of the usual medicines. But 25 per cent are not.

JK: Why not?

AV: The most basic reason is that disease cells sometimes undergo mutations as they multiply. And every once in a while, one of these mutant cells stops reacting to the usual drugs. It achieves immunity. There are other complicated reasons as well . . .

JK: Carry on.

AV: Sir . . . I am sure you have spoken to experts regarding this topic? I am not really a specialist . . .

JK: Perhaps. But I would like very much to listen to Aayush Vajpeyi's version.

AV: Okay. So assume that 25 per cent of the TB cells

in your body are drug-resistant. Now, as you consume your normal doses of TB medicine, the 75 per cent begin to die away, leaving the resistant mutations behind. Step by step, the 25 per cent start proliferating inside you. Eventually, what you have is a colony of disease cells that is perhaps totally drug-resistant.

JK: So, what happens to the patient then?

AV: The patient deteriorates. Sometimes he gets better . . . and then he gets worse. He needs larger doses and stronger drugs to defeat these resistant cells. But the drug-resistant strain spreads . . . and strengthens . . . and spreads . . .

JK: Interesting. So Srivatsa was . . .?

AV: A national plan to get to the bottom of this problem. By attacking it at every level—hospitals, clinics, nurses, researchers, pharmacies, pharmaceutical companies . . .

JK: Where does the SMO come in?

AV: One of Srivatsa's core ideas was to change the way in which antibiotics were being used in society. Some people self-medicate instead of going to a doctor. Others stop their doses as soon as they feel better—perhaps to save money—instead of completing the treatment. Pharmacies sell just about anything over the counter, making this problem worse. One of the biggest factors driving the emergence of drug-resistance is the horrible, casual misuse of medicines.

JK: And your job was to interact with society at large and change people's behaviour?

AV: Exactly. Door to door. Talking to people. Visiting hospitals. Talking to staff at pharmacies.

JK: Did it work?

AV: Yes. But no thanks to Srivatsa. Bombay Fever did our work for us. Drug misuse has plummeted since then.

JK: Just to digress for a moment. Have you witnessed a Bombay Fever meltdown? An actual patient undergoing that? Mr Vajpeyi? I asked you . . .

AV: Many times, sir. Many, many, many times. It is . . . the worst thing I have ever witnessed in my life. The worst.

JK: I am sorry. I have only ever seen it in video recordings.

AV: There are videos? I thought every single recording had been . . .

JK: There are some. I am sorry if I upset you. But there will be other questions which will probe the details of the outbreak.

AV: Of course. I understand.

JK: Very good. Can you tell me, in your words, how Bombay Fever came . . .

AV: At first we all thought it broke out at Bandra Kurla Complex . . .

# 5

**4 days before the outbreak**

Amod Patil, who would later become infamous as Subject Zero—the first confirmed Indian casualty in the Bombay Fever outbreak—sat in his parked Hyundai i20. The car was in the farthest corner of the staff parking area outside the ICICI Bank building in Mumbai's Bandra Kurla Complex. It was a little before midnight and there were just three other parked vehicles in the lot.

Patil looked at his watch impatiently. 11.23 pm. *Seven more minutes to go.*

Patil had spent the preceding two-and-a-half hours in the driver's seat, sifting through a stack of office documents. They were mostly proposals and price lists from service providers—caterers, taxi services, printers, housekeeping firms, event managers—the types of companies that would offer their services to a 'new media' start-up.

Patil was bored, sleepy and hungry. He turned around, reached for the back seat, retrieved his gym bag, and tossed it into the passenger seat next to him. As he unzipped the bag, Patil grimaced. The car was filled with the stench of sweat. But Patil was famished and he recalled that he usually carried a few packets of wholemeal crackers in his gym bag for emergencies.

As he munched on a cracker, Patil glanced at his watch again. 11.29 pm.

*Close enough.*

He stepped out of the car and looked around. He then walked past the parking lot, crossed a small service lane, and then the car park by the adjoining building. He strode towards the building's façade, swiped his identity card at the access door, and stepped into a large, oval-shaped lobby.

Here, he asked a security guard, who sat behind a desk: 'Have they left?'

The guard, later Subject 21 or 22, nodded with a smile.

*Brilliant. I have achieved complete secrecy.*

Amod Patil walked towards the elevator, pressed a button, and shivered. The lobby, awash with cold air from the building's massive climate control system, was at least 10 degrees colder than outside.

*What a waste of electricity.*

As Patil waited for the elevator, he pulled out a folded piece of paper from his trouser pocket. Listed on the sheet were thirty-six entries, empty boxes next to each one. On top, in bold, was the title: 'Housekeeping Checklist'.

Amod Patil, the newly recruited admin manager

for *The Indian Opinion,* entered an empty newsroom—small by the standards of most Indian media organisations, with workstations for just twenty-five employees. The company had just started hiring, and all but eight seats were empty. In some cases, office chairs lay cocooned in plastic wrapping.

Patil took a pen from his workstation and held it in one hand, the checklist in the other. He then started a slow and methodical inspection of the quality of work done by the housekeepers who had come at around 11 pm.

Over the previous week Patil had received several complaints about smelly toilets, dirty carpeting and sloppy cleaning. He had decided to inspect the quality of the cleaners' work right after they left. His plan was to take photographs of all the inadequate work, and email this, along with a strongly worded letter, to the housekeeping contractor.

Forty minutes into his inspection, Patil was in a very foul mood. The quality of work in the newsroom itself was appalling. He now had to check both the men's and women's toilets.

*God help me. If they can't vacuum the carpets . . .*

Surprisingly the women's toilets had been cleaned very well.

The men's, less so.

In particular, Patil was bothered by the washbasins. None of them had been scrubbed. One basin had globules of viscous yellow fluid splattered on the mirror behind it.

Patil rolled his eyes.

### 3 days before the outbreak

Past midnight, Patil had ticked off every item on his checklist. Another twenty minutes, and he had sent his email to the contractor.

He got up, slipped the checklist into a drawer, and then popped into the men's room. As he began washing his hands, his eyes kept going to the little splatter of yellow on the mirror.

*What is that? Soap?*

Amod Patil stood straight, pulled a tissue from the dispenser on the wall, and looked at himself as he wiped his hands clean.

Patil was a thirty-two-year-old single man in the prime of his life. He had never felt or looked better. And this was beginning to tell on the way his social life had blossomed over the last three months.

Since moving to Mumbai, Patil had been on dates at least once every weekend. Most of them went very well. Patil always made it clear that he was not looking for anything serious or long term. In fact, he wasn't even particularly looking for sex. He seemed to enjoy the conversation and the company of his companions, and often stayed in touch with them afterwards.

Thus, in a very short time, Amod Patil had nurtured a large social network in Mumbai. Members of this circle would describe him as a nice, hard-working man whose only fault was vanity. Patil was somewhat obsessed with the way he looked.

Later, when they put together his complete medical history, investigators would realise why Patil had been fanatical about staying in shape. For most of his life, Patil had been morbidly obese. It was only after his thirtieth birthday that he had embarked on a strict regime of diet and exercise.

Patil crumpled the paper towel. He was just about to throw it into the empty bin when he stopped. He leaned forward and wiped the yellow splatter from the mirror. He noticed that some of the liquid had dried into a crust. So, Patil ran the used towel under a tap for a moment, and scrubbed the mirror clean. He then balled up the paper again and threw it away.

In the morning, Amod Patil would come to work feeling a little under the weather.

'It is okay,' he'd tell one of the reporters at *The Indian Opinion*, 'it is just a mild cough.'

# 6

**84 days before the outbreak**

The driver who worked for Rapid Cabs, a radio taxi company, slowed his car outside the small, freshly painted guard post. He rolled down his window. Inside the guard post, a policeman sat in front of a small metal desk, on which was a large ledger.

'Destination?' The policeman spat out the words.

'Cusrow Baug,' the taxi driver replied. The policeman carefully wrote this down.

'Passenger name?'

The taxi driver turned around and looked at the passenger in the back seat. 'Sir?' he mumbled.

His passenger sat slumped. His eyes were closed. He seemed asleep. Then, he spoke without moving or even opening his eyes. 'Hormazd Patel,' he muttered before gently coughing twice.

'Hormazd!' repeated the taxi driver.

'Go!' said the policeman even before he had finished writing it down.

The taxi swung out of the Mumbai airport's exit lanes and swerved into the main road outside. Within moments, it was stuck in bumper-to-bumper traffic.

Hormazd sat up, looked at the traffic through the windscreen. He exhaled dejectedly, then coughed again.

The driver had forgotten to roll up his window, and hot, humid air mixed with exhaust fumes streamed into the car.

'Boss, close the window, no?'

'Sorry, sir.'

Hormazd slumped back into the seat. After a few moments, he pulled out his mobile phone, reactivated data, and opened the browser application. He then punched in the words: 'Lausanne Murugan temple woman death'.

Google returned seven results.

Six of these were identical—copies of the same Reuters wire story that stated that two days prior, a woman had died at a temple in Lausanne under mysterious circumstances. Local authorities in the city said they were still investigating. The victim was identified as Kanimozhi Balasingham, a Sri Lankan Tamil refugee who lived in Geneva with her parents. She was a student at the University of Geneva who worked part-time as a cleaner and babysitter. She had just returned to Switzerland after a two-week holiday in Jaffna. The Lausanne police said they had no evidence of foul play and reassured the public, and especially the Sri Lankan community, that there was no reason to panic or worry.

Hormazd read the story once more.

No mention of any Indian tourist. No mention of the iPad or even the trade fair.

The seventh and final search result led Hormazd to a community website run by Sri Lankan Tamil refugees in Switzerland. There was a blog entry on Kanimozhi's death with details on how readers could send messages and money to the grieving family.

Hormazd coughed again.

'Sir, are you okay?'

'Yes, I am fine. Thank you.'

'Where are you coming from—if you don't mind me asking?'

'Geneva. In Switzerland.'

'Wow. How is the weather there? Not like this boiling heat in our Mumbai?'

'No, no. It was very cold there.'

'Is that why you are coughing?'

'Yes, I think so.'

*I fucking hope so, man. I fucking hope so.*

'Take care, sir. There is a viral fever going around Mumbai. My wife and daughter are both ill. The little one hasn't gone to school for four days.'

'Hmm.'

Hormazd was no longer paying attention. He was reading the comments under the Kanimozhi blog post, most of which discussed the circumstances surrounding her death. Several were in agreement that Kanimozhi had been targeted by some anti-Tamil outfit—perhaps a Sinhala agent. Some relayed 'rumours' that Kanimozhi was spotted with a group of 'brown guys' at the temple. A few were convinced that she had been killed by an anti-immigrant Swiss racist group. While such groups usually targeted Muslim refugees, they were happy to pick on anybody who seemed sufficiently foreign.

Few of these commentators, Hormazd noticed, seemed to care for the exact details surrounding Kanimozhi's death.

*How did she die? How did she die . . . like that? It has to be poison of some kind. No disease can possibly kill in this manner.*

Hormazd looked out of the window. They were still on the Western Express Highway. It would take an hour to reach his flat. Possibly longer.

'Boss, I am going to sleep for a bit. Will you wake me up when you are near Cusrow Baug?'

'No problem, sir.'

**In time to come . . .**

The next morning, Hormazd Patel went back to work. For the first two or three days, he was unproductive. His mind constantly went back to what happened in Lausanne. Every few hours he searched for news updates. He even installed a browser extension on his computer that translated Swiss newspaper websites to English.

All too soon, as Kanimozhi Balasingham dropped out of the Swiss news cycle, Hormazd Patel regained his focus.

His cough persisted. But it was mild, never got worse, and eventually Hormazd learnt to ignore it.

And then it got worse.

By the end of his week in India, Hormazd was in bed with a cough, headache and a mild fever. He also felt a dull throbbing pain in his armpits. His mother Siloo Patel was convinced he had an ear infection. She always got an ear infection when she travelled on an aeroplane.

'Hormazd,' she said, seated next to him on the bed, 'why don't you try my medicines for a day or two? If you are still unwell you can go and see Dr Kamat.'

Hormazd agreed. Work was piling up and he was eager to get back to the office as soon as possible.

Siloo went to her medicine cabinet on the wall above the television set in the living room, and looked for three bottles, respectively marked 'Fever', 'Cough' and 'Ear Infection'.

She removed a tablet from each. Hormazd swallowed all three in one go with a draught of water.

Siloo Patel did not know that her 'Cough' and 'Ear Infection' bottles both contained drugs with identical compositions. She had just given her son a massive dose of the antibiotic amoxicillin.

Within hours, Hormazd Patel began to feel better. Instead of visiting Dr Kamat, like he should have, Hormazd decided to continue consuming mother's cocktail of drugs for the next eight days.

On the thirteenth morning after his return to India, he felt perfectly fine. The cough, fever and ache in his armpits had all subsided.

Siloo's drugs had eradicated most of the malignant organism that had colonised Hormazd's lungs. Most—but not all. Even as Hormazd got better, a small remnant of the disease inside him began to grow. Slowly.

Unbeknownst to anybody, Hormazd Patel had become the carrier of a new, immeasurably more potent mutant strain of the bacteria that had reduced Kanimozhi Balasingham to a bloody puddle on the grounds outside the Lausanne Murugan temple.

# 7

**3 days before the outbreak**

Nabeel Karimudeen, founding editor of *The Indian Opinion*, and its oldest employee, walked into the conference room at exactly 10.54 am. He settled into the chair at the head of the table. On the wall behind, a large, flat-screen LCD display played a montage of six TV news channels—four Indian, one American and one British. The screen was a mess of scrolling text and talking heads.

The display had its audio output turned down to zero at Karimudeen's express bidding. If any employee of *The Indian Opinion* wished to watch a news channel, he was expected to do so at the PC with earphones. Allowing even a second of what Nabeel called the 'noxious vomit that is broadcast news' to seep into the newsroom was bound to provoke an instant and brutal response from the founding editor.

Nabeel placed a Moleskine notebook on the table and opened it to a page that had been marked with an old, fading Air India boarding pass. He then began to go through the notes he had made earlier that morning during his drive to work.

Slowly, six of the remaining seven members of *The Indian Opinion*'s staff began to shuffle into the conference room and settle into chairs. Each person set the mobile phone to mute and then placed a notebook on the table.

At precisely 11.00 am, Nabeel Karimudeen spoke.

'Good morning. I'll just quickly go through some notes I made this morning . . .'

Amod Patil scrambled into the room, coughed sharply twice, and then sat down. Nabeel looked at him. It was unlike Amod Patil to be late.

'Amod, are you okay?'

'Yes, sir. It is just a mild cough. I am fine.'

'Are you taking anything for that?'

'Yes, I had medicines at home.'

'Please see a doctor before you take anything strong, Amod,' said Janani Ganesh, the deputy editor.

Nabeel continued: 'As I was saying. My morning notes. Just a few minor things before we get to the World Financial Forum. Tushar, can you follow up on why they still haven't released the GDP numbers for this quarter? It is unlike the current dispensation to be sloppy with such things.'

Tushar Jain nodded and immediately reached for his notebook.

'See if there is any bad news they are trying to dress up. Namita, what are you busy with right now?'

'I am working on that Ethiopian food story . . . the new restaurant near the airport . . .'

'Oh, yes. Good story. But finish it soon? We need to build a bank of feature stories. Something to keep traffic coming over weekends?'

'Will do. I'll file it tonight. And then we can chat tomorrow morning after the meeting?'

Nabeel nodded.

'Mr Pradip Saha, have you done anything productive over the last few days?'

Everyone laughed. Nabeel constantly picked on the young economist who was the website's senior editorial writer. Pradip was an excellent essayist.

'Any luck at all with getting Mehta to write for us, Pradip?'

'Not yet. But we're getting there. It isn't an issue of money. He is just far too committed to *The Indian Express*.'

'Tell him we don't want exclusivity. Pay him more. Show him circulation figures for *The Indian Express*. Do whatever it takes. Get him. We need him.'

'On it.'

One by one Nabeel exhausted his list of story ideas. One by one the reporters around the table solemnly made notes in their own books.

Finally, Nabeel brought up the big event. In three days, the India Summit of the World Financial Forum (WFF) would take place in Mumbai. *The Indian Opinion* had been chosen as 'exclusive online media partner'. The appointment had been something of a media coup. It had raised eyebrows and made some senior editors all over Mumbai and Delhi very upset.

Two things had convinced the organisers. First, Nabeel had a brilliant track record as a reporter and editor. Second, one of the venture capitalists who backed *The Indian Opinion* had made phone calls to some very important people at the WFF headquarters in Geneva.

'I cannot emphasise this enough. This is our big break. If we can pull off the India Summit . . . boom! It may not blow our traffic off the charts. But it can make us a lot of money and establish credibility. Janani will commission and edit all the stories. But I will keep an eye on everything. *Everything*. Don't screw this up, guys.'

Nabeel then looked at Amod.

It was highly uncommon for morning meetings at newsrooms to involve anybody from the non-editorial side of the business. But Nabeel's team was so small that he had to involve all employees. He couldn't let Amod and the marketing manager feel that they weren't a part of the team.

'Amod?'

Amod, who had been holding his fist to his mouth all through the meeting, suddenly exploded in a fit of coughing. He apologised and informed everyone about his late-night raid. 'I've given the contractor three days to improve his ops, or ship out.'

'Awesome,' said Nabeel.

Next, it was the marketing manager's turn. She gave a brief overview of revenues in the usual vague terms. 'Overall,' she said a few minutes later, 'things are looking okay. Not great. Just okay. As long as our headcount stays small, we should keep making money. Hopefully Lufthansa will renew their campaign this week.'

'Very good. Thanks all. Everyone can leave except the leadership team.'

Everyone chuckled. The leadership team currently comprised just two people: Janani Ganesh and Nabeel Karimudeen.

After the team left, Janani closed the door. 'How did the interview here with Hormazd go yesterday?' she asked Nabeel.

'Very well. Well, under the circumstances. He was running a fever and had a bad cough.' Nabeel looked through the glass walls of the conference room. Amod was chatting with Rochelle Mendonca.

'Anyway. So yes. I think he is most likely on board. We need someone senior who . . . who understands features. Namita is great. But she needs guidance. Hormazd is a good guy. Hope he joins us.'

Janani nodded, a neutral expression on her face. 'How does that leave us in the manpower department?'

'Not very well,' Nabeel said. 'If Hormazd comes

on board that is a big chunk of my hiring budget gone.'

'Hope it works out, I guess.'

'Hmm.'

Nabeel got up and Janani followed. Suddenly, she stopped. 'Wait. There is one more thing. I should have brought it up before.'

'Go on.'

'Have you seen this SMO thing on Facebook?'

Nabeel looked at her blankly.

She continued, 'Okay, so there is this SMO guy, part of that Srivatsa scheme.'

'Srivatsa? The health thing?'

'Yeah. He has pissed off a whole bunch of people. Apparently walked into a building full of Muslim families and insisted he speak to men and women.'

'Cue: social media meltdown?'

'Yep. I want to pick it up before the TV guys do. I think there is a good story here, Nabeel. A proper story about public health.'

'Sure. Use your editorial judgement. And report the heck out of it.'

'Of course.'

Both journalists left the conference room and went to their respective workstations. Janani's seat was towards the end of the newsroom. Nabeel had his own office. He walked in and closed the door behind him.

Shortly before lunch, Rochelle Mendonca knocked on Nabeel's door. She had an idea that would eventually change everything. 'Sir, I was wondering ... since we are the exclusive online partner, can we also do short online videos from the Summit? Something quirky and cool?'

Nabeel thought for a few moments. 'Like what?'

'Quick takes by the speakers. Chats in the lobbies and corridors. Walk and talk. Things like that.'

'Sounds good, Rochelle. Two things. Don't do something the TV guys will do. Please. None of that crap. Secondly, don't get into trouble. Be subtle. I don't want the WFF people to come back with contracts and agreements in case the TV guys get pissed off.'

'No problem.'

'Take our GoPro cameras with you.'

'Also . . . I was thinking of taking somebody with me as a cameraperson. So that I can do interviews on camera as well?'

'No way, Rochelle. We have six journalists in this office. I can't spare everybody for the WFF. Other things may actually happen elsewhere in the world, you know . . .'

'I know, sir. I was wondering . . . could I take Amod with me?'

'Amod? Did you ask him?'

'He is cool with it if you are.'

'Fine. Give it a shot. Just make sure he isn't coughing so much when he is filming. I'll call the WFF security office and get his name added to the press list.'

'Super. Thanks, boss.'

Rochelle walked over to Amod's workstation. He looked at her with a tense expression. She gave him the thumbs up.

He punched the air.

# 8

**Justice Kashyap Commission of Inquiry**

*Reference: PS 4/PI 17/Maha/Session 4*
*File type: Raw transcript of interview, audio recording*
*Location: Provisional Lok Sabha Complex, Port Blair*
*Security clearance level: 2*
*Note: This recording features two voices*

JK: Do you mind if I ask you a few personal questions?

AV: That will really depend on the nature of these personal questions, sir. Excuse my . . . frankness.

JK: Of course. In general, you are free to not answer questions you don't want to. I cannot force you. At least not in this interview.

AV: Very well.

JK: How old were you at the time of the outbreak? And how long had you been an SMO?

AV: I was almost twenty-nine years old. I had been an SMO for three months.

JK: So this was your first job as a civil servant?

AV: It was my first job of any kind.

JK: Did you appear for the civil services examination right after your MBBS?

AV: After my MBA.

JK: Oh yes . . . you have an MBA as well . . . tell me Aayush . . . why an MBA? And then, why the civil services? All this seems . . . pardon me for putting it like this . . . aimless. It all seems so aimless.

AV: You are not completely wrong.

*Laughter.*

AV: I was born into a family that expected every single member to have a degree in medicine. And not one person rebelled—whether it was my great-grandfather or me. We are all doctors. We own a chain of hospitals across Western India.

JK: Ah yes. The Vajpeyis of Topaz Healthcare.

AV: Exactly. So we were expected to either work as doctors in one of the Topaz branches or help run the hospitals. That is what all of us did. That is all we ever did.

JK: I gather from your tone that you are not a fan of this business.

AV: No, I am not. I love medicine. And healthcare is important. But I hated working in those hospitals. I hated having to see it as a business model with sales targets and profit margins. All that . . . somehow debased the idea of being a doctor.

JK: So you decided to pursue an MBA?!

AV: Yes. Well, my disenchantment was only a part of the problem. I also pursued an MBA because it was the toughest entrance exam in the country that I was eligible to appear for.

JK: You like examinations?

AV: I *love* them. I love everything about them. The preparation. The tension. The endless nights. The physical challenge. The mental stress. The wait for the results. The euphoria.

JK: The euphoria? You always fare well in exams?

AV: Always.

JK: Perhaps this explains what you did during Bombay Fever? Did you view that as an exam, too? As a problem to be solved? A puzzle to be broken?

AV: Perhaps. Maybe that was how I approached it in my mind. But it was not an exam that left me feeling euphoric. Bombay Fever was not a test, sir. It was a tragedy.

JK: Did you lose anyone to it?

AV: Yes. Bombay Fever claimed a lot of people I knew. I lost an uncle and my sister just about avoided meltdown. Topaz Healthcare lost 286 employees.

JK: Hmm. And—to get back to our original point of discussion—after your MBA?

AV: I immediately began preparing for the civil services examinations.

JK: No campus placement?

AV: I had an offer from A.T. Kearney, Singapore. Healthcare consulting. Never joined.

JK: Why not?

AV: I had found one more horrendously difficult examination I could sign up for. Besides, the family would have never let me work for anybody else in the private sector. They were prepared to make an exception for the civil services provided I swore to come back and join Topaz later.

JK: Did you fare well in the civil services exam, too?

AV: I did okay. All India rank 72.

JK: Not bad at all. And so, you were picked to become an SMO right after the probationary period . . .

AV: I was in the first batch of fifteen SMOs picked for Srivatsa.

JK: According to your service record, you were in trouble right through your stint as an SMO. Right till the day you were packed off to Wellington.

AV: In a manner of speaking. I kept pissing off people. Before the Fever. During the Fever. After the Fever.

JK: So, New Zealand is a punishment posting?

AV: Of course, sir. I think that is obvious.

JK: But they can't fire you either, can they?

AV: No, sir. I guess not.

JK: Because you've become a national hero?

AV: Because I was associated with the real heroes.

JK: True, true. Anyway . . . so, the controversies that assailed you as an SMO . . . one of them was the Al Amin Complex outrage?

AV: That is correct, sir. Two or three days before the outbreak.

JK: Tell me what happened.

## 9

**4 days before the outbreak**

The Rapid Cabs taxi driver had never seen such an ill passenger before. Hormazd Patel was in the back seat, doubled over, his head between his knees. His bouts of coughing were more intense and frequent than they had ever been before.

His eyeballs and earlobes felt as if they were on fire.

*How did I fall ill all over again?*

The last time Hormazd Patel had felt so unwell was after he had returned from Switzerland. But his mother's antibiotics had cured him then. This time, even those tablets weren't working.

He coughed almost the entire way home from the office of *The Indian Opinion*.

Later that night, when the driver washed his car, he did not notice the fine spray of yellow fluid on the floor, near the back seat. The yellow was flecked with minute particles of congealed red.

'How did your interview go?' Siloo asked Hormazd with some anxiety.

Hormazd was a good, hard-working employee.

But he did not interview well. He often got nervous and self-conscious. And now there was this cough.

'Shall I call Dr Kamat?'

'Yes. I feel terrible. And your medicines aren't working, Mamma.'

Siloo Patel got up from the sofa in the living room and shuffled towards the bedroom. She came back with a cordless phone. She, too, had a cough now.

It was 6.45 pm by the time Siloo got through to Dr Nilambar Kamat on his mobile phone. The doctor was on his way to a wedding in Goregaon. 'The clinic will be closed tomorrow,' he told Siloo, who sounded distraught. 'But I will be back day after. Don't panic, aunty. Tell me what is going on.'

Siloo Patel gave him a detailed description of the symptoms that afflicted both her son and her. Nilambar was perturbed but tried to hide it from his voice. 'Siloo aunty, why don't both of you take some cough syrup and paracetamol for the fever? If the symptoms persist, this could be TB or pneumonia. But I sincerely doubt it. Must be a bad throat infection. Give me a call tomorrow around lunch with updates.'

He hung up after repeatedly urging the old woman to contact him if the patients' condition deteriorated. Nilambar was still thinking of the Patels when he arrived at the wedding hall in Goregaon. Then he forgot all about them.

The doctor was right to have been perturbed.

But his diagnosis was inaccurate. Hormazd and his mother did not suffer from either tuberculosis or pneumonia. Instead, they had been attacked by a mutant, hitherto unknown form of deadly bacteria.

*

*As Hormazd lay on his living room sofa, coughing up flecks of yellow mucus, a battle raged inside his body.*

*For nearly three months, a drug-resistant strain of bacteria had slowly formed colonies along the mucous membranes in Hormazd's respiratory system. There, latched on to a host, the bacteria had multiplied by the hundreds and then the thousands. When strong enough to wage a terrible war, the bacteria began a three-stage attack that would culminate in the destruction of the host.*

*In the first stage of this invasion, the drug-resistant bacteria did not target Hormazd at all. Instead, it swooped down on the bacteria that already lived inside the journalist. It destroyed the competition.*

*Each human body is home to millions upon millions of microbes. They thrive in the mouth, on the skin, in the gut, between the toes, on the teeth, around the rectum . . . everywhere. Some research suggests that there are ten times as many microbial cells in a body as there are human cells—but nobody knows for certain. Nor do we know what all of them do. Some do nothing at all.*

*What we do know is this: as long as this mysterious universe of microbes is in balance, the human being that hosts them enjoys good health. His organs function normally, his fluids maintain an optimum mix of constituents, and his constitution is stable.*

*This equilibrium is vital. Violate it and the human body can collapse with shocking speed. Thankfully, this is much harder than it sounds. The body has numerous layers of defence to prevent invasion by harmful bacteria. The first of these is the community of pre-existing bacteria already in the body. As soon as an invader approaches, existing microbes line up to protect their turf. Therefore, if an invading pathogen must succeed in its fatal mission, its immediate job, after securing a foothold inside the body, is to control or consume pre-existing bacteria.*

*When Bombay Fever acquired a critical mass inside Hormazd's body—later, researchers would estimate this to be at about 20,000 cells—it unleashed its fusillade—a wave of toxins that would annihilate competitors, leaving room for Bombay Fever to monopolise nutrients and control the host.*

*By the time Hormazd had completed his interview with Nabeel Karimudeen, his respiratory system was awash with toxic proteins generated by Bombay Fever bacteria. These proteins went on a rampage—destroying the microbe communities in his lungs. Hormazd's body responded as it did to any infection—by producing mucus. Hormazd began to cough. As he coughed up this mucus, he ejected millions of copies of Bombay Fever bacterium into the environment. Most of these particles died shortly thereafter. But not all of them. Some of them lasted just long enough to find a new host.*

*Such as Amod Patil.*

*As Hormazd lay on the couch, and as Siloo Patel spoke to Dr Kamat on the phone, Bombay Fever had already moved to stage two. In this stage, the infestation, now in the millions, began to flood Hormazd's blood stream with the same toxic cocktail of proteins. This time these toxins didn't hunt down other bacteria. Instead they drove Hormazd's immune system insane.*

*Stage three: Hormazd's body began to reject itself.*

## 3 days before the outbreak

'According to you, what are the top three sessions at this year's India Summit? That nobody should miss?' Rochelle Mendonca asked the question, and then pointed a pencil-thin microphone at Sophie Perramond.

Perramond, the World Financial Forum's press officer, and one of the half-dozen WFF press officers stationed at the Somerset Hotel in Mumbai's Marine Drive, didn't even have to think. The forty-eight-year-old veteran of more than a dozen India Summits, answered immediately, smiling at the GoPro camera. 'The India-China session on day two will be amazing. I don't think we've ever had such a high power group of Indians and Chinese on the same stage at the same time. We are expecting sparks to fly. Also, on day two, there is a session on free speech that I think will draw a lot of people. In fact, we are thinking of moving it to the main hall if the demand stays high. And finally, without a doubt, the opening session on day one where we ha . . .'

Amod Patil coughed so hard that he dropped the GoPro camera to the floor.

'I'm so sorry . . .' he blurted out, flecks of mucus flying out of his mouth, as he bent to pick up the camera.

Rochelle tried to help him up, gently prising the camera from his grip. 'Why don't you go to the restroom and clean up? I'll finish this and meet you at lunch.'

Amod nodded, looked apologetically at Sophie, and walked away.

Rochelle pointed the camera at Sophie. 'Shall we try again?'

Amod staggered to the bathroom, flung open a door, and bent over the toilet bowl, his hands on his knees. The intense fragrance of a lemongrass air-freshener permeated the toilet. He inhaled once or twice deeply, and then coughed up a gob of mucus.

He spat into the bowl. Just as he reached for the flush, he noticed the streaks of red in the yellow.

*Fuck. What a time to fall ill. I need to find a doctor in this city.*

Rochelle was already eating her lunch by the time Amod walked into the ballroom allotted to the WFF for a staff and media buffet.

'You look terrible,' she said.

'I feel fuck all,' Amod replied. 'Do you know a good doctor? I have to see a doctor, man. I think I'm coughing blood.'

'What? Go home, Amod! Fucking mad or what?' Rochelle picked up her mobile phone and sent Amod a text message with her doctor's phone number.

'Yeah. I think I will eat something and leave. But I will be here tomorrow, Rochelle. 100 per cent.'

Amod picked up the plate from the head of the buffet line and waited for the queue in front of him to move. Aware of the open trays of food around him, Amod took an extra paper napkin. He covered his mouth when he coughed.

The paper barrier was feeble. With each exhalation, each cough and each clearing of his throat, Amod unleashed an invisible jet of bacteria into the environment around him.

All around, the bacteria clung to clothes, food, skin, table linen, carpets and furniture.

As Amod pushed some macaroni and cheese

around his plate with a fork, he realised that he wasn't hungry at all. He left his plate on a table and went home.

At that instant, there were sixty-four people in the ballroom. Over the next few days, most of them would die, along with hundreds more staff, guests and visitors who swarmed the hotel.

Bombay Fever would kill them all.

But not all of them *had* to die. Some of them could have been saved—if only researchers working under extreme pressure hadn't made a tragic error.

# 10

**2 days before the outbreak**

Janani Ganesh squirmed in the chair as she wiped her forehead with a soaked handkerchief. She sat in a narrow, dingy, grey corridor. Several chairs for visitors had been placed in a row, with their backs to the wall, outside a closed door. Someone had taped a sign—produced by an ancient dot matrix printer—to the entrance. It read: 'Srivatsa: SMO Team Mumbai South Residential'. The printout had faded to the cement grey of the corridor's unpainted walls and ceilings.

Up and down the corridor, several windows had been thrown open. They offered no relief. Instead, gusts of hot air, laden with dust, periodically blew into the corridor and swirled around—first coating Janani with a sheen of perspiration, and then a fine layer of Mumbai dirt.

Janani looked at her watch and sighed. She had spent the entire morning waiting for a meeting with the outrageous SMO.

It wasn't the waiting itself that bothered Janani. She didn't care. She would have preferred one of those air conditioned waiting rooms at Mantralaya with soft chairs and 'lowest bidder' coffee machines—but she was no stranger to heat, sweat or unpainted cement. In her career, Janani Ganesh had spent far too much time waiting outside government offices.

Sometimes, she felt that the discomfort helped sharpen her senses and refine her questions as she cornered her prey.

What bothered her that morning was the time— the longer the SMO took to turn up, the greater the likelihood that a TV channel or newspaper would sniff out the controversy and break it online or on social media. Once that happened, there was no point in covering the story with any degree of nuance or sophistication. The rising tide of manufactured outrage would capsize all boats.

The door cracked open. Aayush Vajpeyi stepped out and stretched a palm in her direction.

'Hello I am Aayush Vajpeyi. You must be Miss Ganesh.'

Janani was impressed.

*They really are getting young guys to work for them these days.*

She shook his hand.

'Follow me,' Aayush said, before turning around and walking down the corridor. She could see patches of sweat on the back of his shirt. He led her to a staircase at the end of the corridor and they walked down together.

'What is this place?' she asked. 'I found the address on the Srivatsa website. But this looks . . .'

'Incomplete. No? It looks incomplete to me. As if they just lost the will to spend any more money on this building.'

'I was going to say minimal. But you're right. Nice place to work?'

'Terrible. We have no air conditioning. Anywhere.'

'Why not?'

When they reached the ground floor, Aayush walked out of the main entrance and crossed the road outside; Janani followed. They then went to a little fresh fruit juice shop. Aayush ordered a chikku milkshake and Janani reluctantly called for a mosambi juice, but only after insisting she pay for both.

When the waiter left, Aayush began to talk.

'So this used to be a Planning Commission building. For a long time. Forty or fifty years. Everything was designed back in the day when this kind of brutal interior design was cool. Le Corbusier. IIM–Ahmedabad. Brick. Concrete. Scary bullshit. Now it just looks like a godown designed by a drug addict.'

Janani smiled.

*Must be one of those guys—seems all nice and then suddenly ends up being sexist or racist or something.*

'And it used to have excellent air conditioning. But when they disbanded the Planning Commission, they ripped everything useful out, especially the ACs, and gave it all away to state government offices in Mumbai.'

'A fine example of decentralisation.'

'The finest. Until, a few years later, they allocated the unused building to our team, and refused to install air conditioners because, as per their records, the building already had AC units!'

Both of them sipped their drinks through straws. Aayush drank in long slurps, inhaling and exhaling deeply between mouthfuls.

'So, how can I help you?' he asked when his glass was empty.

'What happened at the Al Amin Complex?'

Aayush dropped his head and sighed loudly. 'Do you know how Srivatsa works? Or what an SMO's responsibilities include?'

'Not really.' This was not entirely true. But Janani liked her targets to talk as much as they wanted to.

Aayush briefly explained the focus of the programme—eradicating drug-resistant strains of diseases—and how each SMO in India was in charge of running the initiative within a designated administrative unit. Some SMOs had to oversee entire districts, while others, like Aayush, dealt with small segments of metropolitan cities.

Initially the plan had been to rotate SMOs between rural and urban postings. That way, the government hoped, these young civil servants would be thoroughly exposed to India's numerous healthcare challenges. Perhaps this would also help propel a bidirectional flow of good ideas between cities and villages.

But there was another, less openly discussed reason for this rotation programme. It ensured that the SMOs didn't have to spend all their time in some remote rural district with no internet, television or water supply. That was the surest way, Srivatsa's planners felt, to force new recruits to quit the service.

Once the programme started, however, the rotation plan was shelved. Not because the planners or administrators didn't want it, but because most of the SMOs chose to stay put. 'I don't think there is any other civil servant who gets as close to the private lives of the public as the SMO,' Aayush explained. 'And that is because we build strong personal bonds with the community.'

Initially, when the Srivatsa programme started, there was resistance. Many households didn't even let SMOs into their doors. Several pharmacies thought that Srivatsa was a smokescreen—an attempt to conceal sales tax investigations. Eventually, as SMOs uncomplainingly persisted with their regions, the results began to show. With their help—and their tremendous insights into the social aspects of drug usage, healthcare awareness and patient-doctor relationships—the government began to capture remarkable health data.

Janani felt a thrill run through her as she listened to Aayush. The scandal at the Al Amin Complex was not the real story. The real story was Srivatsa, the SMO and all this healthcare data being gathered.

But she had to be careful, Janani thought to herself. She had to stay vigilant. For all she knew, Aayush could be planting a story to divert attention from the brewing outrage over his behaviour at the Al Amin Complex.

Rather forcefully, she interrupted the SMO. 'All this is great. Super stuff. But you still haven't explained this Al Amin business. The outrage.'

'I was just going to, Janani. There is no "business" or "outrage". It is just a misunderstanding.'

## 3 days before the outbreak

Daphne Dolker was due to visit Al Amin around 2 pm and speak to all the families at a joint meeting. That was a part of her job as an SMO—one joint meeting, followed by door-to-door visits, and then, periodic reviews.

The Al Amin Complex was located on Shahid Bhagat Singh Road in Mumbai's 'Ward A'. Daphne and Aayush were the two SMOs who jointly handled the ward. This was somewhat unusual. As a rule, SMOs were exclusively in charge of regions. If Ward A was an exception—despite not being particularly big or populous—it was because it housed numerous VIP personalities—military personnel, judges, ministers and diplomats. So, two of the most highly regarded SMOs, one male and one female, were allotted to it. Both were asked to do their jobs with 'enhanced sensitivity'.

Over time, Daphne and Aayush arrived at an effective working relationship. Daphne took care of most of the homes and schools, while Aayush oversaw everything else.

Three days before the outbreak, Daphne fell ill. She asked Aayush to step in for her at all meetings, including the one at the Al Amin Complex—predominantly occupied by middle-class families.

At 2 pm, Aayush stood before a group of thirty-odd women, all of whom expected to see Daphne. The husbands, presumably, were at work.

Aayush went through the drill with practised ease. He had made identical presentations hundreds of times before, in front of all types of audiences. He cracked the same jokes and made the same gestures. Everything went along smoothly until he brought up the idea of door-to-door visits for healthcare surveys.

An old woman in the front row put up her hand. 'Who will be doing these visits, sir?'

'One of the two SMOs. Daphne or me.'

'Sir, I don't think it is appropriate for you to visit the colony during the day when only ladies are there,' the old woman said frowning.

'I understand, madam. But sometimes, Daphne is unavailable and we have to share responsibilities.'

A younger woman wearing a headscarf spoke up. 'I'm Amina Khan and I agree with Mrs Fernandes. This is not a good idea. We are willing to cooperate. But you should also understand our situation. Why don't you come in the evening after 8 pm when our husbands are around?'

A murmur of approval went through the crowd. Aayush exhaled deeply.

*This is why Daphne should be doing this.*

'Madam, I totally agree with you. Daphne will come 200 per cent if she is able to. But if she can't . . .'

Amina shook her head. 'No, no. Do one thing. Why don't you bring someone with you from the police station then? There are female constables at the Azad Maidan station. Bring one of them.'

It was a scorching day and the meeting had been organised in the building's covered car park. This kept the sun out, but not the heat. Aayush was exhausted.

'What is wrong with people like you? No, really. Why is your thinking so orthodox? So medieval? Can't you listen to what you are saying? Here I am trying to help you . . .'

'How dare you!' Amina shouted. The voices grew in pitch. Someone pulled out a smartphone.

Mrs Fernandes stood up. 'Sir, you please apologise right now.'

'No, I will not!' Aayush said, still looking at Amina. 'Disease is a serious problem. Healthcare is not some joke. We are here to help you. But instead of cooperating, you people . . . you people remain old-fashioned and ignorant and . . .'

Before Aayush should say another word, one of the security guards from the building walked up and firmly led him away. Several women shouted at Aayush. He shouted back. Calls were made to the police.

A few hours later, a blurry video clip of the meeting was uploaded on Facebook.

### 2 days before the outbreak

'You realise that the clip makes you look . . .' Janani started to say.

'Like I am shouting at a Muslim woman. And blaming *her people* for their orthodox approach,' Aayush completed her sentence.

'Yes. But you weren't?'

'Exactly. It was all stupid, really. Totally my fault. I shouldn't have shouted like that.'

Janani felt a little deflated.

*Fucking useless controversy. But I will still have to cover it.*

'Listen, Aayush. Why don't I help you deal with this?'

'How?'

Janani outlined her plan. She would spend a few days with him as he went about his work. *The Indian Opinion* would then publish a piece profiling Aayush Vajpeyi and the success of the SMO programme.

'Maybe I could call it: "The Social Medical Officer: The Most Important Civil Servant You've Never Heard Of". What do you think?'

'Sounds great. But I have to get approval first.'

'Obviously. But let us start anyway? Why waste time? I will keep all my notes to myself till you get the permissions you need.'

Aayush stirred the shards of ice in his glass with the straw.

'Okay. But when patients interact, you have to use anonymised health information. And run the story by me before you publish it.'

'Done. Let us start tomorrow?'

Aayush pulled out his mobile phone and looked up his calendar. 'I have a review visit tomorrow at a housing complex. At 9 am. And then a bunch of meetings with pharmacies.'

'Great. Which complex?'

'Cusrow Baug.'

'Excellent,' said Janani. 'Let us hope nothing outrageous happens.'

Aayush smiled as they got up to leave.

# 11

**1 day before the outbreak**

At 9.00 am, just as Janani Ganesh met Aayush Vajpeyi on the street outside Cusrow Baug, Mandeep Ahuja nervously paced up and down the lobby of the Somerset Hotel. Even as he closely observed every small detail—the arrangement of the flowers, the polish on the balustrades, the volume of the piped music—the Somerset's general manager was worried.

An unusually large number of his employees had called in sick. And most of them from a single department.

On the average day, Mandeep expected around ten staff members across all the hotel's numerous departments to file a request for sick leave. This number spiked sometimes, especially after wedding season, when staff members worked themselves ragged. Even then there were rarely more than fifteen employees absent.

This morning, Mandeep was informed that twenty-six of his staff members had stayed at home with coughs and fevers. Of these, twenty-one were waiters who worked in the party catering department.

This was an alarmingly high number. Mandeep immediately called a meeting of all the department heads. He asked them to keep an eye out for any further signs of illness. He also asked the janitorial staff to inspect the party catering kitchens and double down on health and safety measures.

Then, he called up the event management company that coordinated the India Summit. He asked if any of the delegates had fallen ill or if the Summit staff members had failed to turn up for work. His contact at the company had no idea; she promised to check and get back. 'But don't hold your breath, Mandeep,' she said. 'This is not a good time for such questions.'

With just twenty-four hours left for the India Summit to kick off, everyone involved was swamped with last-minute assignments. Calls went unanswered and emails were ignored.

Around noon, Mandeep called the event managers again. They had no further information.

So he left his office and walked over to the south-eastern wing of the hotel.

This entire section—rooms, restaurants, gyms, shops, offices, banquet halls, ballrooms—had been cordoned off behind three levels of security. The first was a private security agency that had been contracted by the hotel. They manned the various entry and exit points. The second security line belonged to the Mumbai police force. All delegates, speakers, journalists, visitors and hotel staff were expected to wear special colour-coded WFF passes, on the basis of which a team of sixty policemen controlled access to various sections of the 'Summit Zone'. The final line of security was run by a team from the elite Special Protection Group (SPG)—the officers dressed as always in suits and sunglasses. This line, comprising X-ray machines, walk-through metal detectors, sniffer dogs and chemical sensors, would only be activated intermittently.

Generally, these men and their paraphernalia would be secreted away. But exactly forty-five minutes before any session featuring a high profile personality, the team of dour, cheerless men would quietly reappear to form this third innermost cordon. They would switch on all the machines. The Mumbai police force would then empty the Summit Zone of visitors and allow sniffer dogs to sweep the area. Afterwards, attendees had to file back into the rooms through the detectors and sensors and past the dogs. It was a tiresome, time-consuming system that invariably ruined Summit timetables. But it was not open to negotiation.

Mandeep glided through the first two lines of security control, flashing his all-zones all-access pass, and then walked past the unmanned metal detector. He entered the main ballroom, the nerve centre of the Summit, and looked around. The hall was abuzz with people and activity. A few minutes later, he spotted Sophie Perramond.

'Do you have a minute, Sophie? I have something urgent to discuss.'

'Hello, Mandeep. Tell me. Has anyone been troubling you?'

'Not at all. I was wondering . . . you see, some of my waiters fell ill with what looks like a flu or viral fever of some kind. I just wanted to make sure everything and everyone here is fine?'

Sophie smiled. 'Everything is perfectly okay, Mandeep. Must be the first few victims of conference flu!' Sophie's comment was a somewhat tongue-in-cheek reference to a handful of complaints—coughs, colds, headaches and stomach upsets—that commonly afflict delegates at conferences.

'I think so, too,' Mandeep replied. 'Still. No harm in checking. Everything is coming along nicely?'

'Very nicely. Now, please, I need to double-check all our press kits. If you need anything, just come by.'

'I shall. Will you please keep an eye out for . . . *extreme* conference flu? Just in case?'

Sophie grinned. 'Will do.'

Mandeep smiled and turned around sharply. As he walked back to the main hotel lobby he reassured himself. *That must be it. No need to panic. Everyone will all be okay.*

Nonetheless, Mandeep placed two phone calls.

The first was to a manpower supply company which often helped the hotel with stand-in waiters and cleaning staff.

The second was to the hotel's medical consultant. The genial physician with a tremendous moustache occasionally dropped in at the Somerset to check on unwell residents who paid an exorbitant service charge for his expert opinion and complete discretion.

'Doctor, can you do me a favour? Could you perhaps move into the hotel for the next week or so? I will arrange for all expenses, of course.'

'Is this for the Summit? I am sure they have made their own arrangements.'

'They have. But I would very much like it if you are here. To take care of the staff and maybe help with emergencies. It will put my mind at ease.'

'I understand. You can count on me. I will be here, bags et al, at 8 pm. Let us have a drink together?'

'Sure thing. Thank you, doctor.'

'My pleasure. Don't worry, Mandeep old chap. Nothing is going to happen. Everything is going to be perfectly fine.'

### 1 day before the outbreak

At 9.00 am, as Mandeep paced up and down the lobby of the Somerset, Rochelle Mendonca paused to catch her breath in the Summit Zone. She was irritated. She had managed to secure an interview with a controversial American economist. But there was no sign of Amod Patil or his GoPro camera. He wasn't at *The Indian Opinion*'s office either. And he wasn't picking up his phone—each time she tried contacting him, the call went to his voicemail.

'Hey. This is Amod. Leave a message.'

'Amod this is Rochelle. How are you now? Is your cough better? I hope it is. I've been waiting at the Somerset since 8 am. Dude, are you coming? If you aren't, can I send someone to your house to pick up the camera? I have to do online interviews, yaar. Call back.'

'Amod. Call back. Please. Please.'

'Yaar, this is totally unprofessional. I don't mind if you are sick and can't help. But at least tell me, no?'

Around 9.45 am, Rochelle gave up on Amod Patil. She recorded the interview on her mobile phone. She then uploaded the video to her corporate cloud account, and phoned a colleague in office to edit and upload it to the website's special India Summit page.

She then asked Nabeel to send someone to the hotel with a camera.

Finally, Rochelle Mendonca called Amod Patil again.

'Hey. This is Amod. Leave a message.'

'Fucker, this is Rochelle. I am both angry and scared now. Please call back. Are you okay?'

Amod Patil was not okay.

Amod Patil was dead.

**1 day before the outbreak**

'Strange,' said Aayush Vajpeyi around 10.35 am, as he followed Janani out of their eleventh meeting at Cusrow Baug.

'What is?' Janani asked, not really paying attention. She was frantically scribbling, recording vivid observations in a notebook on the meeting between the SMO and a beautiful, middle-aged Parsi woman who used to be an Air India stewardess.

'The number of people in this building who have coughs . . .'

'Yeah, I noticed that. But it must be the viral fever going around. One guy in my office has had a cough, too.'

'I wonder if it could be something more serious.'

'Hopefully not,' said Janani. 'Given that we've just spent several minutes each with all of them.'

Aayush grinned. 'It doesn't always work that way. Not everything spreads so quickly. Diseases are complex.' He walked towards another flat. 'Our next family is the Patels. Old woman and one son. Hormazd Patel.'

'Wait, Hormazd Patel?'

Aayush looked at the printout in his hand again. 'Yup, Hormazd Patel. Profession . . . journalist. You know him?'

'Not really. But he recently interviewed with our company. Has a great reputation.'

Aayush rang the bell by the door. A few seconds later, he knocked. The front door of the adjacent flat creaked open. An old woman, who identified herself as Diane, stepped out. 'I don't think they are home. Haven't seen them for two days.'

'But I checked with the security guard,' Aayush mumbled as he flipped through his printout. 'He said that all the residents are in town.'

The old lady shrugged her shoulders. 'Even I was wondering. Maybe I should have a look? Wait for me.' She went back indoors, coughing gently.

'Aayush . . . the lights are on inside.' Janani was looking at a glass panel above the door.

It was a line that Aayush would never forget. It marked the moment when he would first confront the horrors of Bombay Fever.

Diane returned with the spare key to the Patel home.

As soon as the door opened, Janani, Aayush and Diane were hit by a powerful stench. It was like nothing they had ever experienced before. There was not a soul in the living room. But the television was still running and the ceiling fan was spinning slowly. Aayush walked into the bedroom and Janani followed. There, they saw two bodies.

Hormazd lay on the bed, his head on the pillow. Siloo lay on the floor. Their bodies were soaked in congealed, stinking blood that looked like minced chicken livers. And there was so much of it. Each body seemed to have spontaneously ejected all the blood it contained.

The skin on both corpses had broken out into deep purple patches. As if the outermost layers had detached from the flesh underneath.

'What the fuck . . .' Janani said.

Aayush was stunned for a moment. And then, he heard Diane enter the room. She began to scream.

Simultaneously, Aayush received a WhatsApp message on his phone. It was from the SMO who took care of another ward, and was addressed to the 'Mumbai City SMOs' chat group: 'Guys, I hear many people at the airport medical post are suffering from severe cough. Anything in your wards? Wondering if this is something serious?'

# 12

**1 day before the outbreak**

As soon as his assistant placed his luggage in the closet and left the room, the man dressed in the stiff Nehru jacket, trousers and shoes sat by the edge of the bed. He then took a deep breath and fell backwards on to the mattress. He looked up at the ceiling, placed his palms on his stomach, relaxed and began to speak to himself: 'Ladies and gentleman. It is a pleasure to be here. I vividly remember the very first . . .'

There was a knock on the door.

'Come in!'

A man dressed in a nondescript suit, white shirt and tie cracked the door open and poked a head in.

'Sir, did you ask for something?'

'No, Prakash. I was just practising.'

'Oh. Sorry, sir. I didn't realise . . .'

'No matter. Please close the door.'

Just as Prakash's head vanished, the man on the bed called after him. 'Prakash!'

'Sir?'

'When is my next appointment? How much free time do I have?'

'Two hours, sir. After that, you have a private dinner with Mr Alex Winchester . . .'

'Thank you.'

*Two hours. Not a lot of time*, Nitin Phadnavis thought. He could perhaps polish the final draft of his speech tonight, go for dinner, come back, and practise it in front of the mirror. If he still wasn't 100 per cent satisfied with the draft, he could ask one of his staff members to work on it overnight and smoothen the rough edges.

In any case, he would give it one final review before breakfast the next morning.

*And at 11 am . . . show time . . .*

Nitin Phadnavis sat up and looked around. He spotted the little kettle and the coffee-making kit on a shelf next to the large flat-screen television.

He got up from the bed and walked over to the closet. A few minutes later, he returned with a small drawstring bag. He emptied its contents on to the shelf in front of the kettle—a large plastic spoon, an AeroPress coffee-making device, a little Ziploc bag full of coffee filters, and a small jar of Monsoon Malabar coffee powder that he himself had ground that morning.

Coffee was one of Nitin's obsessions. He drank at least three cups a day and insisted on making each one himself. His staff, especially his chef, found this habit bewildering. But Nitin would have it no other way.

As he watched the decoction bubbling inside the AeroPress' chamber, Nitin began to speak to himself again. But this time in a low voice. Prakash Rao, the man in the suit who stood outside his door, was jumpy. There was no need to alarm him once more.

'Ladies and gentleman. It is a pleasure to be here. I vividly remember the very first . . .'

He didn't like it at all. How were his vivid personal recollections relevant? This wasn't about him. Or, at least, not directly.

Nitin waited for the last drop of coffee to drip into the cup. He took a small sachet of milk from the shelf and tipped in its contents. He stirred, then drew the cup close. He closed his eyes as he sipped hot, rich, satisfying coffee.

*No, I have to change the opening. I can bring in myself and my memories later. No reason to waste time. I have to come straight to the point.*

Nitin quickly changed into a pair of jeans and a polo shirt. He sat down at the writing desk and pulled eleven sheets of printed paper out of his valise, along with a pencil. In between sips of coffee, Nitin Phadnavis began to rework the text for the sixteenth time that week. He slashed paragraphs, and drew long, looping arrows as he moved chunks of text around.

Sometime later, as Nitin wondered if he really needed to quote both Gandhi and Wilde, his mobile phone rang. Only six people in the world had that number and Nitin always picked it up.

'Hello, Papa!' the young girl's voice came tumbling out.

Nitin smiled. He spoke to his daughter for a few minutes and then asked Mythili to pass the phone to her mother.

'Are you nervous, Nitin?'

'I am always nervous on days like this.'

'But you shouldn't be. This is a bulletproof announcement. It is going to be a success even if you forget all your lines and read the whole thing from a printout.'

'I know, I know. But still. This is such a huge moment. I want everything to proceed flawlessly. From start to finish.'

'I get that. Just don't make *great* the enemy of *good*. Don't become obsessive.'

Nitin laughed. There was little he could hide from his wife of thirteen years. And she was correct. He had to draw the line somewhere.

'You're right.' Then, hastily, he added, 'Whatever I have by the time I go to bed tonight . . . will be the final draft. No more tweaks. No more worries.'

'Good. And remember it will go well. Anything else on the agenda?'

'Here? Nope. I don't think so. Back tomorrow night as promised.'

'I'm glad.'

'I'll see you soon then.'

Shortly before 8 pm, Nitin Phadnavis summoned his personal assistant. 'Read this,' he said, handing the woman his heavily marked printout. 'Give me a fresh copy before I go to bed, along with notes you may have. I don't want to make changes after that.'

Kiran Nagori nodded.

'Also . . . can I go for dinner like this?' Nitin stood in front of her and spread out his arms. He rotated slowly.

'Absolutely not, sir. Please don't keep asking me this every day. The answer will not change.'

'Nonsense. One day I will resign from this job because of the dress code. Give me fifteen minutes.'

Kiran bowed her head and left smiling.

Nitin stood in front of the mirror in the walk-in bathroom. He stripped down to his underwear. He looked at the reflection of his stomach.

*Still gaining weight. This job is going to kill me.*

He changed into a fresh Nehru jacket, trousers and shoes, and strode out of the door exactly on time. Prakash Rao and Kiran Nagori were already waiting. The corridor outside was deserted. The lift at the other end was wide open.

Prakash marched in first, then Nitin, and finally, Kiran. The lift slid down several floors, then stopped. When the doors opened, Nitin saw another member of his staff waiting for him. 'Please follow me, sir,' the man said. The group walked down a long corridor, took a detour through a staff exit, then navigated another long corridor before stopping before an emergency door.

Nitin waited for his staff members to get the all-clear via their concealed microphones. A few moments later, the door swung open and Nitin Phadnavis walked into a magnificent dining room. It was empty except for a single table. Alex Winchester stood next to it.

Nitin strode towards him purposefully. Kiran walked right behind and nudged him lightly. Nitin stopped. She stepped around him, stood halfway between both men, and spoke in a formal tone. 'Sir, I present to you Her Majesty's Principal Secretary of State for Foreign and Commonwealth Affairs Alex Winchester.'

Then, she turned around nimbly. 'Prime Minister Nitin Phadnavis.'

Alex leaned forward as he shook hands with Nitin. 'It is an honour to dine with you, prime minister.'

'The honour is mine, Alex. I just wish we weren't so . . . alone.'

Alex laughed politely.

Both men sat down. Nitin asked his staff to leave.

A few moments later, waiters began to appear with food and drink.

Both men ate quickly, but between courses spoke at some length. They were old friends but also, occasionally, respectful adversaries.

'Prime minister, my staff tells me that your speech tomorrow is being broadcast live on national television?' Alex asked as he sipped his coffee. Nitin was tapping the top of his cardamom and saffron crème brûlée with the back of his spoon. The image in the bathroom mirror suddenly came rushing to him. He placed the spoon down.

'Yes, Alex, I have some important things to announce.'

'I see. I look forward to this speech. I am intrigued.'

'As you should be, Alex. But I promise you it will only be good news.'

As soon as Alex finished his coffee, Kiran reappeared at the table. She had a printout in her hand. Nitin glanced at her and then at Alex.

'Alex, I must leave now. Let us catch up when you are back in Delhi? Next week?'

'Yes, prime minister. And good night.'

Both men got up. Alex stood by the table as Nitin was herded away by his staff.

Back in his room, Kiran asked Nitin for a favour. She wanted him to 'shake hands' with someone. Nitin agreed, a tinge of weariness in his voice. Ten minutes later, she returned with a gentleman in a suit. 'Sir, this is the general manager of the hotel, Mr Mandeep Ahuja. I told him that you wished to thank him for his hospitality.'

Nitin shook Mandeep's hand vigorously. 'Thank you very much, Mr Ahuja. Your arrangements so far have been excellent. Dinner was very enjoyable.'

Mandeep beamed. 'I am happy to hear that, sir. If there is anything at all the Somerset can do to make your visit more comfortable, please . . . do ask me personally.'

'I will. Thank you. I am sure we are all going to enjoy our brief stay here very much indeed,' said Nitin Phadnavis.

# 13

**Outbreak + 0**

On the morning of what was later designated as Day Zero of the Bombay Fever outbreak, several events happened at approximately the same time.

At the Somerset Hotel, Mandeep Ahuja learnt that none of the twenty-six employees who had called in sick the previous day would be coming to work. Most of them were not returning phone calls or text messages. He had already made arrangements to temporarily hire fifty wait staff.

**Outbreak + 0**

Having convinced herself that Amod Patil was probably just very ill, Rochelle Mendonca decided that she would shoot videos, file stories and tweet updates from the India Summit all by herself. Shortly before the inauguration, she sent Nabeel Karimudeen a text message asking him to check on Amod Patil.

**Outbreak + 0**

At Cusrow Baug, two crises began unfolding simultaneously. Aayush Vajpeyi was involved with both.

Aayush had spent the previous evening and most of the waking hours of Day Zero assisting a team of policemen at the Patel flat and filing a First Information Report. He asked the policemen to treat the crime scene very carefully and avoid touching the bodies. They ignored his advice.

On Day Zero, after having slept briefly in the neighbour's living room—partly to keep the rattled woman company—Aayush made four phone calls.

The first went to Daphne Dolker, his fellow SMO. She did not respond.

Next, he called the public health post in Ward A and asked to speak to one of the public health workers. He ordered the person at the other end of the line to urgently send a sampling team with test kits to Cusrow Baug. He wanted to take blood and mucus samples from all the residents and rush them to the labs in Andheri. Overnight the number of residents reporting coughs had increased. Some of the cases were deteriorating rapidly. The conventional public health system didn't really work within an SMO's purview. But Aayush knew enough people in the ward to pull rank or call for favours.

His third phone call was to Dr Ratnakar Joshi at the National Institute of Virology in Pune. Ratnakar was the lead rapid responder for outbreaks in India's western zone, which included Mumbai and Pune; an expert in tropical diseases; and one of India's leading microbe hunters. He had delivered a series of lectures on epidemics to trainee SMOs, and later, Aayush had struck up a friendship with the handsome, bookish man.

'Hello?'

'Hi, doctor. This is Aayush. I don't know if you recall—we met during the SMO training camp in Bangalore . . .'

'Oh, yes. Mr Topaz Healthcare . . .'

'Doctor, I wanted to ask you for a favour.'

Aayush explained what he had seen in the Patel flat. He told Ratnakar that the police investigators were certain that foul play was involved. One sub-inspector had suggested that perhaps the Patels had been poisoned.

'You mean, like one of those KGB things where they poke people with radioactive pointy umbrellas?'

'Doctor, I am serious. I've never seen bodies bleed like this. Or the blood congeal in this manner. I've taken some photos. Could you look at them?'

'Sure. You have my email address?'

'Yes. Also . . . and excuse me if this sounds nuts . . . but a lot of the Patels' neighbours have very bad coughs. I am not saying these things are related . . . but . . .'

Ratnakar promised to look at the photos. He also agreed to follow up on the blood and mucus tests that Aayush had ordered at Cusrow Baug.

After hanging up, Aayush emailed the pictures he had taken on his phone to Ratnakar's email address.

Aayush's final phone call was to the SMO who had sent the WhatsApp message the day before regarding the health scare in Mumbai's airport: Sati Rout.

'Sati? Sorry I couldn't respond to your message last night. You won't believe what is happening.'

'Aayush . . . can I call you back? We have a crisis here at the airport.'

'Is it the cough?'

'Yes. It is getting much worse.'

'Same story here.'

### Outbreak + 0

At the office of *The Indian Opinion*, Nabeel Karimudeen had just finished the morning meeting when he had a visitor. It was the client manager from the housekeeping agency. Convinced that he had lost the contract, the manager now came to apologise to Amod personally, and offer a 15 per cent discount for the next six months of service.

Since Amod was missing, the client manager was sent to Nabeel's room. The editor reluctantly agreed to talk to him.

'Look, I don't want to get involved with these things. Amod takes a call here. So he will get back to you in a day or two,' Nabeel said dismissively.

'Sir, please sir. I can extend that discount for another six months. Sir, please.'

'You don't understand. This is not my decision to take . . .'

At that moment, Nabeel received the text message from Rochelle.

'Give me one moment,' he told his unwelcome visitor.

Nabeel called Amod several times. Each time it went to his voicemail.

He looked at the client manager. 'Have you heard from Amod over the last day? Emails? Phone calls? Anything?'

'No. In fact, that is why I came down here. I thought he was giving me the silent treatment.'

Nabeel thought for a second.

He turned to the visitor. 'Sorry. But as you can see we have no idea where Amod is. Can you give me a few days? Don't worry about your contract. Just ask your fellows to clean properly.'

The manager thanked Nabeel profusely. He got up to leave.

'Funny thing is that some of my cleaners have also gone missing,' the client manager said as he picked up his bag, motorcycle helmet and windcheater.

'Oh?' Nabeel responded. Suddenly, he felt a knot in his stomach.

'Yes. The same guys who screwed up here. Anyway . . . I was going to terminate their services. So, in a way, I think this is a blessing in disguise.'

'I very much doubt that,' Nabeel said.

## Outbreak + 0

Back at the Somerset, Prime Minister Nitin Phadnavis spent the morning rereading his speech. He then made coffee, had breakfast, met his staff and attended the inaugural ceremony of the India Summit. He was the chief guest. Next, he retired to an antechamber to prepare for his 11 am speech.

Sharp at 11, the ballroom in the Somerset erupted in applause as Nitin Phadnavis walked in through a side door, up a few steps, and on to the stage. The ovation continued for several minutes. Eventually, he had to shout over the noise: 'Please! Please, ladies and gentlemen! Please.'

Another minute passed before the audience sat down and settled into silence.

'This is an unexpected honour. So you will forgive me if my remarks appear unprepared and incomplete.

'During the inaugural address, I had the privilege of revealing that in the last quarter the Indian economy had grown by an unprecedented 11 per cent.'

Someone in the audience shouted, '11.02 per cent!'

Everyone laughed.

'Indeed, 11.02 per cent. I now stand before you to announce that this year onwards India will become a net donor nation. I can say with some confidence that within the next thirty-six months India will reduce all incoming foreign aid to zero. Finally, and I think this is more significant, I can also now reveal that India has officially met and surpassed two of the eight Millennium Development Goals we had committed to at the UN's Millennium Summit in 2000. India is the first and, so far, only nation in the developing world to do this.'

Applause again. Nitin gestured for silence.

'Thank you. I was scheduled to return to Delhi tonight to be with my family. But my staff and many of you insisted that I stay back for the events and the special celebratory dinner tomorrow. I agreed only after the general manager of this hotel reluctantly allowed the government to foot the bill. I think my government can at least afford this much right now.'

Laughter.

'I just want to point out one thing here. These achievements are by no means of the government alone. They are testimony to the calibre of Indians everywhere and across all walks of life. If you must celebrate someone, celebrate the millions of public sector employees who help run this nation. Salute our magnificent private sector that creates jobs and wealth for our people. And thank each and every Indian who, through sincere work and generous taxes, has made this happen. I ask all of you to raise a toast to the people of India.'

A few minutes later, once the applause had died down and Nitin had descended from the stage, he pulled his personal assistant aside.

'When can I get back to Delhi?'

'Day after morning. I'll arran . . . arrange for the plane . . . s . . . soon, sir!' She slurred as she spoke.

'Are you drunk, Kiran?'

'A little bit, sir,' Kiran said, looking away in embarrassment.

'Not on beer, I hope?'

She held up a champagne flute. Nitin nodded in approval.

'Look, we have to be back first thing the day after tomorrow,' he said. 'I have to prepare for that cabinet meeting on the bloody dual-citizenship project.'

'Yes, sir. Will be done.'

Nitin looked around. Several people, among them a few ambassadors and India Summit speakers, were milling around for a quick chat. But Nitin's security guards held them back.

'Where is Prakash? I was hoping we could get him to finally have a drink.'

'Oh, he has gone to see the hotel doctor,' Kiran said. 'Suddenly developed a very bad cough.'

'Anything serious?'

'I doubt it.'

'Good. Now let me leap into this den of vipers.'

'Sir?'

'Kiran, we just told the world that we are ready to donate international aid. What do you think will happen now?'

'Best of luck, sir.'

Nitin sighed. He then turned around sharply, a crisp smile on his face, and approached the ambassador of Laos. Behind him, Alex Winchester waited his turn. Alex coughed a few times into a handkerchief.

## 14

## Ward A

Ward A in Mumbai stretches across an area of 12.5 square kilometres. It is bound by the Colaba 'military area' to the south and by Carnac Bandar Bridge to the north. Along the eastern edge, it is bordered by the dockyards. To the west is the Arabian Sea.

The ward is home to 2,10,929 residents. However, several times that population flows in and out of Ward A over the course of an average working day. The itinerants comprise office workers, domestic servants, tourists and travellers who change trains and buses.

The ward is criss-crossed by thirty-nine major roads and 135 minor ones. It is serviced by four police stations, two railway stations and two bus depots at Colaba and Backbay. There are no functioning cemeteries.

For a number of reasons, most of them to do with the district's history as a centre of power and wealth, Ward A is reasonably served by healthcare facilities. It is home to no less than seventeen private hospitals and nursing homes, five municipal dispensaries, two municipal health posts and a municipal hospital.

That, in any case, was the official estimate at the time of the outbreak. Unofficially, there were at least another two dozen nursing homes in Ward A.

And it was one of these unauthorised nursing homes that became the first healthcare facility in Mumbai to be swamped by Bombay Fever cases.

## Outbreak + 1

At 7.30 am, Nurse Jacintha John settled into the swivel chair behind the reception desk at Tripoli Hospital. She switched on her computer and printer, unlocked the cash box, and then pulled out a little book of numbered paper tokens. While the two doctors would only arrive around 9.00 am, it was not unusual for patients to drop in early to pick up a token.

Ten minutes after she had settled in, just as Jacintha was opening a packet of Horlicks biscuits for breakfast, the first patient of the day appeared. He had a very bad cough that seemed to bring up blood.

Token number two was a follow-up case. The patient had recently recovered from mild food poisoning and was back for a routine check-up.

By the time the first doctor arrived at 8.45 am, there were fourteen people in the waiting room, twelve of whom had severe coughs. This did not particularly surprise Jacintha. It was not uncommon for outbreaks of viral fever, dengue or flu to sweep through the locality.

By noon, the situation had escalated. Patients were flowing in faster than the doctors could deal with. Jacintha ran out of one token book and started another. The waiting room had twenty-five seats, but it now had around forty patients waiting. Some were standing outside the main door, in the front courtyard.

The phone on Jacintha's table rang. She picked it up. It was Dr Anil Bansal, the younger of the Bansal brothers.

'Jacintha, how many patients do we have waiting?'

'Thirty-eight, doctor.'

'How many of these have cough with blood?'

'I have to look at the register. But I think around thirty.'

'Do any of these patients know each other? Any groups?'

Jacintha looked at the crowd around her. Every few seconds, somebody wheezed.

'Let me check, doctor.'

She understood the logic guiding the doctor's question. She picked up a notebook and a pen, and stepped out from behind the table.

Suddenly, Nurse Jacintha John hesitated. She reached for a drawer and pulled out a small bottle of hand sanitiser. She slipped this into a pocket in her white uniform.

## Outbreak + 1

At the Chhatrapati Shivaji International Airport, Sati Rout was facing a similar problem. The health centre at the airport was now running at full capacity. The doctor on duty and both the nurses were grappling with a dozen cases of bloody coughs. Most of the patients were passengers, though three were airport staff.

It was just Sati's luck that she had chosen to visit the airport on Day Zero of the outbreak. Since the complex was home not only to a health centre, but also three pharmacies, Sati had hoped to make the standard Srivatsa pitch at all four locations and keep an eye on the cough epidemic she had heard about. Instead, she had been compelled to help with a mounting crisis. Overnight she had seen enough to call a meeting with the airport's chief executive officer. She had to wait till noon on Day One of the outbreak to get an appointment.

'Sorry, but there is no protocol for this kind of thing,' the airport CEO, a South African expatriate, told the SMO.

'Why not?'

'You don't understand. Airports react to external health problems. If there is an Ebola outbreak or some SARS type problem we know how to respond. But diseases don't start from here. We don't have a plan for a health crisis originating from the airport.'

'What do you mean? Diseases can start from anywhere.'

'Possibly. But I maintain: it is highly unlikely that an epidemic will erupt from the airport. We have high hygiene standards everywhere. From the air you are breathing to the food you eat in the restaurants. Everything is checked and double-checked every day. We even sanitise bathroom doors every hour, just in case a passenger doesn't wash his hands. This is one of the most sanitary buildings in Mumbai. In India.'

Sati was in no mood to waste time. 'Perhaps. But you don't see my point. You have a dozen passengers in the health centre suffering from identical symptoms. You don't exactly know what is wrong with them. You have to do something. You cannot afford to take a chance here.'

'Why don't we wait and see if something happens? Maybe it is just a cough?'

'What if it isn't? What if it is a terrible flu of some kind? Yesterday I spoke to a friend of mine who works in town. He mentioned some form of cough there. This could be related. What if Mumbai airport ends up exporting hundreds of infected passengers and creates an international incident?'

The CEO looked startled. 'But that could mean shutting down the airport . . .'

'Not right now. Maybe later. But not now.'

'What do you suggest I do?'

Sati thought for a second. 'Did you have a protocol during that Ebola thing a few years ago?'

'Yes. We had a screening system for incoming passengers.'

'What happened if someone was picked up by the screen?'

'I don't recall exactly what we used to do. I need to check.'

'Please check right away,' said Sati.

## Outbreak + 1

At the National Institute of Virology in Pune, Ratnakar Joshi looked at his smartphone as he ate his lunch. He had devoted the morning to lectures, team meetings and some video calls. He was exhausted, and the phone offered an easy diversion.

Suddenly, he came across the email from Aayush Vajpeyi with the Patel photos.

The previous evening, on Day Zero of the outbreak, Ratnakar had tried opening the high resolution images on his phone and had failed. He had then decided to download the images at home. This, he promptly forgot to do.

Over lunch he noticed that the phone had eventually downloaded the images after all. He began to flip through seven pictures.

*Good god. What the hell . . .*

Ratnakar stopped eating and looked again. This

time he paid close attention to the details of the skin and the congealed blood. He tried to look at the eyeballs, but the photos were not clear enough.

*Where have I seen this kind of bleeding before . . .*

And then he suddenly remembered.

*Can't be. Impossible. It just can't be.*

He immediately called Aayush.

'I really can't tell anything concrete from the pictures,' started Ratnakar. 'But it reminds me a lot of Marburg virus.'

Upon hearing those words, Aayush felt the ground under his feet fall away.

'Oh my god, what do we do?'

'Don't panic. This is just on the basis of a photograph. Nothing could be less scientific. I want to personally take some samples. Where are the bodies?'

'At the police mortuary. Should I tell them to isolate the bodies or something?'

'No. That will just cause panic.'

Ratnakar looked at the clock on the wall. 'Okay, listen. I will leave Pune right now and drive over there . . . should reach in another three hours or so. Will you please talk to the police and get me access?'

'Done.'

Aayush hung up and went back to helping the health worker take samples from the Cusrow Baug residents. He tried to remain calm. But mentally he was overwhelmed.

*If this is Marburg . . . fuck ho gaya boss.*

# 15

## Beta Protocol

On the evening of 21 May 1974, three days after India's first nuclear bomb test at the Pokhran Test Range in Rajasthan, Indira Gandhi had a visitor in her office.

Rameshwar Nath Kao was a striking man who had a propensity for wearing tinted spectacles. It gave him an air of mystery. Which was just as well because Kao was chief of the Research and Analysis Wing (RAW).

Founded in 1968 by Kao, RAW is India's external intelligence agency. In other words, RAW runs India's international network of spies, and R.N. Kao was the country's first spymaster.

While the existence of the agency is a matter of public record, not much is known about the people who work for it or what it actually does—which is precisely as Kao intended. Not surprisingly, startlingly little is known about Kao.

The meeting in 1974 was anything but unusual. Kao was one of the few people India's paranoid prime minister truly trusted. They met late almost every day in the prime minister's office (PMO), after she had exhausted all her other commitments.

Indira Gandhi liked to go over the day's events with Kao. She did all the talking, while he did all the listening. When she asked for advice what she really wanted was validation—and since Kao was not a yes-man, he rarely spoke unless he had anything to report.

'Do you know what they are up to? Surely they will respond?' the prime minster asked Kao.

'Yes. The Pakistanis will carry out a test at some point. They are working on it.'

'Well. I think we've made our point. Can you stop them?'

'I can't stop them. But I am making it very difficult for them.'

'Very good. So I met this gentleman from Arthur D . . .'

'Indiraji, we need to talk about something urgently.'

The prime minister frowned. She didn't like being interrupted. But then, Kao rarely interrupted her. It had to be something urgent.

*Why can't I just enjoy this moment for a few more days?*

'Go on, Rameshwar. Ruin my mood.'

Kao pulled out a file and placed it on the prime minister's table. 'Whether we like it or not, the Pakistanis will now carry out their own tests. And if they can't do that, they will acquire nuclear weapons from somewhere. Two days ago, I asked my boys to put together a set of scenarios for a possible Indo-Pak nuclear exchange. They came up with several. Twenty-three of them to be precise. I've made single page summaries of all them here.' He pushed the file across to the prime minister.

'What do you want me to do?'

'Each sheet has a list of initial targets in both countries that will be destroyed in a particular scenario. I want you to have a look at them.'

Indira Gandhi called for a cup of tea and then spent a few minutes going through each sheet. 'A lot of people will die irrespective,' she said. Indira Gandhi spoke so softly that Kao at first thought she was speaking to herself.

'That is the nature of nuclear warfare. Can you see what will happen to New Delhi in each scenario?'

She flipped through the sheets again. 'It gets attacked every single time. In each scenario.'

'Exactly, prime minister. So if Delhi is destroyed by a thermo-nuclear weapon, where will you run the country from?'

'I suppose we will activate the same wartime plan that we did in 1971?'

Indira Gandhi was referring to the Bangladesh liberation war. During that crisis, an emergency backup office for the prime minister had been established at the naval base in Visakhapatnam. The office was never used and later dismantled. But that remained the government's protocol in times of war—a swift relocation to an office somewhere in one of the naval bases in the south, far away from the border with Pakistan or China.

'That also won't work. In sixteen of the twenty-three scenarios most of our naval bases will come under attack, too.'

The prime minister smiled. Kao did not.

'You have a plan, Rameshwar. Tell me about it.'

'Prime minister, I think it is time we started considering an alternative headquarter.'

Kao's plan involved building an impenetrable complex of offices and control centres. This 'alternative headquarter' or AHQ would be fully equipped to function as an emergency seat of government the moment New Delhi confronted the threat of war or natural disaster—in short, anything that could materially imperil the stable functioning of the government. It was not, Kao pointed out, an original idea. Several countries all over the world already had fully functioning AHQs.

There were three crucial factors to be kept in mind when India pushed for her own AHQ, Kao continued.

First, it had to be built and maintained in complete secrecy. Knowledge of its existence had to be restricted to a limited operating crew. This crew would ensure that the AHQ was ready to host all critical government functions in a matter of hours, if not minutes. Not even the prime minister, Kao pointed out, could be aware of its location until such time that the AHQ had to be operationalised.

Indira Gandhi nodded grimly. 'So something like the PEOC in Washington,' she said, 'except that not even the head of state knows it exists.'

'Precisely.'

The PEOC—the Presidential Emergency Operations Center—located deep underground, beneath the East Wing of the White House, is shrouded in secrecy. But it is believed that the structure is designed to withstand a nuclear hit.

'Our idea for the AHQ differs from the PEOC in one way,' said Kao. 'It won't be located in Delhi at all.'

This was the second crucial factor in Kao's plan. It was all very well locating the PEOC under the White House. The chances of Washington being physically overrun by Russian troops were dim. Not so for New Delhi. The PMO was a day's drive from the Pakistani border and a short flight away on a Red Army bomber for the Chinese.

'The AHQ has to be located somewhere else. If it has to be a meaningful safe haven in a time of crisis.'

'I assume you've studied this, too, Rameshwar?'

'I have.' The spymaster pushed a sheet of paper across the table. It was a map of India with four marked points.

The prime minister looked at this, and the moment she did, the sheet vanished into Kao's briefcase.

'And what is the third factor?'

'A procedure for activating the AHQ.'

This, Kao explained, was the most crucial part of the programme. It was not enough to just build a world-class operations centre. All this would come to nought if the centre was used improperly.

The trick was to activate it at exactly the right moment. Open it up too soon and you blow its cover, making it vulnerable to attack. Flip the switch too late and there may not be a head of state or seat of government to save.

The prime minister understood what Kao was getting at. 'This means that nobody in the actual government should be taking that call.'

Kao nodded. 'Not anybody in the government or in the military.'

'So what do you have in mind?'

'I am working on a plan, prime minister. But I want to know what you think of it.'

Indira Gandhi sipped her tea—cold and acrid—and winced. The events of the preceding three days played on her mind. Pokhran or 'Sleeping Buddha' had made the Americans very upset. The Russians were miffed. The Chinese and Pakistanis were obviously livid. The French sent a telegram of congratulations and then, to Indira Gandhi's great displeasure, chose to withdraw it shortly afterwards.

*India will always be alone.*

'I like your plan, Rameshwar. I think you should proceed with . . . what do I call it?'

Kao looked around the PMO. 'This is the Alpha of the Indian government. All our powers emanate from here. So I have decided to call this,' he pointed to the file, 'Beta Protocol.'

'Interesting. Keep me posted?'

'I will.' Kao got up and walked towards the door.

'Rameshwar?'

He turned around.

'You didn't ask me which of the four locations I wanted for the AHQ.'

Kao smiled. 'I do not wish to burden the prime minister of India with such trivial matters.'

Then he turned and left the room.

## 16

**Outbreak + 1**

Just after 10 pm—though by then Dr Anil Bansal of Ward A's Tripoli Hospital had lost track of time—Nurse Jacintha John walked into the consultation room.

Anil was seated, his forehead on the table in front of him. He was exhausted.

'Doctor, are you okay?'

'Yes,' he said without lifting his head. 'Send the next patient in.'

'No more, sir. All finished.'

Anil sat up. 'Really?'

The nurse nodded.

'How many did we do today?'

'Eighty-six.'

'It felt like 800. Dr Arvind?'

'He finished ten minutes back. He has already gone home. Doctor, you should also return home now.'

'Yes. Finally. Give me ten minutes to clean up.'

Jacintha trotted back to her chair behind the reception desk, stretching as she walked. Never, in all her years as a nurse, had she experienced a situation quite like this. Usually the Bansals had thirty patients, a day, forty on a bad day.

She was relieved it was over.

But Jacintha was also worried. Of the eighty-six patients the two doctors had treated that day, roughly sixty had come in with coughs. The cough apart, the symptoms seemed to vary a great deal. Some spat out blood, some didn't. Some had fever, while others seemed to be developing dark skin rashes. One patient, a taxi driver, had severe stomach pain. Whatever this disease was, it wasn't one of the usual suspects.

*Must be something new. This city is always creating new ailments. Always finding fresh ways to give doctors business.*

Jacintha began to work through her daily winding-up ritual. She cleared her desk, emptied the rubbish bins, switched off all the air conditioners and double-checked the cash register. She was just about to take the cash box to Dr Anil when the main door flung open—pushed with such force that it swung all the way around and crashed into the wall.

Jacintha shoved the cash box into a drawer and pushed it shut. She reached for the glass paperweight on the table.

A young man in an autorickshaw driver's uniform staggered backwards into the waiting room, dragging another man in his arms. Just as the door swung shut again Jacintha noticed an autorickshaw waiting outside. It had been driven right over the kerb and into the courtyard.

The driver gently placed the sick man on the floor. The patient was dressed in a waiter's uniform that was soaked in sweat, blood and urine. 'I think he is dying,' said the driver. 'Please do something. *Please.*' The sick man, his eyes partly shut, coughed feebly. A thick red fluid dribbled out of his mouth. He moaned, semi-conscious.

'Dr Anil!' Jacintha screamed as she ran towards the consultation room. 'Dr Anil!'

Through the blood-soaked fabric of his shirt, the embroidered logo of the Somerset Hotel on his chest pocket barely showed.

## Outbreak + 1

It was close to 11 pm when Sati Rout finally found the time to return Aayush Vajpeyi's call. She rang up Vajpeyi from a phone in the airport manager's office.

She quickly brought him up-to-date with what had been a traumatic couple of days at the airport. It had taken several calls to finally get through to the staff that had run the old Ebola cell at the National Centre for Disease Control (NCDC) in New Delhi—even so, the information gathered remained patchy. Sati had been frustrated by two factors. First, it was hard finding all the paperwork from the 2014 Ebola crisis.

The airport's recent sale to a private equity company had wreaked havoc on the archives. Second, the airport manager, who could guide with protocol, kept being pulled away by a VIP's security guard. Someone very important had had to reschedule a private plane.

'VIP? Who? The CM?' asked Aayush.

'No idea,' said Sati. 'Could be the PM. I asked the manager. He wasn't supposed to tell.'

'Oh, damn. Hope your crisis winds down tomorrow. Otherwise, Phadnavis will only make things worse.'

'Aayush, I think it will get better.'

Aayush was surprised by his colleague's optimism. At Cusrow Baug, several patients had shown no signs of improvement. In fact, some were getting worse with blood in their mucus, skin rashes, and high fever. And now, Diane, the Patels' neighbour, had a rasping cough, too.

In the airport, on the other hand, the patients seemed to be stabilising. Some of them still had coughs, but nobody was getting materially worse. In fact, a few had been discharged from the health centre.

'But we've kept some patients in quarantine. At least until the NCDC decides to do something. What about you? Getting any help?' Sati asked.

Aayush told her about Dr Ratnakar Joshi's visit. The virologist had taken samples from the cadavers of the Patel family. He had then picked up mucus and blood samples from Cusrow Baug residents and driven back to Pune.

But Aayush left out Ratnakar's hypothesis—that the city was potentially confronting a Marburg virus epidemic. There was, he reckoned, no reason to cause alarm, least of all when so much was still conjecture.

'Maybe we are panicking for nothing,' said Aayush. 'Maybe these outbreaks aren't even related.'

Just at that moment an airport employee rushed into the airport manager's office.

'Sir . . . Rahul Bhandari . . .'

Rahul Bhandari was one of the airport staff members who had been treated for a cough and then discharged.

The employee looked around for the manager, then blurted out, 'Where's sir? We just got a call from field team. They found Rahul's body. There has been a horrible accident!'

## 17

**Justice Kashyap Commission of Inquiry**

*Reference: PS 4/PI 17/Maha/Session 4*
*File type: Raw transcript of interview, audio recording*
*Location: Provisional Lok Sabha Complex, Port Blair*
*Security clearance level: 2*
*Note: This recording features two voices*

JK: Can you explain why you didn't immediately see the connection between the crisis at the airport and Cusrow Baug? If you and Ms Rout had instantly worked this out . . .

AV: I wish we had, sir. In hindsight, it feels as though we wasted a lot of time in the beginning.

JK: Please let me finish my questions. Interruptions make for very messy recordings and transcripts.

AV: Sorry, sir.

JK: So, yes. Why didn't you instantly connect the two events?

AV: For a bit, I did think they were connected. I thought the same outbreak had hit Cusrow Baug and the airport.

JK: But then you changed your mind . . .

AV: Yes. Because the passengers at the airport started getting better. They started responding to drugs. Most of them were discharged.

JK: But at Cusrow Baug nobody was getting better?

AV: Precisely. Nobody there got better. Most of them got worse. Most of them would eventually die of the Fever.

JK: Do you think this was an opportunity missed? Could we have made the connection faster?

AV: No, we couldn't possibly have made that connection with certainty at that stage.

JK: Why not? Surely—despite the variance in the response to the drugs—two outbreaks of cough in two different parts of the same city would be related in some way?

AV: Not at all, sir. Not always. Not in a city like Mumbai. And especially not in airports. Such things can often be completely unrelated.

JK: I don't understand. Can you please explain?

AV: I will try, sir. First of all, a communicable cough can be symptomatic of a range of problems—from a simple sore throat to a chest infection to something life-threatening. You could have two entirely unrelated outbreaks of respiratory diseases in two housing colonies just a kilometre apart in Mumbai. The patients may all have similar symptoms to start with and then things will suddenly diverge afterwards.

The bigger a city is . . . the more people come and go . . . the more disease conditions there are . . . the more complicated these outbreaks become. So we have to be very careful before drawing conclusions.

JK: And you mentioned airports?

AV: Yes. Airports complicate things further. Airports, railways stations, bus terminals. These are all ideal places for vectors to propagate diseases.

JK: Can you please explain what a vector is? For the record? And can you please refrain from technical terms henceforth?

AV: Of course, sir. A vector is any agent—human or animal or insect—that carries and transmits an infectious patho . . . an infectious disease-causing microorganism.

JK: And why are airports especially difficult spaces to assess?

AV: Because they can often exaggerate the prevalence of a disease. Let me . . . let me explain that with an example, sir. During summer vacations, lots of children travel out of cities with their parents. They go to their ancestral villages or to hill stations. They often overeat. Then, when they travel back home— or reach the airport or railway station—they show signs of dysentery or allergies. So, if you work in an airport health centre during summer vacations . . . you may think there is a dysentery epidemic in the country. There isn't. You are just selectively seeing a particular type of passenger.

JK: This must make it very . . . confusing to work in an airport at the time of an outbreak.

AV: Yes. But the first job of an airport during a health crisis is containment. Keep sick people in, if there is cause to believe that the home country is witnessing an outbreak. Keep sick people out if the outbreak is in another nation.

JK: And how did Mumbai airport perform at this task during the Bombay Fever crisis?

AV: It failed on both counts, sir. It couldn't keep Hormazd Patel out. And it couldn't keep Altaf Ali or Rachel Soanes in. But we were saved by that accident at the airport. If it weren't for that . . .

JK: Yes. Rahul Bhandari's death? So when did you actually make the connections and solve the mystery surrounding his demise?

AV: A couple of days after Dr Ratnakar Joshi's death.

JK: This is the doctor who died in Pune?

AV: Yes, but not from Bombay Fever.

JK: Oh, yes. I remember now. Poor guy. So, when did you finally work out the environmental aspect of Bombay Fever's propagation?

AV: That would come even later, sir. And we didn't join the dots. That was Dr Bansal's work . . .

# 18

**Outbreak + 1**

The airport perimeter patrol jeep had turned turtle on the runway. A trail of debris extended from the point where it had bounced off the grass, crashed into a concrete pump house and tumbled on to the tarmac.

Sati and the airport manager stood by the strip of gravel that bordered the grass. Both were waiting for the emergency response team to finish its work.

Sati looked around. She realised that all the planes were stationary. 'You've shut down the airport?'

The manager nodded. 'Just when I was beginning to think your virus bullshit was over.'

'So he just passed out?'

The manager looked at the point where Rahul Bhandari had lost control of the jeep. 'I have no idea,' he said. 'Has to be. Why would he want to do something like this? It makes no sense.'

'Maybe he was trying to drive into a plane?' Sati asked.

After being discharged from the health centre, Rahul Bhandari—who worked for the private security company that patrolled the airport's borders—had immediately gone back to his job. Technically speaking, the perimeter didn't need human presence. Every inch of the fence that surrounded the Chhatrapati Shivaji International Airport was under constant surveillance through a system of cameras, sensors and a fleet of micro drones that flew in a strict formation high above the airport wall.

But nobody wanted to take a risk. Jeep patrols had been a fixture at the airport for decades, and new technology wasn't going to change that.

The patrol fleet consisted of six duty jeeps and one backup. At any given point, three jeeps would patrol the seventy-six-kilometre-long circuit. Every four hours, the drivers would bring their jeeps back to the fleet centre, just as three other jeeps would leave with fresh drivers. The returning drivers would then take an hour's break before being assigned 'standing' security jobs at the terminal.

'No chance. Each of these drivers is vetted personally by our head of security. Rahul had a spotless service record.'

Sati nodded glumly. 'Maybe you should check the drones to see if they have captured a video? Is there a camera on the jeep?'

There were three cameras on each jeep—one facing forward, one backward, and one pointing at the driver. After extricating Rahul's body, and filing a case, these cameras were to be retrieved for inspection.

Sati asked the manager if she could have a look at the camera tape pointing at the driver—just in case the crash had something to do with the cough outbreak.

The airport manager exploded. 'Look, as far as I am concerned, the cough nonsense is finished. I have other things to worry about. You've wasted enough of my time. You think Rahul coughed so hard that he drove the jeep into concrete? Please!'

'But you can't just ignore his health record. At least let's wait for the NCDC to get back to us? Let us get some test results?'

'I'm done with this! Do whatever you want. I need to figure out how to deal with the present crisis!' He pointed at the wreckage. 'This logjam of planes!' He pointed at the sky. 'And finally, I must attend to that one over there!' He pointed at a plane in a hangar a few hundred meters away. It was a twin-engine Boeing 777-300ER painted in the familiar red, yellow and white of India's national carrier. The particular plane's call sign was AI-1.

This is the call sign and flight number of any Air India aircraft that is scheduled to carry the prime minister of India.

## Outbreak + 1

'Sir? Sir!'

Nitin Phadnavis stirred in his sleep. He opened his eyes, removed his earplugs and sat up. His personal assistant stood in front of him. A single table lamp threw a weak beam of light around the room.

'What time is it, Kiran?'

'Close to midnight.'

'What is it?'

'There is a potential problem with your flight to Delhi, sir.'

Nitin swore loudly. He then apologised to his assistant. 'What happened?'

Kiran told him about the accident at the airport and the lockdown. Planes were now being diverted to other airports. For the time being, nobody was flying in or out of Mumbai. She told him that the situation was complicated by the fact that the jeep had crashed close to AI-1.

'Damn. I assume somebody has already sounded out a terror alert?'

'Yes, sir, the SPG is on alert.'

'Excellent. So what do I do now?'

'There is a process being followed, sir. First of all, the SPG and the air force have to give the all-clear. If they do, I will arrange for a jet to take you from the private airstrip in Juhu or from the naval base. For now, I think you should go back to sleep, sir. Things will be clearer in the morning.'

Nitin slipped back under the sheets.

'Also Kiran . . . any idea of the Arsenal score?'

'Sir, they lost to Bournemouth 2-1. Bielik scored.'

Nitin pulled the sheets over his head. 'Can this day get any worse!' he mumbled.

## Outbreak + 2

Around 2.30 am, Kiran and Prakash completed briefing the prime minister's entourage. They would all stay put in the hotel till they got more information. While the terror alert was being processed, they would carry on as usual. The prime minister would use his room as a makeshift office and the rest of his staff would use the hotel's business centre—which the Somerset had freed up for them.

Next, Kiran read out the prime minister's altered schedule for the next day. The cabinet meeting would go ahead without him. 'I will try to patch him through the business centre videoconferencing facility. But I will first have to make sure that it is 100 per cent secure.'

A few minutes later, as the meeting broke up, Kiran approached Prakash. He looked exhausted.

'How are you, Prakash? How is your cough?'

'Better. The hotel doctor is an insane old man. But his medicines worked. I am feeling better now.'

'Good to know. The PM was asking about you.'

He nodded in gratitude. 'Chalo, we have an SPG meeting now. I'll see you in the morning.'

# 19

**Outbreak + 1**

The waiter's name was Nelson Castellino. He was an only son born into a family from Mangalore. His father used to own a small hotel in Hampankatta, near Light House Hill. The hotel and most of the family's savings were lost in a series of terrible stock market investments by the father. Now the family got by on the money Nelson sent home each month, after working back-breaking hours in a five-star hotel.

The twenty-four-year-old man now lay dying on the floor of the waiting room in Tripoli Hospital. The driver, who had deposited him there, had fled.

'Doctor, what do I do? I don't know what to do!' Jacintha lost her nerve as she knelt on the floor next to the moaning man.

'Arrey, let me at least figure out what is happening to him.'

Dr Anil Bansal had no idea what was happening to Nelson. So, he surveyed him from head to toe, mentally cataloguing a list of all the symptoms he could read. Perhaps he could then collate everything and arrive at a plan of action.

'Jacintha, keep his mouth open and make sure he is breathing.' The nurse ran into the consulting room and came back with a packet of disposable gloves and a tongue depressor. She pulled on the gloves, tilted the man's head backwards, and then used the depressor to keep his airways clear.

As Anil studied the patient, he made a mental note of his situation: Nelson had fever. He seemed to be floating in and out of consciousness. His pupils had dilated. His nostrils were blocked, rimmed with dried blood and mucus.

The thick fluid streaming out of the side of his mouth smelt putrid, like bile, and seemed to be a mix of mucus and blood with other fluids. It was unusually thick and lumpy. Nelson's tongue was swollen and tender to touch—as though it were filled with liquid.

All over Nelson's skin were dark patches. Anil pushed at these with his fingers. He recoiled. They weren't bruises. He could feel the patches move beneath his fingertips. 'This is blood.'

Anil ripped open the waiter's rancid-smelling shirt. He gasped. The man's entire chest was covered with a mosaic of the same blood-filled patches.

*All this blood? Where is it coming from?*

Nelson's heart rate and pulse were low. And his breathing was highly irregular. He wheezed loudly as he inhaled and exhaled. His fingers were splayed out and locked stiff, a phenomenon that would later be known as 'jazz hands'—a dreaded sign of Bombay Fever's onset.

Anil inspected the patient's fingernails. He rubbed the nail on the right index finger. The nail lifted off the nail bed completely. There was no resistance at all. And the patient didn't even seem to notice. Anil, stunned, carefully placed the nail on the floor next to him, and resumed his check.

Nelson's trousers were soaked with blood, urine and faeces. There was an unusual amount of blood streaming out from his rectum. It had drained down the legs of his pants, past his ankles and into his shoes, where it congealed.

Dr Anil Bansal was baffled. So, he decided to do whatever he could to stabilise the patient and then call for help.

Jacintha got up and ran to the storeroom to pick up some fluid bottles and an IV kit.

Suddenly, Nelson went utterly quiet. He stopped breathing. He arched his back and his eyes opened wide. He seemed to be looking straight at the doctor. Just as he appeared to be going into a convulsion, Nelson vomited. A thick jet of blood and mucus, teeming with millions of particles of Bombay Fever bacteria, exploded on to Dr Anil's face, clothes and upper body. The doctor, shocked at the force of the flow, tumbled backwards. He then heard a faint popping sound.

Nelson bled out through his bowels.

Jacintha had gone away for less than a minute. By the time she returned, it was all over. Nelson Castellino was dead.

Dr Anil Bansal cowered in fear. It was as if the patient had melted into a puddle.

*

*Bombay Fever was a new destructive force that the body's immune system had never seen before. All attempts at a counter-strike—such as the production of mucus—had failed miserably. The immune system raised the body's temperature with a fever. This worked with many common pathogens—elevated temperatures are known to annihilate invaders. Somehow, this only helped make Bombay Fever more lethal. The bacteria began to pump even more toxins into the body.*

*Provoked by this growing threat, the immune system, now panicking, began to respond with greater force. It unleashed stronger cells to attack not just the toxins but the bacteria itself. Even as the host's body began to chip away at the colonies of invading bacteria in the mucus membranes, it began to destroy small groups of Bombay Fever cells. As they disintegrated, the remnants of these cells washed into the blood stream. Usually, these remnants are harmless and flushed out of the system, or are incorporated into* the complex network of biochemical reactions that go on endlessly within the body.

Unfortunately, this was not true in the case of Bombay Fever. One of its remnants—researchers later discovered it came from the bacteria's cell wall—was a piece of protein with a remarkable capacity to latch on to anything it came by—bacteria in the gut, stomach lining, the liver or cells that belonged to the host. Once the protein found a foothold, it tucked itself in.

Next, it convinced the host's immune system that any cell with these protein markers was a copy of the invasive microorganism. The hapless patient's body, pouring everything it had into the desperate battle against Bombay Fever, turned against itself. Cell by cell, organ by organ, the host's immune system destroyed the very body it was meant to protect.

Amod, Hormazd, Siloo, Nelson had all been killed by their own immune systems.

It was finally here. Bombay Fever. The drug-resistant super-disease that public health experts in India had been dreading for decades.

Now, they had to deal with its full, brutal, relentless force.

# 20

**Outbreak + 2**

Altaf Ali and Rachel Soanes had been on the last two flights to leave Mumbai airport before the lockdown. Both had boarded with bad coughs. Bacteria, numbering in the millions, had carved out colonies in their respiratory systems well before they had arrived at the airport. In both cases, the pathogens were preparing for the second stage of the disease—a barrage of toxins.

Altaf did not pay any attention to his cough. He was a heavy smoker who routinely puffed through two dozen cigarettes every day. Whatever was left of his health had been battered by three decades of working for a construction company in the Persian Gulf. This had left him with a permanent tan, deeply creased skin, a prematurely bald head, and a disproportionately large paunch. There wasn't a day when Altaf didn't wake up with aches, dizziness or nausea. To his mind, a cough, even a bad one, hardly counted.

Altaf's prime concern was getting back to work as soon as possible.

When he had joined the Gulf company in the late 1980s, it had been one of the largest public works contractors in the region. They built air bases in Saudi Arabia, installed radar stations in the United Arab Emirates, and maintained oil platforms off the coast of Qatar. At first, Altaf had been hired as a mason on daily wages—the lowest paying job in the entire organisation. He was a part of an army of Indians, Pakistanis and Bangladeshis who built rooms, offices and barracks in the middle of the desert. The turnover within these teams was very high—more than two-thirds of the men didn't make it past the first six months.

Altaf ploughed through his first two years without taking a single day off. By then he had lost his sense of smell and taste. But he was promoted to foreman with a proper monthly salary, some health benefits and a month's annual leave that could be forfeited in lieu of pay.

It was another three years before Altaf asked for leave—this, for his mother's funeral. She was buried on a Monday and he was back at the labour camp in Ruwais that Saturday. In his thirty years in the company, Altaf had only claimed eleven months of leave.

In more recent years, his organisation had fallen on hard times. The decline began with the Gulf War of 1991. Altaf's company was owned by a family of minor Kuwaiti nobles most of whom were killed or had gone missing after the Iraqi invasion. Much of the company's wealth—cash deposits, gold reserves, share certificates, land deeds—vanished along with them. While the organisation was revived after the war, it never regained its past glory. Thousands of workers lost their jobs.

Altaf Ali kept his. He was by no means indispensable. Yet nobody had the heart to fire one of the company's most loyal employees. The experience, however, left Altaf even more paranoid about his job. He took even fewer vacations, worked even harder and complained even less about the low pay or the brutal conditions.

A while after his flight took off, a stewardess approached Altaf Ali. She waited for him to stop coughing for a moment. 'Sir, we have free rows towards the back. Perhaps you could go there and lie down?'

'No. Here I am okay.'

'Please, sir. You can lie down and get some sleep.'

'I am fine, Miss.'

The stewardess left frowning. A few minutes later, another member of the cabin crew, a man, approached Altaf. This time he spoke to the passenger in Hindi.

'Sir, your cough is making a woman here quite upset. She has small children. If you move to the back, you will get some privacy. Sir, please?'

Altaf got up from his seat, mumbling.

When he was woken up shortly before landing, Altaf sat up and buckled himself in. He was famished, but it was too late to call for some food. And then he noticed the seat back-pocket in front of him. Someone had left him a couple of cheese sandwiches and a bottle of water. Altaf ate quickly, without looking up even once.

As he sat back, somewhat content, he suddenly realised something. His chest still felt heavy, and he could feel sticky patches of mucus along the back of his throat. But he was no longer coughing.

He was pleased.

*Thank god. Finally this horrible cough has healed.*

In reality, Altaf Ali had not healed at all.

## Outbreak + 2

Rachel Soanes had not healed either. Like Altaf, Rachel had also fallen asleep on her Air India flight. Like him, when she was jolted awake before landing, she found that she felt much better than she had in Mumbai. Her cough hadn't gone away entirely, but it was under control. Rachel was pleased about what this meant for her job prospects.

Rachel had been out of work for over two years now. After spending her entire adult career working for the British Broadcasting Corporation, she had been one of several to get laid off during the BBC's cost-cutting spree. Most of the other fired editors immediately found work at one of the private channels in the UK, and the remainder snuck back into the BBC as contract staff or temporary project coordinators.

All of them, that is, except Rachel Soanes. Unfortunately for her, there were no takers in the UK for her set of highly specialised skills. Rachel was an expert in what she liked to call 'public affairs programming'. In other words, she was one of the few journalists in the world who specialised in broadcasting legislative, town hall and city council meetings, and sessions in the houses of parliament. She knew where to place the cameras, how to design graphics, how to package debates, how to highlight the speakers, and how to splice hours and hours of boring footage into sexy little bulletins.

It was important work. It was noble work.

It was also deeply unprofitable and extremely unpopular. Rachel's pet project, the BBC Parliament channel and online video portal, had abysmal ratings. For years, the accountants at the BBC had begged for the entire 'public affairs programming' division to be axed. Successive bosses had held firm in their resolve to keep Rachel's project alive.

Until two years ago.

An unemployed Rachel had flown all over Europe trying to sell her bouquet of skills. But there had been no takers. It wasn't that people didn't care for politics or politicians. They did. But they didn't care enough to actually listen to the debates or watch policies being fashioned or implemented. Anybody could point a camera at a prime minister. And apparently that was the only skill most broadcasters in Europe demanded.

The plane landed smoothly and Rachel let out a sigh of relief. She waited impatiently as it taxied to a stop. When the seatbelt indicator lights went off, a few passengers got up. Most would remain on board for the onward flight to New York. Rachel, along with a handful of others, would disembark.

Two hours later, Rachel Soanes checked into her four-star hotel. The cough was resurfacing—she coughed on her way to the lift, up to the seventh floor, and kept wheezing till she brewed herself a cup of tea. As she sipped on the warm, soothing liquid, Rachel went over her notes from the meetings back in Mumbai. She sighed. It had all been very depressing. Nothing fruitful had emerged. The Indian private sector had little enthusiasm for her non-fiction programming skills.

She looked out of the window at the skyline of this new city that was nothing like Mumbai.

*Maybe this is where I will finally find some work.*

She ordered a small plate of sushi for dinner, and then went to sleep.

In the morning, feeling better, she went to the

lobby, where she was met by the head of a local television channel.

'Good morning Rachel!' he said. 'Instead of talking at the office, why don't we go straight to the location? Why waste time?'

Rachel agreed immediately.

*This is great. He sounds as if I already have the job.*

The large, round building was only ten minutes away by road. But it took another hour for Rachel and the man to get their access badges, run their bags through several X-ray machines, fill in forms, walk through full-body scanners, and finally make it into the cavernous chamber. It was a hot, humid day and the heat seemed to aggravate Rachel's cough. By the time the man walked into the central hall, she was coughing into her handkerchief every few minutes. The silk fabric began to show a sprinkling of droplets of blood.

'And this,' Ranveer Singhvi, editor of Secretariat TV, said looking at the huge space around them, 'this is the Lok Sabha. India's lower house of parliament. The most important room in this country.'

Rachel coughed hard.

# 21

**Outbreak + 3**

Around 11 am, on the third day of the outbreak, Dr Ratnakar Joshi finally decided to take time off. He'd spent the last forty-eight hours travelling between cities and working in his laboratory at the National Institute of Virology. Except for a brief hour-long nap the previous afternoon, he'd toiled non-stop. He was exhausted and hungry. Despite the air conditioning that blasted through the room, his clothes reeked of sweat. Joshi got up from his chair, walked through a series of decontamination chambers and then into a brightly lit hallway outside the lab.

As he approached the staff canteen, the bug-hunter pulled out the mobile phone from his pocket. He called Aayush Vajpeyi.

'I was wrong, Aayush,' Ratnakar said with a sigh of relief.

'So it isn't Marburg?'

'Definitely not. It doesn't match any of the pathogen profiles I have for Marburg.'

'Oh, thank god,' said Aayush.

Both men went quiet for a few seconds. They knew

what this implied. Aayush was the first to break the silence.

'So, what is it then, doctor? I've never seen anything like this. But you're the . . . expert.'

Ratnakar silently mulled over the past forty-eight hours. It had not been entirely fruitless.

'It is definitely bacterial. And it seems to multiply quickly. The samples were full of it. Also it seems to deteriorate slowly once it . . . err . . . kills the host. But it does deteriorate. Which is encouraging, I suppose.'

'Okay.' Aayush was disappointed. 'That is not a lot to go on . . .'

'I know, I know. I need more time.'

Aayush went on to explain the events at the airport and how Sati had called up the Ebola team.

'This Sati . . . is she sensible?'

'Absolutely. She isn't an MBBS. But she shone during her training period.'

'Good. What is the scene at the airport at this moment?'

'Nothing like Cusrow Baug.'

'How bad is it there?'

Aayush exhaled with such force that Ratnakar was startled by the static on his phone.

The SMO, who had visited Cusrow Baug five days in a row, explained the peculiar situation there. In total, he said, thirty-eight residents had shown similar symptoms: bad coughs, mild fever and lethargy. A few had stomach aches and diarrhoea. Aayush had recommended some standard medication to ease the cough and antipyretics to fight the fever.

'Did this work?' Ratnakar asked as he waited for his idli, sambar and coffee. The food arrived cold and he sent it back to be microwaved. He then listened carefully to Aayush.

The patients at Cusrow Baug responded to the drugs in one of two ways. Most of them, after consuming the medicines, went back to their flats, slept and woke up feeling better.

Seven patients, however, began to crash. Their coughs and fevers got worse and their mucus and stools carried blood. Two residents, both retired corporate executives, developed dark rashes all over their chests.

'What kind of rashes?'

'I only had a few moments to examine them before the ambulance picked them up. But it looked . . . like they were bleeding in patches under the skin.'

'Didn't the Patels . . .'

'Yeah. Their bodies showed similar symptoms.'

Ratnakar sipped his coffee grimly. He couldn't be completely certain. But it looked like whatever had killed the Patels was now beginning to take some of the other residents down as well. Ratnakar used a napkin to dab the coffee sticking to his moustache.

'And nothing like this is happening at the airport?'

'No. Nothing. Everyone there has stabilised. A couple of passengers have been kept under observation at the health centre. The NCDC guys should have a look at them.'

'They haven't reached yet?'

*Typical*, Ratnakar thought to himself.

'Mumbai airport has been shut down, doctor. You didn't know?'

Aayush explained that Rahul Bhandari had been treated for a cough and had gone back to work—only to crash his patrol jeep. Ratnakar asked Aayush to repeat the story but didn't allow him to finish it.

'Aayush, where are you right now?'

'I am at Opera House. I've called an emergency meeting of all SMOs and health officers . . .'

'You have to do something for me right now . . . before your meeting,' Ratnakar said, already jogging towards the main exit of the building. 'I have to look at Bhandari's body ASAP. I am leaving Pune right now. Ensure I can examine it.'

There was something mysterious about the way this bacteria operated. Dr Ratnakar Joshi could not quite put his finger on it. But as he approached his WagonR and switched on the ignition, he felt like he'd found a piece of the puzzle.

## Outbreak + 1

'What the hell do you mean—get rid of the body?' Dr Anil Bansal clutched on to his iPhone and

screamed at his brother. In his other hand, he held
a large bottle with two litres of strong bleach. He
poured the solution on to the floor of the waiting area,
where Nelson's disintegrating body had lain an hour
ago. Jacintha rubbed the bleach into the bloodstained
linoleum with a mop.

Earlier, Jacintha had helped Anil wrap the body in
clean sheets. The doctor had then rolled the corpse in
the plastic tarpaulin they used to cover the courtyard
during the monsoon rains. They placed the body on
the floor in Arvind Bansal's consulting room, turned
on the air conditioner to full blast, and locked the
door.

By the time they were done, Jacintha's clothes
were soaked with Nelson's blood. She begged to be
allowed to leave. She couldn't wait to have a shower.
But the doctor politely refused. He asked her to stay
back just long enough to help him clean the clinic.

'Look, you know we don't have a licence,' Anil
said. 'If somebody comes looking for that boy and
sees the blood on the floor . . .' She agreed reluctantly.
'Afterwards you can go back home and wash yourself
clean. You will be fine.'

But Anil was secretly afraid of something else.
What had killed the waiter? What disease slayed in
this manner? And how much of it was in the patient's
blood? If the disease spread through blood or fluids,
Bansal was certain that the nurse and he had little

chance of surviving. But at least he could prevent an outbreak within his clinic.

'Okay, look. I will call you when I am done cleaning.' He hung up on his brother, slipped the phone into his pocket, placed the bottle of bleach on the reception desk, and picked up another mop.

'What did Dr Arvind say?' Jacintha asked.

'He wants us to close the clinic today, get rid of the body, and pretend as if nothing happened.'

Jacintha stopped mopping and looked at him. 'How do you get rid of a body, sir?'

Anil shrugged. But he had a feeling that his brother knew exactly how.

A little later, Jacintha wrapped herself in a spare sheet, got into an autorickshaw and made her way home.

## Outbreak + 2

Jacintha reached her residence. There was a power failure. In darkness, she bathed, changed into a nightdress, and then packed her soiled uniform into a garbage bag. She left this bag outside her front door. Jacintha then went to sleep.

Two hours later, the nurse, still asleep, began to cough.

If anyone had slipped a thermometer into her mouth, they would have seen that she had a mild fever. Further, if anyone had lifted her nightdress and looked at the small of her back, they would have spotted a tiny rash, no bigger than a thumbnail.

At around 5 am, a reed-thin man, dressed in a faded khaki shirt and trousers, picked the garbage bag outside her door. He flung it into a barrow, where it fell on top of several other bags of refuse from other flats.

Later, as he loaded the refuse into a small truck, he paused when he picked up Jacintha's bag.

*Old clothes? Anything useful?*

He ripped the bag open and pulled out her uniform with one hand. He instantly gagged. He flung it back into the truck, quickly rubbed his hands down the front of his shirt, and then walked down the road. He had sixteen more buildings to visit.

## 22

**Outbreak + 1**

Dr Anil Bansal watched through the glass door as the nurse got into an autorickshaw. He suddenly felt an inexplicable sense of loss.

He stood silently for a few minutes. Then he went to the storeroom, pulled on a clean white overcoat, switched off the lights, and carefully stepped out of the clinic's front door. He didn't want passers-by to see his blood-splattered clothes. Once outside, Anil reached for a long metal rod, slotted it into a hole by the side of the front door, and rolled the pale blue shutter, until it was three-fourths of the way down. Then he slipped under, went back into the clinic, and turned on the lights.

Something had to be done. Unlike his brother Arvind Bansal, Anil had no intention of getting rid of the body and pretending that the whole thing had never happened.

As far as he knew, there was a strange outbreak sweeping through the local community. And then, there was the poor waiter. It had been a horrible death. He had undergone an ordeal Anil had never seen or even heard of before.

The doctor wasn't sure if the events of the day were related. Could a cough, even an infectious one, kill people like that?

He had to do something. Tell someone. But how?

The Bansal brothers used to work together at a 'luxury' hospital in Bandra. They were both general practitioners with an uncanny ability to fleece rich hypochondriacs. They were good-looking, educated, had a soothing tone of voice and, above all, exuded a certain aura of efficient harmlessness. Rich, bored Mumbaikars, especially the parents of celebrities, were ardent fans of the Bansals' brand of benign medical care.

They made a lot of money for both the hospital and themselves. Until, that is, the elder of the Bansals, Arvind, had an affair with one of his patients. This caught the attention of the paparazzi for two reasons. First, this patient was a critically acclaimed film star who had been happily married for many years with two teenage children. Second, the patient was a forty-six-year-old man.

The scandal was quickly hushed up at great cost to both the hospital and the brothers. The Bansals instantly became unemployable at any of the city's major health centres. They were eventually forced to open Tripoli Hospital illegally. This meant that a significant portion of the clinic's meagre monthly earnings went towards ensuring that nobody asked too many questions.

The threat of criminal charges and financial ruin loomed large over the brothers. But they went about their jobs diligently and remained hopeful. Every decade or so, city authorities regularised hundreds of unlicensed facilities. Usually this cost nothing more than a steep fine and a registration fee. As long as the brothers didn't get into trouble in the interim, and developed a quiet reputation for competence, they hoped that Tripoli, too, would be legalised.

Patients bleeding on the floor of a waiting room and dying didn't help Tripoli's cause. Arvind had a point.

Anil entered his consulting room, shut the door behind him, and slumped into a chair. The space was so cold his teeth began to chatter. He carefully considered the options before him. And then he called his brother.

'Just shut up and listen to me,' he said before Arvind could speak. 'I have a plan.'

Anil wanted to call up a friend who worked at a 'legitimate' hospital nearby and was aware of the Tripoli's situation. She would handle things discreetly. He would inform her about the cough outbreak, then lock up Tripoli, and leave a sign outside asking patients to go to his friend's hospital instead.

'Why Anil? Just shut the hospital, no? Say there is some family emergency . . .'

'You don't get it, Arvind.'

'Help me get it.'

'What if the cough is some kind of outbreak? What if there is some horrible disease that killed that boy?'

Anil couldn't alert the authorities himself. But his friend could. If a sufficient number of the Bansals' patients landed up at her hospital with coughs, she had reason to report the outbreak herself. If nobody turned up, there was no crisis and they could all just forget about it.

'What about the body?' Arvind asked.

'I will take him to her hospital and . . .' Anil suddenly felt a sharp obstruction in his throat. He coughed.

At the other end, Arvind felt his heart stop.

'Anil . . .' Arvind said, his voice breaking.

'Please, Arvind. Calm down. The room is bloody cold, that's all. So . . . I will take him in my car to her hospital and she can tell them I saw him lying on the road near my flat. I tried helping him. But he died. Her hospital will call the police, register a case, tell the relatives and all that.'

'Boss . . . what if they think you killed him?'

'You can't kill someone like that. You can't. You have to see his body.'

'No, thanks. Okay, fine. Once you call your friend and get rid of the body, will you come home? Please?'

'I'll be there in an hour or so. Let me call her now.'

Anil disconnected the call and coughed a few times. Each time his throat felt a little worse.

*Fuck.*

He looked at the corpse, shook his head vigorously as if to clear his thoughts, and dialled his physician-friend who worked at the legitimate hospital. When she took the call, he could hear chaos in the background.

'Anil, I have to call you back. We are swamped here.'

Just before she hung up Anil heard the distinct sound of several people coughing.

*What the fuck is going on?*

Anil changed his plan. The body would have to wait in his brother's room for the time being. There was no point in taking the corpse to her hospital right now, given how preoccupied his friend seemed. Instead, he would simply shut his clinic, leave a sign redirecting all patients, and go home. There he could sit and worry properly about his cough.

Anil shut his room's door. He walked into the waiting area. He switched off all the lights except one, double-checked the drawers, cast his eyes over the faint outline of blood on the floor and then picked up a large bunch of keys from the reception desk.

For the second time in the day, someone stumbled into the clinic just as Tripoli was being shut.

There was a loud noise as the shutter was pushed back up.

'Hello, *koi hai*?'

'Yes . . .'

A man slipped his head through the shutter.

'My children have a very bad cough. They have been coughing since last night. Can you please look at them?'

Anil switched the lights back on and ushered the man in. He was followed by three small children—a boy and two girls. Flecks of blood rimmed their small mouths.

# 23

**Outbreak + 3**

Nitin Phadnavis was perilously close to losing his composure and poise.

The prime minister of India had a reputation for equanimity. Nothing—not even the worst political scandal or the most embarrassing foreign relations faux pas—seemed to affect him. He handled it all with his signature smile, optimism and ability to 'stick to a plan' no matter what. After a particularly bruising Security Council debate, the Greek prime minister had famously referred to Nitin as the 'Smiling Assassin'.

It hadn't been a complimentary quip. But Nitin liked the nickname and it stuck.

Inside the Somerset's business centre there wasn't a hint of a smile on the prime minister's face. Thanks to his grounded plane and the terror alert still in force, the prime minister had already spent longer at the hotel than he had desired. Sure, he had been kept busy—his staff had managed to hook up a videoconference facility with his cabinet in New Delhi—but Nitin knew his physical presence in the capital would have made all the difference. It would have turned a frustrating, inconclusive session into a decisive one.

When his team informed him that there was still no clarity on his return to New Delhi, the prime minister exploded. 'What the hell! I don't understand!' He sat behind a desk inside the largest conference room available. It had previously been set aside as a press room for the Summit. Nobody objected, publicly at least, when it was allotted to a stranded prime minister.

At the other end of the table, Nitin's staff stood looking glum. Most of them were worn out. Some seemed ill. One or two occasionally coughed.

'Surely there has to be a way to get me to Delhi. I am the prime minister of India, damn it! Find me a plane, a helicopter . . . *something* . . .'

Nitin scanned the people in front of him. 'Where is Kiran?'

'Sir . . . she has gone to see the doctor,' Prakash said. 'She has a bad cough and fever.'

'Didn't you have the same problem?'

'Yes, sir. Same thing. Cough and fever. But I've been well since. She should also be fine soon.'

'Good.'

Nitin leaned back and stretched his arms up in the air. 'So what do I do now? Does anybody have a plan? Anything?'

An SPG officer spoke up. 'Sir, I am currently

talking to the city police commissioner. The all-clear to take you to the private airstrip in Juhu—whether it is by copter or car—is still pending.'

'What is holding up the all-clear?'

'The same. Security, sir. As long as the terror alert is still active we can't take the risk of driving you down the roads or flying you to the airbase. Hopefully, we should get the all-clear in the next few hours. Everyone is working on this, sir. Getting you home is our top priority.'

Nitin smiled grimly. He picked up his phone and flicked through his calendar. 'Okay. Can someone please put me on a call with the home minister? I want the home secretary to be present.'

One of his staff members nodded eagerly and rushed out of the room.

'Also, I need someone to do me a couple of favours. Kiran normally takes on this kind of thing . . .'

Prakash raised his hand.

'Prakash, can you bring me my coffee maker and my coffee? And ask the hotel to send me a kettle please?'

Prakash pulled a small notebook and pen out of his suit pocket.

'Also can you get me a couple of white full-sleeve shirts in size 44? From one of the shops here?'

Prakash looked up. 'Umm . . . which brand, sir?'

'What brands do they have?'

'Zegna and Brioni, sir,' somebody said.

Nitin reached for his wallet and pulled out a card. He handed it to Prakash. 'Buy two from Zegna and put this on my personal credit card please.'

Nitin then thanked his staff and asked them all to get back to whatever work they could get done under the circumstances. The chamber quickly emptied until only Prakash was left.

'Sir, may I have a word in private with you please?'

'I hope so. I trust this room isn't bugged,' Nitin joked.

'It isn't. I checked,' Prakash said without humour.

'What is it?' Nitin asked, as he went through the papers on his desk.

'Sir, there is one other problem in addition to traffic and security.'

Nitin looked up.

'Sir . . . we've received reports . . . very early reports . . . of some kind of disease outbreak.'

Before Prakash could say another word, there was a knock at the door. Nitin looked at his trusted SPG team leader. The latter nodded.

'Come in!'

It was the staffer who had rushed to arrange the call with the home minister. 'Sir, the call has to be postponed.'

'Why?'

'The home minister is sick, sir. He has been admitted to AIIMS, sir.'

The SPG team leader turned around and spoke to the staffer: 'Does he have a cough and fever with some rashes?'

The staffer had a look of utter astonishment on his face. 'Yes . . . but how did . . .'

Nitin Phadnavis felt the bottom of his stomach lurch.

'Sir, may I step outside for a second? With this gentleman?' Prakash Rao asked. 'I need to make some calls . . .'

Phadnavis nodded his head absent-mindedly, his thoughts elsewhere.

Prakash stepped out, and asked the staffer to repeat everything he knew about the ailing home minister. A deep furrow ran across his forehead. He thanked the staffer, waited for him to leave, and then walked down the corridor till he found a quiet corner by the lift lobby. Prakash leaned against the wall behind him, took a deep breath, closed his eyes, and thought.

Prakash Rao was arguably one of the world's best-trained fighting men. But training men and women to fight was easy. Rao himself had seen scrawny little boys and girls turn into ruthless, remorseless fighting machines prepared to take a bullet if the job demanded it. They had been drilled—and drilled for weeks and months—until their minds and bodies had come to be driven by just two instincts—an instinct to kill and an instinct to die.

But training a man to think was an entirely different matter. A few weeks before his appointment as head of the prime minister's personal security team had been formally announced, Prakash Rao had been ushered into a meeting with the head of RAW and the outgoing SPG team leader.

As he stood in the corridor of the Somerset Hotel, Rao replayed in his mind that strange consultation and the secret training sessions that had taken place afterwards. It had all been quite extraordinary—but also elegant and beautiful.

Prakash knew, of course, that he had only been shown a tiny glimpse of the mystery that was Beta Protocol. Indeed he had been explicitly told not to worry about what the specifics entailed. That was not the point of his involvement. Prakash Rao's job was strictly to assess risk—to figure out when things got bad enough.

A suspected terror attack on the prime minister's plane. A mysterious illness that seemed to have struck Delhi and Mumbai—even, quite possibly, the very hotel the prime minister was staying in. Rao had seen enough.

Prakash pulled out his phone. He dialled a number that immediately routed him to a recording machine. He waited for the beep, then said: 'This is Prakash Rao. Please call me back.' He put his phone away. The job was done, Prakash thought to himself.

The number Prakash had called was registered in the name of a call centre company called Nuance 24/7. This company did not exist. As soon as Prakash left his message, a computer server automatically picked it up and matched it against a database of half a dozen voices. Once a match was established, the server—through Prakash's phone—established a connection with a tiny health monitor embedded in his right arm just above the elbow. The monitor instantly sent back a packet of health data. The computer scanned this data and looked for a range of markers. When all markers were deemed normal, the server sent prerecorded messages to three human beings and a computer server.

The server then erased the message, shut itself down, and went to sleep.

Prakash Rao had just initiated Beta Protocol.

## Outbreak + 2

As usual, Altaf had done everything by the rules. He kept his seatbelt fastened till the lights went off. He got up from his seat only after the plane came to a complete stop. He thanked a cabin crew member by the door as he disembarked. On stepping on to the air bridge, he walked briskly, his head bowed, his mind already intent on getting back to work.

*Wonder if they've finished installing all the toilets . . .*

Altaf followed the signs to the immigration check, and dutifully stood in queue for 'Category L Work Visas'. It was the longest of all the lines in the large, cold, well-lit hall, and the one that moved the slowest. But Altaf didn't mind—it was standard practice at this airport to herd all the labourers, masons, plumbers, carpenters, painters and other low-wage workers through a separate, more rigorous immigration check.

In the past, workers like Altaf hadn't even been allowed inside the main arrivals terminal. Instead they were sent to a separate 'Labourer Visa' section where they had to spend hours in appalling conditions, waiting to be let into the country. Anyone who complained had their visa cancelled on the spot. Many troublemakers were bundled into a plane back home.

Now, things had improved considerably—perhaps because the Western media had suddenly 'discovered' the condition of migrant workers in the Persian Gulf. Not only did this cause the closure of the 'Labourer Visa' section, but it also led to the visa category getting renamed—Category L was far more refined. Workers, while still having to deal with long queues, no longer had to spend hours cooped up inside a sweltering, concrete box.

'As-Salaam-Alaikum,' Altaf greeted the uniformed man inside the glass cubicle. He slipped his passport through a rectangular slit in the glass. The immigration officer nodded as he collected it. He glanced at Altaf and then at the photo in the passport. He swiped the travel document through an e-reader machine.

'Which company?' the man asked in Arabic.

'Bin Ali Group. Construction Division,' Altaf replied in fluent but thickly accented Arabic.

'Where is your visa?'

'Page 24.'

'Where is your work permit?'

Altaf slipped the plastic work permit card through the glass slit. The officer placed the card on a reader. He glanced at the computer screen in front of him and frowned.

'Is there a problem, sir?' Altaf asked.

The immigration officer typed frantically. 'Did they terminate you?'

'What . . . I was on leave, sir. I have worked for Bin Ali for thirty years.'

'But your work permit is invalid.'

Altaf had been holding back a cough. But the shock of the immigration officer's comment got the better of him. He exploded into a coughing fit. He was now also running a mild fever.

'Your work permit was cancelled three days ago,' the officer continued.

'But that is impossible . . .'

'It is true. You have to go back to India.'

'But . . .'

'Please come with me.'

The officer got up and stepped out of the cubicle. Behind Altaf the other passengers began to grumble.

'*Yaar, nakli passport ho kya?*' somebody asked. 'Fake passport?'

Ten minutes later, Altaf found himself inside a familiar room. He hadn't been inside this squat, grey building for years. But it hadn't changed one bit. The walls and ceilings were still bare. There was no hint of air conditioning and the entire room—the erstwhile 'Labourer Visa' section—stank of sweat, rotting food and fuel. It was crammed with 'labourers' in various stages of being processed. Along one long side, there were a dozen or so rooms. Every few minutes a policeman came out of one of these rooms and mangled a passenger's name.

'Krishnan Kutty!'

'Kalluparambil Jose!'

'Felix Fernando!'

In one corner, a small group of passengers sat on the floor inside a fenced-off area. A policeman stood watching them. They were due for immediate deportation.

'Please wait here,' the officer told Altaf.

'Where, sir?'

'Anywhere. Sit on the floor. Just wait. Someone will call your name.' He then turned to leave, but Altaf ran up to him.

'Please, sir. I have worked in this country for so long. No problem. No passport problem, no visa problem, no drinking problem. Nothing, sir. Please help me. Please don't deport me. Thirty years, sir.'

The officer stopped. Altaf coughed so hard that a gob of mucus flew from his mouth and splattered on to the floor.

'Are you okay? What is wrong with you?' the officer asked, recoiling.

'Just a cough.'

Taking pity on the obviously ill passenger, the officer asked Altaf to wait. He went away into one of the rooms and then returned a few minutes later.

'Okay, you go to that phone. Call your HR manager or passport officer at Bin Ali. Tell him about the work permit problem. Then ask him to call this number. If he can clarify matters with my colleague, we will call you and let you go. No problem. Okay?'

Altaf thanked the officer profusely and ran to join the long line in front of the telephone booth. An hour-and-a-half later he got his turn with the phone.

All his calls went unanswered—whether these were to Bin Ali's HR department or passport and visa section. He then tried calling the company's main telephone number and received an automatic message in Arabic: 'This number is no longer active.'

Altaf didn't know what to do. This had never happened before. Even when they had fired all those other employees and shut down sundry divisions, they ensured that they always renewed his work permit and Category L visa. Surely this was all a misunderstanding.

Altaf decided to wait for a few hours and try again. This meant finding a little corner in the room seething with humanity, waiting, then going back to the telephone queue.

## Outbreak + 3

It was Altaf's fourth attempt at getting through to the Bin Ali offices—when he found himself behind a Filipino man. The Filipino, when it was his turn, spoke in rapid Tagalog.

Altaf remained hopeful. But now he also felt very ill. The fever raged, his cough was worse, and his stomach was beginning to ache very badly.

The Filipino man's call was brief. He left looking pleased and smiled at Altaf as he ran towards one of the rooms.

Altaf tried his long list of numbers. None worked. So he dialled home. He wasn't sure if the free phone could make international calls, but when his wife answered, Altaf smiled. He spoke briefly without mentioning the problem with his work visa. He promised to call her again over the weekend.

Altaf walked away from the phone, and scanned the room, seeking a few inches of space. He found a corner by the wall, near the deportees' cell. He sat down and pulled out a thin blanket from his handbag.

He spread it across the floor, then sat down, leaning against the wall.

Altaf coughed and coughed, but none of the other passengers seemed to care. The fever, meanwhile, was beginning to make his eyes heavy and the back of his neck ache. His fingers were growing stiff, the knuckles ached when he bent them.

Altaf briefly considered asking one of the policemen for help. But then he decided against it. He opened his bag, took out a couple of Crocin tablets, and swallowed them dry. He settled against the wall once more and chose to wait for a couple of hours before making another call to the Bin Ali offices.

As he ran his palms over the back of his neck, Altaf suddenly felt a lump under his right ear. It felt like a large, flat boil. Like some fluid had bubbled up under his skin. But even as his mind began to worry over this new development, his eyes began to droop. Altaf was exhausted. He fell asleep.

Nine hours later, one of the security staff noticed that there was some kind of thick liquid oozing out of the man sleeping on the floor next to the deportees' cell. When they stirred the blanket they noticed that Altaf Ali, now long dead, was bleeding slowly. His skin was covered with a mosaic of rashes and his fingernails seemed to fall out at the slightest touch.

As the medical crew came to pick up his body, 300 Category L workers watched with little interest.

All of them kept waiting for their names to be called out.

## 24

**Outbreak + 3**

It was around 10 pm when Ratnakar Joshi obtained samples from Rahul Bhandari's remains.

It had taken him several hours to work his way through a maze of bureaucracy and get the approvals required. Given that the terror alert was still in force and Rahul Bhandari was being investigated, Ratnakar found access to the remains much harder to secure than ever before. The Patels had died in their homes. Bhandari, at least theoretically, may have been trying to drive a jeep into AI-1.

It had also taken Ratnakar longer than ever to collect samples. The doctor had driven down from Pune with a sophisticated sample storage system. Conscious of the fact that the bacteria deteriorated once the host died, Joshi wanted to slow this process down as much as possible with one of his latest acquisitions.

The MultiSampler was based on a simple idea—that it is difficult to estimate the ideal conditions for storing pathogens. Some pathogens prefer warm environments while others prefer cooler conditions.

Some microbes stabilise in acidic environments while others prefer alkaline surroundings. Yet others liked a narrow combination of all these factors.

The MultiSampler took some of the guesswork out of the investigative process. All Ratnakar had to do was insert a vial of blood or a tissue sample into a machine the size of a laser printer. The machine instantly atomised the sample, divided it into forty equally sized sub-samples, and then injected each into forty tiny vials. These vials were then stored inside various chambers in the machine and maintained at forty slightly different combinations of temperature, acidity and other factors.

Expectedly, the majority of these samples would prove to be worthless. This is why the MultiSampler always retained four 'baseline' samples—one in distilled water at room temperature; one in a 'body temperature equivalent environment'; one, frozen; and one that remained in its original form at room temperature.

But every once in a while the MultiSampler threw up a surprise—it discovered a unique environment that seemed to stabilise the sample or even encourage growth. For bug-hunters like Ratnakar Joshi this could often save hours and even days when it came to fighting a disease.

Ratnakar had been lucky. As soon as Rahul Bhandari's body had been removed from the wreckage, it had been placed within the airport in a cold storage facility that was usually used to stow coffins in transit. This helped slow the deterioration. As Ratnakar injected a sample from Rahul Bhandari's remains into the MultiSampler, he reminded himself—in the worst case scenario, he had 'baseline' samples to work on. On the other hand, if even one of the forty environmental iterations returned a positive result . . .

Ratnakar shook his head. That was just wishful thinking. Yes, MultiSamplers were powerful, useful machines. But over the last twelve months, ever since they had been deployed at research facilities all over the world, Ratnakar didn't know of a single incident where they actually returned a statistically significant 'positive' at the first attempt.

'So, this is the MultiSampler,' Sati Rout said as Ratnakar watched the large touchscreen in front of the device. 'It doesn't seem very sophisticated. In fact . . . it looks like a . . .'

'A laser printer, right?' Ratnakar spoke without looking away from the screen.

'Exactly!' Sati said, grinning.

'That is what everybody says. It looks exactly like one of those old Brother DCP-1512 printers. It is a little bit heavier though. And much, much more expensive.'

'How much?'

'You won't believe this . . . but over two crore . . .'

'Seriously?' Sati walked over and ran her fingers over the machine. 'Is it worth it?'

'Kind of,' Ratnakar murmured. He went on to tell Sati that the machine could potentially save substantial amounts of time when new outbreaks had to be identified. But, he admitted, there was a knack to using it properly. And that knack lay in choosing the right mix of vial environments.

'You mean forty vials aren't enough?' Sati asked.

'Of course not. There are thousands and thousands of possible environments the machine can generate. You could run the same sample through fifty settings . . . even two thousand different environments, without getting a single positive. And mind you, each setting can, at times, take up to twenty-four hours to complete processing.'

Suddenly there was a flash of comprehension on Sati's face. 'Ah! So you run it once, check the results, eliminate some conditions, carefully choose a new set of forty conditions, run it a second time . . .'

'And you do that over and over again till you get a result,' Ratnakar completed Sati's sentence. 'It is like a video game.'

Sati nodded thoughtfully and said, 'And eventually the machine will win.'

Ratnakar shrugged. 'Not always. This game can end in different ways.'

'Like?'

'You could run out of samples. Or you could simply run out of time. And everybody dies.'

## Outbreak + 3

'Can you please turn up the volume on the TV?' somebody said.

'One second!' Mohan Thomas shouted as he got up from behind the cash register and stepped around the ice cream freezer. He then walked to the flat-screen TV perched on the back wall of Expressway Cool Bar. Mohan reached up and held a button down till the television channel was loud enough to be heard over the incessant din of the twenty-four-hour restaurant and the intermittent rumbling of the traffic on the highway outside.

'*Aur upar karna!* Louder.'

Thomas sighed and increased the volume again.

He briefly glanced at the screen, half expecting to see a cricket match. But he looked away when he noticed that the TV was tuned to a news channel. Mohan ambled back to the cash register, and resumed his watch over the restaurant, customers and staff. Every few minutes a large group of travellers pushed the door open and walked in. A gust of hot, dusty air followed them, before the door swung shut again, and the air conditioner expelled the brief spike in temperature.

When Mohan Thomas first started work at the

Expressway Cool Bar, back in 2002, it had been one of the more upmarket eateries on this stretch of the Mumbai-Pune Expressway—with air conditioning, waiters in uniform, clean toilets, female wait staff— and a killer Pune-style vada pav that soon became known simply as the 'ECB'.

Since then, Mohan's fortunes had diminished. Dozens of hotels and restaurants had opened up along the Expressway stretch, squeezing margins and siphoning off customers. First the female wait staff went, and then the clean toilets. Only the waters in uniform and the air conditioning remained.

Many travellers still stopped over for his famous 'ECB', but they usually parked outside and sent their drivers to pick up packets. The good money no longer sought out Expressway Cool Bar.

On TV, a news anchor spoke to Janani Ganesh.

'Ms Ganesh, at this point do we know how many people have died from this disease? How many are suffering? What do we know at this stage? Is Mumbai under threat? What are the authorities doing?'

Janani seemed surprised at the speed with which the questions were flung at her. 'Anita, what we know at *The Indian Opinion* is this. Over the last forty-eight hours, dozens of patients all over South Mumbai have approached hospitals and clinics with bad coughs, mild fever and a strange rash. We do not know how many. But at *The Indian Opinion*, we think that the number is between 300 and 400 so far. And this is only increasing.'

'And you are saying that it started in Cusrow Baug? And that people have died? Our viewers need to know what is going on. Please tell us . . . why are the authorities trying to hide this?'

'It is too soon to say this, Anita. I can personally confirm that there is a major outbreak of some kind in Cusrow Baug. I can also confirm that a family of two has been found dead in the locality. As far as I know, the authorities are responding to this in their usual way. There is nothing to suggest that they are trying to hide this.'

'Thank you, Janani. If the authorities are not trying to hide an epidemic, why have they not responded to our request for inputs? I would like to tell viewers that we have repeatedly asked the state minister of health and the Mumbai health department for a response. They have asked for more time. You can decide what you want to make of their reluctance.'

Mohan Thomas sat up in his chair.

'Janani, in your explosive blog post today you also wrote that one of your own staff members may have died of this plague . . .'

Mohan Thomas winced at the mention of the plague.

'It is not a blog, it is an online news website. Yes, it is true that one of our staff members was found dead at his residence. We believe he had a very bad cough before his untimely demise. But, Anita, we don't know what this disease is. So it may be best not to give it a name before we hear from the authorities . . .'

The anchor looked at the TV screen and said, 'If the authorities are listening . . . why are you doing this to the people of Mumbai? This mystery plague . . . it is already killing people. Do you care? After a commercial break, we will continue speaking to Janani Ganesh here.'

There was a blast of music followed by a graphic—a giant syringe—that split the screen in two. Zooming in were the words: 'New Plague in Mumbai?' Below, in smaller type: 'How Many Will Die This Time?'

In Expressway Cool Bar, on the outskirts of Pune, Mohan Thomas felt a flame of rage rise up again inside him.

## Outbreak + 3

At the office of the Srivatsa programme near Opera House, Aayush Vajpeyi watched Janani Ganesh on the screen in utter shock.

Sati Rout and Ratnakar Joshi were still in the mortuary at Mumbai airport when the report was aired. They would learn of Janani's TV appearance long after the broadcast.

### Outbreak + 3

Inside the business centre at the Somerset Hotel, the prime minister of India missed the live broadcast. But he was shown a recorded clip of the bulletin a few minutes later. He knew he had to act promptly.

### Outbreak + 3

In New Delhi, Rachel Soanes missed the bulletin entirely. She was busy doing her research—grasping the ins and outs of the Indian political system—despite her bad cough and mild fever.

### Outbreak + 3

In the newsroom of *The Indian Opinion*, Nabeel Karimudeen couldn't believe what he was seeing on TV.

'I told her so many times,' he muttered to himself. 'I told her . . . we should have waited. I told her . . .'

# 25

**Outbreak + 3**

Oblivious to Janani's appearance on the TV channel
and the chaos that now ensued, Ratnakar Joshi
calmly went about his work—as always, quickly
but assuredly. He tapped the touchscreen of his
MultiSampler a few times until the machine's
embedded software displayed a single-screen
summary of its operating parameters.

Sati peered at the screen over his shoulder.

'As you can see,' Ratnakar said, 'the machine is
powered by a high density, high redundancy hydrogen
fuel cell.' He was working to a tight schedule, but
Ratnakar enjoyed showing off his gadget to this
bright, young medical officer.

'Fuel cell . . .?' Sati asked hesitantly.

'It is the same technology that Toyota uses in
those Mirai cars. Just much more compact, much
more powerful, and much more expensive. And
bloody heavy.'

'How long can it run?'

'Depends on how many vials you are processing.
On a full load of forty vials, like now, it will probably
last between twenty-four and thirty-six hours.'

'And after that?'

'The software kicks in. It is pretty smart, you know. When the power bank is down to around six hours, the MultiSampler quickly analyses all the vials and automatically determines which ones show signs of growth.'

Ratnakar explained that the results of this quick analysis were stored on the on-board solid-state memory drives. Then, when the power bank dropped to three hours, the software automatically began to discard inferior samples, and redirect the power to focus on high potential vials.

'From that point onwards, the machine begins to reassess the situation every thirty minutes. It will keep discarding vials till it is left with just the best five environments and the four baseline samples. When the power is down to one hour, the software will switch to ultra-low power mode. It will record a final summary of all results until that point, route every last electron of current to the tiny baseline frozen sample, and then shut itself down.'

Sati looked at the MultiSampler in wonder. 'And what happens after that?'

Ratnakar shrugged. 'The whole thing will just die. If you don't insert fresh cells soon enough, the only thing you will have are those quick analysis results. Which is better than nothing, but not by much.'

Sati nodded solemnly.

'Okay. Now enough of the lecture, Sati. Help me carry this to my car.'

Both struggled with the weight of the machine, but eventually managed to gently place it inside the boot of Ratnakar's car. The virologist strapped the MultiSampler into place with a couple of wide nylon restraining bands, and then placed several rolled-up cloth sheets around it.

'Done,' Ratnakar stretched his arms above his head. He yawned and walked towards the driver's seat. 'Chalo, I will now . . .'

'One second, doctor,' Sati said as her mobile phone began to vibrate. She glanced at the screen.

'Hello Aayush, I was just helping doct . . .'

Sati stopped mid-sentence. Ratnakar noticed her face turn pale. He stood by the driver's side door, waiting for the call to end.

'Okay,' Sati said after a few minutes. 'Right away. I will bring Dr Ratnakar as well. He has a MultiSampler with him. Sure. Oh no. Okay. Bye.'

'What happened?' Ratnakar asked.

'Doctor, change of plans. It's all a mess.'

## Outbreak + 3

Sati had cause to worry. She had just heard that the NCDC was on its way. Ratnakar Joshi and a tight-knit group of SMOs would have to liaise with the incoming team as soon as it reached.

The NCDC was bound by World Health Organization regulations when it came to responding to outbreak alerts, and its Emergency Response Procedures or ERPs were a double-edged sword.

Yes, ERPs helped nations respond to emergencies optimally and uniformly. The procedures reduced panic and mitigated the chance of premature government misaction. They also helped keep the global community informed, so nobody was caught unawares when an outbreak jumped international borders.

On the other hand, the moment ERPs were initiated, premature headlines became par for the course. These blaring breaking news stories inevitably led to domestic panic and international travel sanctions.

Not surprisingly, some governments—not wishing to jump the gun—waited far too long to raise the alarm. Sati remembered how administrations in West Africa had tried to secretly contain the 2014 Ebola outbreak and delay invoking ERPs. Precious time was lost and thousands of patients died by the time the World Health Organization got involved.

## Outbreak + 3

Within minutes of Janani's appearance on the special news bulletin, Sophie Perramond's telephone started ringing continuously. At first the World Financial

Forum's press officer had no idea why so many delegates wanted to immediately cancel their sessions and check out of the hotel. There were events and panel discussions still scheduled for the final day.

The first thought that popped into Sophie's mind was that there had been some kind of terror attack or military coup. Perhaps something had happened in China? That had always been Sophie's nightmare scenario—to have a Chinese government collapse during a WFF event.

At around 11.30 pm, she switched on her TV and began to flip through the news channels. CNN. Nothing. BBC. Nothing. Al Jazeera vaguely mentioned a growing health crisis in India's financial capital on a scrolling marquee, but nothing else.

She turned to the Indian news channels. They were running non-stop with news of a mystery outbreak.

There was no question about what Sophie had to do next. The Summit was off. She had to get out of Mumbai as soon as she could.

Just then there was a knock. It was the general manager of the hotel, Mandeep Ahuja. He looked forlorn. He had a bad cough and his eyes had sunk into his head. Sophie instantly retreated into her room. She backed into the armchair farthest away from Mandeep and sat down.

'There is chaos downstairs,' the general manager said. 'Everybody is checking out. Chaos. I have no taxis, no cars . . .'

'I know, Mandeep. I think we should not stop them. Under the circumstances.'

'Yes, but Sophie, you don't understand,' Mandeep said. He coughed. 'The airport is closed. There are no flights out of Mumbai. Where will they all go?'

'Mandeep . . . do you mind stepping outside . . .'

'Pardon . . .'

'Please step outside. Please. Your cough . . .'

'This is nothing, Sophie. I have bronchitis. Have always had it. Since childhood.'

'Sure. But please. I am requesting you.'

'Okay. I will go to my office and call you then.'

A few minutes later her landline rang.

'Since the airport is closed . . .' Sophie started as soon as she picked up the phone, 'how can I get out of Mumbai?'

'I . . .' Mandeep thought for a few moments. 'The best way . . . is to drive to Pune and take a flight from there. The Pune airport is still open. But if you must leave, leave now. Before all the tickets get sold out.'

'Can you find me a taxi? Anything that will take me to Pune?'

'But what about the Summit?'

'Forget about the Summit, Mandeep. Somebody else can take care of it. The Summit is finished. We can settle things later. Right now I need something that will take me to Pune. Anything, Mandeep. Please.'

'Let me figure this out. I will call you back.'

Forty minutes later—during which time Sophie spent every second frantically packing—Mandeep called again.

'I have a jeep ready downstairs. We use it to carry staff to outdoor catering events. It will take you when you are ready . . .'

'I am ready now.'

As Mandeep watched the white Maruti Gypsy drive out of the service exit of the hotel, he coughed hard a few times. Under his shirt he felt uncommonly warm. He touched the back of his right palm to his forehead. He had fever.

*When will I ever grow out of this childhood bronchitis?*

He turned around, walked back into the hotel, and then to the lobby.

## Outbreak + 3

Unlike all the other people in the Somerset Hotel, the prime minister's entourage wasn't panicking. Or at least it seemed that way.

Soon after stories of the mystery disease hit the news channels, Nitin Phadnavis summoned a meeting of his entire staff. Everyone attended—except for his personal assistant who was still very ill. No one else in the team, for the moment at least, presented worrying symptoms. Nitin thanked them for not instantly fleeing like everyone else. He then asked them to work out of the hotel for another twenty-four hours—after which, irrespective of the terror alert status, he would make arrangements to fly them to the capital.

Nitin then attended an emergency cabinet meeting in Delhi via video. It started poorly. Half the members were missing. At least four of them, including the still ailing home minister, were undergoing medical check-ups. His minister for health and family welfare was present and had come prepared. She quickly presented an outline of the government's ERP for disease outbreaks. The NCDC team was on its way to Mumbai, she said, and would coordinate with the state health department and a rapid response team at the National Institute of Virology in Pune.

'How will the NCDC team get here?' Nitin asked.

'I am not aware of the details. But I believe they are flying down to the airstrip in Juhu. It is part of the ERP. They always assume that the main airport is a hot zone.'

Nitin thought for a moment. 'I have a call with the director of the NCDC. I'd like you to join me, of course.'

Everyone hung up except for the health minister.

A few minutes later, the director of the NCDC appeared on a large screen in front of Nitin.

'First off, I will fly back to Delhi in your plane once it lands in Juhu. I'll send the plane back—don't worry. Now . . . how bad is the situation?' the prime minister asked without wasting time.

The director of the NCDC was caught off guard by the directness of the question: 'Umm . . . we know very little right now. I just spoke to a Dr Ratnakar Joshi who is in Mumbai.' He then summarised the events of the preceding days.

'Why didn't we raise the alarm before? Why did we have to wait for that stupid channel?'

'Because there is a procedure for this, sir. We cannot raise an alarm unless we know what this disease is.'

Nitin Phadnavis slapped the table with the palms of both hands. The director looked startled.

'I am sorry,' said the prime minister. 'That was not directed at you. I was just expressing my frustration.' Nitin sipped a glass of water. 'Look, I am not a medical professional. I have no idea how severe this disease is. Or even if there is genuine cause for alarm. I trust all of you will do your jobs. This is top priority. We have to start responding to people.'

The director briefed Nitin regarding the next steps in the government's response to the crisis.

After the call, Nitin called the head of his SPG team, Prakash Rao. 'I'm tired of waiting. I don't know if you've heard—I've informed the NCDC that I will fly back to Delhi in their plane once it lands. I want you to make the necessary arrangements for my transport to the airstrip, alert or no alert!'

'I don't think that will be possible, sir.'

'What do you mean?'

Prakash walked over to the door, looked around, then closed it. He approached the prime minister's desk and placed a file on the table in front of him.

'Sir, are you aware of something called Beta Protocol?'

# 26

## Outbreak + 4

The Boeing Business Jet carrying the team from the NCDC landed at the private airstrip in Juhu at 1.35 am. As instructed by air traffic controllers, the plane taxied off the runway and parked inside a low, unmarked hangar at the western end of the strip. The team rushed out of the plane and was bundled into a pair of idling cars. These immediately left for the old Planning Commission building at Opera House.

This was a deviation from standard operating procedures. Usually, as a first step, emergency NCDC teams coordinated with state and district officials at the offices of the state health ministry. This allowed the NCDC experts to gently but speedily assume full control of ERPs in a manner that was politically sensitive.

State governments didn't like seeing Delhi assume control of any health emergency—at least not before the state had a shot at taking charge. After all, if an outbreak spun out of control, local politicians—and not the NCDC—faced the serious risk of national and international humiliation.

But ever since the plague outbreak in Surat in 1994, the central government had refused to loosen its grip over ERPs. States could continue to collect, generate and analyse health data, run testing centres and maintain disease information services, but at the first hint of a serious outbreak, central specialists, usually from the NCDC, had to assume charge of the response.

It had been Ratnakar Joshi's idea to conduct the first meeting at the Srivatsa office. His rationale was simple: this was no time for political pleasantries. Hospitals in Mumbai were choking with coughing patients and news channels were reporting wildly inaccurate rumours about the 'new plague'. Only an urgent, convincing and visible response from the centre would curtail mass hysteria.

'At any given moment, these SMO guys know the health situation better than anybody else. Even the state government,' Ratnakar told the NCDC team. 'Right now I think they know more about this outbreak than any other entity. They have data, contacts . . . we should be talking to them first.'

The NCDC team agreed.

As the cars with the NCDC team sped away, a small group of men surrounded the Boeing Business Jet and established a security perimeter. Prakash Rao boarded the plane, walked up to the cockpit and flashed his badge.

The flying crew looked at him curiously. 'What is this regarding?' the pilot asked.

'You are aware that the prime minister will accompany you to New Delhi?'

'Yes. We have been informed. Are you here for a security check?'

'No. I am here to tell you that your flight plans have been changed.'

## Outbreak + 4

After parking the car, the family walked into Pune's Jamuna Mall and took the elevator to the food court on the fourth floor. At noon, on a working day, the food court was deserted.

The young man asked his parents to sit at a vacant table and then went with his wife to buy lunch. 'Sanjay! Ritika!' the old woman called as she got up and went after them. They stopped and turned around. 'Don't buy anything unhealthy for Papa,' she said when she caught up with the couple. 'He will say yes to everything, especially Chinese. You know how he is. Can you get him soup? Something hot and spicy? For his cough?'

Fifteen minutes later, Sanjay and Ritika returned with two veggie burgers, a portion of roast chicken with French fries, and hot-and-sour chicken soup for Papa. They ate slowly, allowing the old man to slurp his soup between coughing fits.

'You should see a doctor, Papa,' Ritika said.

The old man harrumphed at the suggestion. 'It is nothing. I always get coughs when the climate changes. It will go away in two or three days.'

Afterwards, the family got up and went for a walk around the mall. They stopped at several windows, but didn't enter any of the stores.

'Look, Sanjay,' Ritika said after an hour, pulling him aside. 'Your father looks exhausted. Before he asks to go home . . . let us buy it, na?'

Sanjay nodded and winked at her. Over the next few minutes, he slowly nudged his parents in the direction of a large electronics store on the first floor of the mall. He ushered them inside, and then towards a display of tablet computers. He picked one up and handed it to his father. The old man beamed as he pushed at some of the icons.

'Does it have Candy Crush?' he asked. They all laughed.

'You can install whatever you like after . . .'

The old man exploded into a coughing fit. When he stopped, there was a fine spray of mucus on the tablet screen.

'Excuse me!' A salesman rushed towards the man and grabbed the device from his hands. 'What have you done?' he continued in Marathi as he watched the screen in disgust.

The store manager, who was watching the news

on a flat-screen television, ran towards them. 'Don't touch that!' he screamed. He picked up a plastic bag from behind the counter, and held it in front of the salesman. The salesman looked at the bag in confusion. 'Put it inside. The tablet.' The salesman dropped it into the bag. 'Now, please go, wash your hands. Immediately.'

Then the manager turned towards the old couple. 'Sir . . . madam, excuse me but have you come from Mumbai?'

Ritika intervened. 'My husband's parents live in Mumbai. They came for . . .'

'Please don't mind, madam, but all of you have to leave the store. Immediately.'

'What do you . . .'

The old man coughed harder. The manager recoiled. 'Get out! Get out!'

'Excuse me, Mr . . .' Ritika stepped forward, coming between her father-in-law and the store manager.

'Throw that man out of the store before he spreads that plague!' the manager screamed at the security guard. 'Don't you people watch the news!'

Customers, who until then had been silent onlookers, immediately scrambled out of the store. Many of them ran with their mouths covered.

The security guard grabbed the old man by his arm and pulled him towards the exit. Sanjay ran after him. A scuffle began, until all three tumbled out of the store and on to the parapet outside. As Sanjay and the security guard began to push and shove each other, the old man leaned against the railing overlooking the ground floor atrium. He began to heave up gobs of mucus. His wife rushed to his side and slowly led him to the escalator. Just as they were about to step on, Sanjay and the security guard, still scuffling, pushed the old couple. The man and woman tumbled over, crashing into the metal steps and the side panelling.

The bodies jerked down the escalator and hit the ground floor.

For a moment nothing happened. Then a trail of blood began to trickle out of the bodies.

Somebody who was standing on the first floor and looking down shouted, 'That man has the plague! Don't touch him. Don't touch him! Run.'

Dozens of customers bolted away.

## Outbreak + 4

In the morning, the preliminary meeting at the Srivatsa office went according to plan.

First on the agenda was to duplicate the standard World Health Organization outbreak response team line-up—an epidemiologist, a microbiologist, a general practitioner and a nurse. Ratnakar would function as the team leader and microbiologist. Two NCDC team members would take on the roles of an epidemiologist and a general practitioner. That left the nurse.

'Why don't I help out for the time being?' Aayush offered.

'Are you sure? There is a risk involved. Also, this isn't really a doctor's work,' one of the NCDC experts said.

'No problem, sir. And, in any case, the rapid response team is going to start at Cusrow Baug. I can help.'

'Ratnakar? You are okay with this?'

'It is an excellent idea. In any case, I was hoping to have Aayush help us as much as possible.' Ratnakar flashed a thumbs up at the SMO.

The next item on the agenda was a communique for immediate release to the press. Someone from the NCDC printed out a template.

Ratnakar got up from his chair. 'Guys, you don't need me for this. I'll drive to Pune as soon as possible. It will take me a couple of hours to put together equipment for the rapid response team. No point in wasting time. And I need to plug in the MultiSampler.'

Everyone agreed. Ratnakar walked out of the door, sweat dripping from his forehead, and jogged down the stairs.

An hour later, the NCDC came up with a draft communique that the Maharashtra state health department approved. All that was needed now was for someone senior in the hierarchy to take ownership of the document and sign off against it. A joint secretary in the health department was despatched to the chief minister's house with a freshly printed copy.

Then, the team broke up into groups.

One team called the health minister in Delhi for a briefing.

A second group, largely comprising health officers and SMOs, began to work on a field communication plan. This team had to contact every single hospital, clinic and pharmacy in the city; collect data on the outbreak, possible symptoms, drug responses and signs of successful diagnoses; urge hospitals to respond without panic—for nothing spooked the public more than doctors in a state of alarm; and finally, ask pharmacies to keep an eye on sales—especially of powerful antibiotics.

A third cohort prepared to set up an emergency helpline number. This was not for the public—that would come later. This number would be given out to doctors, health workers and other officials working in the field.

A fourth and final team was assigned the task of tracking public response. What were people saying on TV channels? On social media? The idea was to mitigate outbreaks of panic. With no meeting rooms left at the Srivatsa office, this team placed a line of tables in the hallway outside. A series of laptops and tablets were arranged on this table, each playing a different TV channel. This was meant to be a stopgap arrangement. Either the outbreak would come under control or, if it didn't, the Press Information Bureau in Delhi would set up a special cell.

Within a few minutes, a tremendous barrage of noise from the TV channels began to echo around the entire floor. Instantly someone walked down the row of tables and turned down the volume across all the channels.

Unfortunately, none of the devices was tuned into a nondescript Marathi language news channel: Puneri365. If anyone at the Srivatsa office had switched it on, they would have seen rolling headlines about unrest in Pune. The channel showed an enraged young man wielding a cricket bat. 'We will not let them bring that disease into Pune,' he said. 'If you are in Mumbai, stay there! Don't come here.' He then turned away. Moments later, another camera showed a small group of men rolling boulders across the highway outside Expressway Cool Bar.

At that exact moment, Ratnakar Joshi, who had just dined at a twenty-four-hour outlet of McDonald's, got into his car, and drove on to the Mumbai-Pune Expressway.

# 27

**Outbreak + 4**

Mohan Thomas could still remember every aspect of that day in minute detail.

He had arrived at the airport in Mumbai four hours ahead of his flight. Mohan was dressed in a new denim shirt, the sleeves rolled up, and a new pair of khaki pants. His shoes were also new, and so were the watch on his wrist and the thin gold chain he wore around his neck. The chain was a component of his wardrobe that Mohan was least fond of. But his father had insisted. 'It will make them think that you come from a nice family,' he had said. 'They will respect you. Otherwise they will think you are from some desperate, poor home that can't make ends meet.'

Which was exactly the kind of family Mohan belonged to. Poor and desperate. His father ran a small shoe store in Coimbatore, at Cross Cut Road. It never really made any money. For most of Mohan's childhood the household survived by periodically selling off small parcels of unused farmland around the family home near Palakkad. This caused Mohan's father great embarrassment. For, the land had belonged to the family for at least five generations.

The beleaguered old man pinned his hopes on his only son. No expense was spared for Mohan's education.

When Mohan announced that he wished to become not an engineer, or a doctor or even a chartered accountant, but a chef, his father was secretly heartbroken.

Mohan enrolled at an expensive school of catering and food technology. He studied hard and graduated with fine credentials. But for some reason he was cursed with bad luck when it came to jobs. His first stint as a trainee chef ended prematurely after the restaurant in Ooty was forcibly closed due to licensing violations. Mohan then began work at a four-star hotel in Bengaluru that was meticulous about everything except paying employees on time. Disillusioned by mainstream employers, Mohan joined a large manufacturing company in Hosur as a corporate chef. He was prepared for the worst, but this surprisingly proved to be a very fulfilling job. He enjoyed coming up with interesting menus for the many international delegations that frequented the company. He was paid well and regularly sent a part of his salary back home to Coimbatore.

Just when things seemed to be settling down in his professional life, Mohan faced another crisis. His chief executive officer was fired by the parent company in Germany for accounting irregularities.

Several other terminations followed before a new German CEO was flown down to take control. One of his first decisions was to slash overhead expenses. Out went the entire catering and hospitality department, and Mohan Thomas along with it.

Seven months of unemployment followed—seven months that crushed Mohan's spirit and plunged the family into suffocating gloom. There were no parcels of land left to sell. And the shoe store continued to flounder.

And then, one day, Mohan got a call from his old CEO at the factory in Hosur. He had chanced upon a job for Mohan.

'Where are you going?' asked the customs officer at Mumbai airport.

'Muscat,' Mohan said cheerfully.

'Show me your papers.'

Mohan handed over a sheaf of documents.

'You are joining a cruise company?'

'Yes. I am a chef.'

'Very good. Best of luck, jee. When you become rich and famous don't forget small people like us.'

Both men laughed.

Sometime later, Mohan sat in a chair outside his boarding gate, nursing a cup of milky tea in his hands. The gate would not open for another ninety minutes. Mohan had plenty of time to kill. He sat back in his chair and began to wonder what life on a cruise ship would be like. He would board an empty ship at Muscat and spend some weeks preparing. Then the vessel would take on passengers in Hong Kong and embark on a three-month cruise. Mohan would fly back to Muscat thereafter, rest, recuperate, and board his next cruise ship a week later.

'Excuse me? Passengers to Muscat?' A short, stocky man in an airline blazer stood next to the departure gate. He asked the passengers to gather around him. 'Anybody who does not understand English? No? Good. There is a problem with this flight.'

Mohan inched towards the front to hear the man better.

'As some of you may know, this morning there were news reports of a plague outbreak in Surat. We have received information that several countries may soon announce travel restrictions to and from India. As a precaution, our airline has cancelled all flights from India for the time being.'

The crowds exploded in anger.

'Please! Please listen to me first before you lose your temper. We will refund the full cost of your tickets immediately. Also we will pay you another 15 per cent extra. You can use that to immediately book another flight. Alternatively, we can give you a voucher that you can use with our airlines when travel restrictions to Muscat are lifted. You can have the money or the voucher.'

A part of the crowd went quiet, mulling over the offer. Others, including Mohan, clamoured for clarifications. When would they start flying from India again? What if the other airlines also stopped flights? Could the airline transfer them to other flights right away?

The man in the blazer had nothing to offer besides cash or vouchers. As the irritated crowd melted away, Mohan sidled up to the airline staffer. 'Sir, this plague is in Surat. Why are they stopping flights from Bombay?'

The airline representative shrugged his shoulders. 'I think they are afraid that people will travel from Surat to Bombay with the plague. And then some idiot will board a flight and take it to New York.'

'But . . . they should just stop people from leaving Surat, no? Isn't that common sense?'

The man shrugged again. 'I don't know all that. If you want my advice, take the voucher. In two or three weeks, when travel restrictions are lifted, prices will be very high. Use it then.' He walked away, fending off other customers.

As it turned out, the staffer was right. Travel restrictions were lifted in a few weeks, flights from India resumed, and ticket prices exploded. Mohan Thomas had a voucher, but he didn't have any reason to use it. By then the job on the boat had gone to somebody else. The cruise company wasn't prepared to wait indefinitely for a chef.

While this turn of events hurt Mohan Thomas deeply, it crushed his parents. His father fell ill with blood pressure problems, and died in his sleep a few weeks later. His mother became a shell; she withdrew into herself. Mohan sold the shoe store, deposited the proceeds in his mother's bank account, and left her at her widowed brother's house. Then he moved away. He sent money to his mother every month, sometimes spoke to her on the phone, but he never returned.

He didn't want to be reminded of his choices or their implications.

A series of part-time jobs in Mumbai and Pune followed. Then came Expressway Cool Bar. He joined just when the owners were hoping to spruce up the place and make it family-friendly. Not only did Mohan transform the restaurant's look, he brought in huge crowds with his irresistible ECB vada pav recipe. Eventually Mohan arranged for enough money and a bank loan to buy out the restaurant from the owners.

While the good old days were well behind it, the ECB still made enough money to grant Mohan a comfortable life with his wife and two children.

Shortly after he saw the news bulletin on Puneri365, Mohan made a call home. His wife picked up the phone, but he asked to urgently speak to his daughter.

'Can you move your flight up?'

'Why Daddy?'

'Can you?'

Later that month, Mohan Thomas' elder daughter Sheena was due to fly from Pune to Geneva, via Abu Dhabi, to enrol at a hotel management school. Unlike her father, Sheena didn't want to become a chef. Instead she had applied for, and had been admitted into, a highly rated graduate programme in hotel administration and business management. The course was expensive but not unaffordable.

'Yes, I can. But then I will have to arrange for some accommodation in Geneva until classes . . .'

'I can take care of that. I want you to move the flight up. Maybe this week itself.'

'What?'

'I will explain when I come home tonight. Just call the airlines as soon as possible.'

Mohan watched a clip of a young man with a cricket bat. He turned in his chair and looked out, through the tinted glass panes, at the road outside. A steady stream of cars kept driving down the highway from Mumbai and into Pune.

*Not again. I will not let these idiots ruin my life again.*

He hopped off his chair and called out to some of his staff members.

Mohan Thomas had made up his mind. The authorities weren't doing anything to shut down Mumbai and control whatever new plague now ravaged that city. He was going to do something about that.

## Outbreak + 4

Ratnakar Joshi suddenly noticed the traffic in front of him slow down. He overtook a few vehicles, until he saw a few men by the side of the road, waving pieces of cloth at oncoming cars. He stopped near an exit, next to an old Chevrolet Tavera taxi, and rolled down his window.

'What happened?' he asked the driver standing outside the vehicle.

'It is not safe to go ahead. They are preventing people from entering Pune.'

'What? Who?'

'No idea. Who knows? Some mad chutiyas.'

'Has anybody called the police?'

'I think so. Not me. I don't want to take a risk,' the man said.

Ratnakar Joshi rolled up his window, briefly thought about the device in the boot of his WagonR, and decided to risk it. He started his car and swung back on to the highway.

After a few minutes, he saw a string of men standing across the road. Thirty or forty metres behind them, he could see someone rolling small boulders on to the highway. Ratnakar realised that he had to get through quickly before the lanes were completely barricaded. He pressed down on the accelerator. The needle on his speedometer ticked past the highway speed limit.

Two men holding tree branches in their hands stood on the road in front of him, but jumped aside when the car showed no sign of stopping. Suddenly a large stone crashed into the driver's side window, cracking the glass and startling Ratnakar. He momentarily took his eyes off the road. The WagonR veered to the right and the bumper clipped one of the boulders on the tarmac. Ratnakar swung hard to the left, then lost control of the car. The vehicle narrowly missed another man standing on the highway, bounced over a thin strip of gravel and ploughed into the metal guard rail. The crash barrier sheared through the windscreen and out of the back of the driver's seat.

The car came to a rest, wedged between the railing and the traffic divider.

Ratnakar Joshi was killed instantly.

# 28

**Outbreak + 4**

As instructed, the chief minister of Maharashtra looked straight into the camera. She waited for the teleprompter to start, and then read off a short paragraph. The text made no sense. It was just a sequence of words designed to relax her speech, exercise her mouth, and avoid any embarrassing slip-ups during the live broadcast. 'Thiruvananthapuram,' she said slowly and deliberately. 'Thiru . . . va . . . nantha . . . pu . . . ram . . . Thiruvananthapuram . . .'

'Five minutes to go live!' a voice said from the darkness behind the bright camera lights.

'*Theek hai*,' replied the politician and continued with her speech exercises. Some of the filming crew watched her with puzzled expressions on their faces.

*How can she be so nonchalant about this new plague?*

Nishtha Sharma was anything but nonchalant about the crisis unfolding in two of the largest cities in her state. Everything about this mystery disease shook her. Where did it come from? How many would it kill? When would they find a cure? Why was she the last person to be informed? How did the prime minister know about it before her? Most of all, how would the people of her state react? They would panic, there was no doubt about that. People always panicked. The trouble was figuring what form the panic would take.

This is why Nishtha approached the bulletin she was to read with a spirit of detachment. If her address to the people of Maharashtra conveyed even the vaguest hint of fear or uncertainty, it would only add fuel to the conflagration. She had to deliver her message with complete authority and calm.

Already, she had spent hours working on the original NCDC draft of her message—first finalising an English version, then translating this carefully into Marathi, and finally reworking the Marathi draft till she was satisfied with every word, transition and pause.

Nishtha looked down at the final printout on the table in front of her. It was an unpleasant but restrained message.

In the nine-minute-long broadcast—she had timed it with a stopwatch—Nishtha would tell the people of Maharashtra that an outbreak of an illness had been detected in Mumbai. Authorities in the city and New Delhi had been tracking the illness for some time. However, in the light of recent unsubstantiated media reports, she had decided to directly speak to her fellow Maharashtrians. The disease, she would say, had not yet been identified. Therefore the authorities were currently not in a position to suggest remedies or cures. However, the finest medical minds in India were already in Mumbai, investigating the outbreak with the best technology available.

This first part of the message was more or less accurate. The next part was not.

In this segment, Nishtha would state that, so far, there had been no indication that the mystery illness was fatal or impossible to cure. Comparisons with the plague or with Ebola were completely unsubstantiated. Investigators from the NCDC and the state health department were confident of identifying the disease and recommending treatment schemes within the next seventy-two to ninety-six hours. There was absolutely no need to panic.

Nishtha would then encourage anyone suffering from the illness to seek the medical help they usually did. To conclude, she'd assert, the situation was completely under control.

Nishtha knew it wasn't—her brief telephone conversation with an NCDC expert had indicated as much. They had no idea what the illness was, how it spread, or what drugs to administer.

'One minute to live broadcast!'

Nishtha nodded and looked straight at the camera. She sat up and straightened her neck. She inhaled and exhaled deeply. She waited for the thirty second warning.

Suddenly, there was some commotion in the darkness behind the camera. A man burst out, closely followed by Sharma's personal secretary.

'Madam, you have to read a new speech. The old one is no longer relevant.'

The man placed a printout on the table in front of the chief minister of Maharashtra. As she read it, Nishtha's pulse quickened.

'But when did this happen? How . . . I cannot read this . . .'

'Madam, this is a direct order from the PM. He has seen it. There is no time. You have no choice. You have to . . . before more people get hurt.'

Nishtha felt her composure melt away.

'Thirty seconds to go live!' said the voice from the darkness.

### Outbreak + 4

As Nishtha went on air to deliver the new address, a hastily assembled staff of around 150 people was hard at work at the Srivatsa office in Opera House. An equal number of SMOs and medical officers were coordinating with hospitals and clinics all over the city.

In fits and starts, as SMOs reached out, data on patient numbers began to trickle into what had become the ad hoc command centre. They were many hours away from having sufficient data for the NCDC epidemiologists to work with their mathematical models. But there was just enough coming through to get a sense of how bad things looked on the ground.

Things looked very bad indeed.

In Ward A, all public and private hospitals were inundated with patients reporting bloody coughs, fever and strange rashes. The situation was even worse in Ward D which had ninety-four registered hospitals. Not only were most of them drowning under a tidal wave of emergency cases, but several had also downed shutters and locked gates to avoid dealing with the crowds.

Initially, the NCDC team had asked one of the health department clerks at the command centre to enter admission data and casualty rates into a neatly formatted spreadsheet. But this rapidly proved to be useless. Everybody wanted to see a running total of admission figures, and no one had the patience to stand behind the clerk and peer over his shoulder. Finally, someone put up a blackboard in one corner of the room and started totting up numbers in chalk.

By 9 pm, everyone, especially the NCDC officials, agreed that they were dealing with a major crisis. With data from just over half the wards coming in, they were already estimating 7,500 patients waiting in emergency departments; between 2,000 and 2,500 ailing in in-patient departments; and a death count of between 600 and 700. As everyone looked at these numbers in astonishment, someone walked up to the blackboard and wrote the word 'official' in brackets. A loud, collective gasp ran across the office. The number of dead and dying patients at the hundreds of unlicensed clinics and hospitals didn't even figure in these estimates.

A dozen-strong NCDC team quickly gathered for a meeting. It was decided that three of them would immediately fly back to Delhi and brief the health minister. These three would then go to the NCDC head office and activate various response protocols.

The first four to six weeks of a major outbreak—when attempts were being made to get a sense of the disease, analyse it, identify a treatment scheme and draw up a standardised response strategy—were the most chaotic and least predictable. The NCDC and the entire national network of medical research facilities had to pour every ounce of intellect, ingenuity and invention into identifying an unknown killer.

The three NCDC specialists—who had been informed about the prime minister's plan to use their jet—called the PMO at 10 pm to ask after Nitin Phadnavis' travel itinerary—*did he wish to accompany them? Had he already left?* The PMO brusquely stated that it had no updates to offer.

The specialists then called the airport to check on the plane—it was waiting.

They quickly got into a car and drove to the airstrip in Juhu. Close to midnight, the car entered the airport complex, slipped into the service road by the side of the tarmac, and sped towards the hangar.

When the specialists arrived, the hangar was deserted. There was no sign of the Boeing Business Jet or its crew.

## Outbreak + 4

'How dare you do that to me!' Nishtha Sharma bellowed as she crashed her fists into the table in front of her. A vase of flowers along one end wobbled and fell over. Nishtha dropped into her chair and sat with her eyelids tightly shut.

Her personal secretary stood in front of her, cowering. Next to her, the man who had interrupted her live broadcast watched stone-faced. He waited for a few moments, then spoke: 'Madam, I understand how you feel. What happened was . . . unfortunate. But we did not have a choice. As soon as we realised what was happening in Pune, we had to shut down Mumbai. And it had to come from you.'

'It could not have waited?'

'No. If it could have waited I would not have forced you to change your broadcast.'

'Hmm . . . you realise that I spoke in English? That itself is going to make many people very upset.'

The man nodded.

'Tell me,' she said after a brief pause. 'How bad is this outbreak?'

The man repeated the numbers he'd just received from the command centre on his mobile.

'Hundreds of deaths? My god . . .'

'And it is going to get worse, madam. This is just the beginning.'

'What can we do? Is there any way to stop it?'

'Right now, all we can do is wait for the samples to come back from Pune and for the rapid response team to start working. What you can do . . . what the state can do is maintain law and order somehow. Panic will only make things worse—both for the public and for the doctors trying to figure this out.'

'We will do what we can. But, of course, I suppose the PM is in charge of my state also now?'

The man didn't say anything immediately. 'Madam, I must now go back to our command centre. They need all the help they can get.'

Nishtha waved at him to leave her office.

After the door closed behind him, she addressed her personal secretary. 'I want to speak to the PM right away. I don't care where he is or what he is doing. He cannot treat me in this manner. That is not how things work. I am not his pet bitch.'

The personal secretary scurried away. She returned two hours later looking even paler than she did before.

'Ma'am, he is . . . it has been so hard to track the PM . . . the prime minister has left Mumbai.'

'How did he leave?'

The personal secretary didn't have the specific details, but had gathered that the PM had taken a plane from an airstrip in Juhu.

'Has he gone to Delhi?'

'I don't know.'

'Then ask for the passenger manifest. Pull strings. Do something. Ask favours of your bureaucrat-friends. I want to know where he is and speak to him as soon as possible. Go away and get it done. *Now*.'

## 29

**Outbreak + 5**

According to the manifest filed with the controller at the Juhu airstrip, the Boeing Business Jet carrying the prime minister, his security chief and a small entourage would land in Bhopal at half past midnight. Authorities at the Raja Bhoj Airport had been specifically asked to ensure complete secrecy. The plane was to be met by a convoy of three cars with a driver each. The convoy would then transfer the group to an undisclosed location somewhere in or around Bhopal.

However, these directions were followed with an overeager lack of attention to detail. Raja Bhoj didn't often host the prime minister of India, and the airport manager decided that 'complete secrecy' didn't rule out a small reception committee. When the plane landed, exactly on time, it was met by the three cars, but also by the airport manager in question, a district magistrate and a young female officer with the CRPF. Usually, the officer helped manage security procedures at the airport. That night she stood awkwardly with a bouquet in hand.

The first three passengers to disembark were all members of Nitin Phadnavis' personal staff. Next to follow were two members of the SPG. The reception committee waited for the prime minister. When there was no sign of him stepping out, the airport manager walked up to one of the SPG men.

'Why is he not coming out?' the manager asked. 'Is it because of all this?' He pointed at the officer holding a bouquet. 'I can send them all away.'

'Who is not coming out?'

'The prime minister.'

'He is not here already?'

The airport manager looked dumbstruck. 'No! I was told he was to be on this plane.'

The SPG man seemed puzzled. 'He was supposed to land just before us . . .'

'No other private plane has come. I was specifically asked to make arrangements for the prime minister and his team.'

'Sorry, sir,' the SPG man said. 'I have no idea where the prime minister is.'

India's prime minister had vanished.

### Outbreak + 5

'Has anybody heard from Ratnakar?' asked one of the NCDC reps at the command centre, a little after midnight. 'Can somebody please check up?'

Twenty minutes later, after persistent calls to

Ratnakar's mobile phone, and to the National Institute of Virology in Pune, there was still no news of the man.

Someone suggested that the researcher could be deep inside one of his sterile laboratories working on the MultiSampler results.

Sati, who had just finished setting up a hospital helpline, offered to help locate this most crucial cog in the investigative machine. She first called the IT department at the National Institute of Virology and asked them to find out when Ratnakar had last swiped into the building. She was taken aback by what she heard. She then asked for Ratnakar's residence phone number. Sati's phone call woke up Ratnakar's wife, who also worked at the National Institute of Virology as a research assistant. She hadn't seen her husband for days, she said. But this was far too common, she complained. The man had no sense of day or night when he worked. Sati asked if she had any idea where he could be. She thought about it, and suggested that he had perhaps gone back to Mumbai for extra samples. Or, perhaps, he was stuck in traffic somewhere on the highway, unable to get out of Mumbai or into Pune.

Sati thanked her and hung up. She decided to try Ratnakar's mobile phone number herself. The first half a dozen times the phone just rang and then went to his voicemail. On the seventh try, someone took the call.

'Hello! Ratnakar Joshi? Hello! This is Sati!'

The voice at the other end of the line said nothing for a few minutes. Then, Sati heard a rustling noise. It sounded like a thin plastic sheet or wrapping paper being crushed into a ball.

Then, the line went dead.

When Sati tried again, an automated voice told her that Ratnakar's phone had been switched off.

## Outbreak + 5

'I trust everyone is aware of the chief minister's broadcast last night?' the prime minister asked his cabinet over the satellite video link in the early hours of the morning. Several heads nodded.

In Delhi, Nitin Phadnavis' cabinet was assembled inside the parliament building in a space that was simply known as Room 406. Over the years, various attempts had been made to give it a less mundane name. For some time, it was called the War Room. But that name was dropped after the 'Naval War Room' corruption scandal of 2005, when over 7,000 pages of sensitive defence information from the Navy War Room and the Air Headquarters were leaked by a spy. Various other names were tried by successive governments—Black Box, Spearhead, Astra—nothing stuck. Everyone still called it Room 406.

This was the most secure room in the parliament building, featuring a number of electromagnetic shields, secure communication channels, biometric access controls and state-of-the-art encryption technology. Its existence itself, however, was not a state secret. Everyone who worked in the upper echelons of the government knew of it. And for all its high-tech security, the room was used several times a year. There was even a joint secretary in the ministry for parliamentary affairs whose sole job was to process bookings, schedule appointments and troubleshoot connectivity issues.

The cabinet, assembled in Room 406, had no idea where the prime minister was speaking from.

'All roads in and out of Mumbai are being shut down as we speak,' Nitin said. 'The airport will remain closed till further notice. And so will the ports. I have asked the chief minister to ensure nobody enters or leaves Mumbai for the time being.'

'And she was okay with this?' It was the minister for information and broadcasting.

'I didn't give her a choice,' Nitin said, smiling. Several heads rocked back with half-grins.

Privately, Nitin was deeply troubled about how he had forced this decision on Nishtha Sharma. He had deep respect for the chief minister of Maharashtra. Nishtha was a formidable woman who had overcome impossible hurdles to achieve her political goals. Not only was she the first woman chief minister of the state, but she was also the first 'outsider' to come to

power there. Born and brought up in Lucknow, Uttar
Pradesh and a first generation migrant to Mumbai
at the age of eighteen, Nishtha was swept to power
with an astonishing 64 per cent of the vote share in
the assembly elections.

Nitin would have to call her up later to make
amends, he told himself. 'So, what do we know so
far? Can we all get an update please?' he asked.

On the screen in front of him, the health minister
opened a slim file. She began to read a summary of
the latest data from Mumbai. 'First, the numbers.
We suspect there are around 15,000 cases of this
disease in Mumbai so far. 6,000 patients have been
admitted to in-patient departments in hospitals. Over
800 people have died.'

Several gasped.

'But this number will definitely get worse,' the
minister continued. 'Data is still being gathered across
Mumbai. We have to reach out to many, many more
hospitals and clinics.'

'What is our worst case scenario?' Nitin asked.

'Frankly . . . I have no idea. Anything I tell you
will be a hypothesis. But I have epidemiologists
modelling this right now. I should have a forecast in
a few hours.'

'I should be the second to know—after you.'

'Of course.'

'And what about movement? Any other cases
anywhere else?'

'Too soon to say. There are some cases in Pune, as you would expect. And a couple of staffers here in the parliament complex have been complaining of coughs. Also the home minister is still undergoing a check-up at AIIMS. But we can't say anything for sure till we either identify the disease or at least come up with a list of symptoms—a cough could mean anything and is all-pervasive. I have a rapid response team working on this in Pune right now . . .' she said, referring to Ratnakar Joshi.

'Excuse me . . . sir . . . everybody . . .' the minister for external affairs held up his hand. 'I've just got a message from one of my ambassadors. I think we're about to receive our first international travel notice.'

'Oh no!' Nitin said. 'From whom?'

'Actually . . . it is from the entire Gulf Cooperation Council. The GCC. All of them. UAE, Qatar, Oman . . . the entire lot. They're going to release a joint statement soon.'

'Okay, what do we do now?' Nitin asked. 'Do we have a standard protocol for this?'

'I'll take care of it. Give me an hour,' the minister for external affairs said before excusing himself and leaving the room.

Nitin spent a few moments thinking, until someone at the other end of the connection spoke up. 'Hello, prime minister? Are you still there? I think the screen has frozen . . .'

'No, no, I am here. Our first priority is to understand the scope of our problem. I want eyes on every state, every health department, every health centre. If this assumes epidemic proportions outside Mumbai . . .' He didn't want to consider the possibility. 'We'll meet again in twelve hours. I don't have to tell you—this is the only job we have right now. Nothing else. Thank you.'

Just as Nitin Phadnavis was about to get up from the chair, a new voice crackled over the speaker. 'Sir, this is Sumit Jaiswal . . .' Sumit was the minister of state for home affairs. He was standing in for his sick boss.

'Yes?'

'Can I have a word in private, sir?'

'Sure.'

Both men waited for the room to clear.

'Sir . . . my wife and children are in Mumbai. I spoke to them recently. My children are very ill. I don't know if they are suffering from the disease in question. But can you do something, sir? Please?'

Nitin ran a forefinger along the wrinkle on his forehead and gnashed his teeth. He had been dreading a conversation like this ever since he had ordered a shutdown in Mumbai.

'Sumit . . . you know that is not possible. All of us have family and loved ones in Mumbai. If I had a choice . . .'

'Sir, where are you, sir?' Sumit looked hard at the screen in front of him. The prime minister seemed to be seated in some kind of narrow space, like the interior of an airplane.

'I can't tell you that, Sumit. There is a security protocol in force right now.'

'Sir, but you have left Mumbai, yes?'

Nitin sighed. 'Yes, I have, Sumit. But things are . . . Sumit, I have a job to do. We all have a job to do. And I think we should focus on that now. The sooner we understand this outbreak and bring it under control, the faster we can help your family. I cannot make exceptions right now. We have many MPs from Mumbai. I hope you understand, Sumit.'

'Yes . . . I understand, sir,' Sumit said.

'Thank you so much for seeing my point of view,' Nitin muttered before hanging up.

In truth, Sumit Jaiswal hadn't seen it from Nitin's perspective at all.

## Outbreak + 5

'What do you want?' asked Aayush Vajpeyi.

'I just wanted to apologise,' Janani Ganesh said.

They stood by the side of the road, in the wee hours of the morning, outside a small nursing home in Kalbadevi. Janani had called Aayush and arranged the meeting. Aayush was still livid about her decision to take the story to the TV channels.

'Too late for apologies, Janani,' Aayush said, wiping his forehead with a filthy handkerchief. 'All you had to do was give me one call. One phone call. And I would have given you access to anybody in the government to confirm that we were handling things well. We could have managed this.'

'You would have made this disease go away? Don't give me that, Aayush. We saw it with dengue, swine flu, leptospirosis. The government always lies about outbreaks. Every single time.'

'And now look at what you've done!' Aayush said, pointing at the riot police standing outside the hospital. 'Maybe there is a reason why governments downplay things. People are idiots, Janani . . . look at what happened in Pune . . . human beings were murdered.'

'So what if they are idiots? People still deserve to know if their lives are in danger.'

Aayush didn't say anything. A part of him agreed with her. But over the last few days he had seen too much chaos. The public and private health infrastructure in Mumbai was now well past breaking point.

At the command centre, a row of blackboards had been arranged to keep track of the numbers—figures were spiralling out of control. What made things worse was that there was still no clarity on how to respond. Feedback from doctors, hospitals and nursing homes had been confusing. In some cases, patients entered the hospital bleeding profusely—displaying symptoms beyond the ken of any medical practitioner. In other instances, those ailing seemed to react to drugs and stabilise. The third lot of patients were the most mysterious—they'd get better with the drugs administered at the hospital, go back home, and crash after a few hours. Why did drugs work in some cases but not in others? So far, everyone seemed clueless.

And it didn't help that the team at Opera House now confronted another puzzle: where in the world was Ratnakar Joshi?

'Did it help? The stunt?' Aayush asked.

'What do you mean?'

'Did it help your website? That was the point of it all, no?'

Janani shrugged and looked away from him. 'We got fucked. The initial explosion of traffic took our servers down. By the time we got them back up, everyone else was running our story with our pictures. Now we get some traffic from link referrals. But otherwise . . . fucked.'

'Oh, well . . .' Aayush began to say, trying to sound sympathetic.

'Besides, we've closed the office. Everyone is afraid they'll catch something.'

'It is all such a mess.'

'How bad are the fatalities?'

'Are you trying to get another story?'

'No, Aayush . . .'

'Horrible. Last I checked, we were at 800 deaths. Usually things slow down for a bit at this stage— people stay at home instead of venturing outdoors. The next few days are critical. If an outbreak remains out of control for beyond a week . . . or ten days . . .' Aayush let his words trail away.

He was about to say something when his phone rang. It was Sati.

'Aayush . . . I just spoke to a mobile riot control room jeep. They mentioned an incident on the Expressway.'

'More violence?'

'No, no. They've identified Ratnakar Joshi's body. His car had crashed into a divider. Died on the spot.'

'Oh my god!'

'The MultiSampler . . .'

Aayush bit his jaw so hard, the sides of his face behind to bulge. 'Is it damaged? Or broken?'

'No. It is missing. It was not in the car. It is gone.'

## 30

## Beta Protocol

When he first drew up a plan for Beta Protocol, India's great spymaster based it on three *core ideas*— deception, control and resistance.

Rameshwar Nath Kao knew that in the future, there'd be other wise men and women who'd wish to update Beta Protocol to incorporate new technology and tools of political control. Kao was many things: ruthless, intelligent, obsessive, secretive, even a misanthrope. But there was one thing he was certainly not: impractical. Kao knew that he had little power over his successors, and their attempts at updating Beta Protocol as they saw fit. But when they did try tinkering with the most secret of Kao's many secrets, he wanted them to keep intact his core ideas.

Beta Protocol was, above all, a tool of deception. The entire point of the project was to ensure continuity of political control. Irrespective of the nature of the threat that confronted India's people or government, Beta Protocol had to guarantee that the prime minister could be immediately moved to a safe location that was immune to enemies, foreign or domestic. This meant that the Protocol, when activated, had to deceive not only an enemy nation or nations, but also everyone in India.

When the moment came, Kao stressed in his plan, the prime minister had to vanish into thin air.

From that point onwards, till Beta Protocol was terminated, his or her location would be known only to a tiny group of Beta Protocol operatives. Thus, Phase One of Beta Protocol set into motion steps to create that moment of magic—when one of the most closely watched individuals on the surface of the planet slipped into the shadows.

Next, Kao wrote, came control. Once the prime minister had been secretly transported to a secure location, he or she had to instantly assume control over a government that, in all likelihood, was facing a moment of intense crisis. There would be no time to forward calls, enter passwords or hook up computers. There was no point in creating a system to ensure continuity if ministers or generals had to wait for hours to speak to the premier. Kao insisted that Beta Protocol had to include a system for seamless, instantaneous communication and control, even if a prime minister arrived at a secure location with nothing but the clothes on his back. Computers had to work, phones had to ring, and files had to be available. The expense involved in creating such a system would be considerable, Kao admitted, but also non-negotiable. Hooking up this secure location into the national telecommunications grid was the primary focus of Phase Two in Beta Protocol's activation.

Finally, and most importantly, came the small matter of resistance. It didn't only matter how quickly and discreetly the prime minister was transferred to a secure location, or how smoothly the instruments of government were activated. If the location itself was vulnerable to attack, Beta Protocol would find itself resting on very brittle foundations.

Initially, Kao was committed to building a secure location resistant to anything short of a direct thermonuclear strike. But then, as Kao's team began to model potential scenarios during a hypothetical cross-border war, they began to weigh the impact of biological and chemical weapons. What if sarin gas were used? What if canisters full of odourless, tasteless VX gas were dropped? What was the point of building an impenetrable bunker under hundreds of tonnes of rock and concrete, if the prime minister opened a tap, and drank a glass of water contaminated with Anthrax spores?

Kao suddenly realised that his original plan for the Beta Protocol safe house had been grossly inadequate. He had to start all over from scratch.

Three years after that original meeting with Indira Gandhi, Kao once again found himself in the PMO. This time, the person in the chair on the other side of the table was different, and so was the tone of the meeting.

Morarji Desai, who defeated Indira Gandhi in the 1977 elections, was deeply mistrustful of Kao and RAW. Desai suspected, perhaps correctly, that Indira Gandhi had used the agency to spy on her detractors and opponents. As soon as he took office, he initiated an internal investigation to see if this was true.

Kao was well aware of this. He knew that there were few people in all of Delhi whom Desai trusted less than him. So he had come prepared with a compromise.

Morarji Desai broke the awkward silence and spoke first. 'Kao, do you know that Zia-ul-Haq called me again today?'

Kao nodded.

'So you know what he wanted. Is that man mad? Why does he keep calling me all the time? Now, he wanted an Ayurvedic remedy for baldness.'

Kao smiled.

'If I had an Ayurvedic remedy for baldness, do you think my head would be like this?'

Kao's smile widened. He almost chuckled. 'Sir, he is calling you to soften you up. To make you think he is your friend.'

Morarji Desai nodded with a smile.

'Sir, he is also waiting for a mistake.'

Desai frowned. 'Mistake? In what sense?'

'That you will reveal something secret. Something confidential. Nothing important, but just enough to help his intelligence staff.'

'I am smarter than that, Kao. I know you hate me. But you know I am smarter than that.'

'I do not hate you.'

Desai got up from his chair and walked over to a chest of drawers. There was a jug of water on top of it. He poured himself a glass. 'So why did you want to meet me?'

'Sir, I want you to read this file. I would like your thoughts on it afterwards.'

'Leave it on my table. I have many things to do . . .'

'No, sir. This is not a file that can wait.'

Desai walked back to his chair, sat down and picked up the file Kao pushed across.

Twenty-five minutes later, he placed it down, and looked at Kao. He didn't speak for a few moments. Then he said: 'This is a sad world we live in, Kao. Where a democratically elected leader has to deceive his own people for their own good.'

'You disagree with this proposal, sir?'

'Of course not. I think your Beta Protocol is a work of genius. I am sure there is plenty missing from this report. But I think you should go ahead with it. Why didn't you get it finalised under Mrs Gandhi?'

'It took me over a year to draw up a plan I was happy with. And then I thought it would be inappropriate to get something like this approved during the Emergency.'

'Inappropriate or inconvenient, Kao? You were afraid that along with all the secrets that would tumble out after the Emergency, your Beta Protocol may also accidentally slip out . . .'

'There was an element of that fear as well, sir . . . yes.'

'So what do you want me to do?'

'Pay for it.'

'How much?'

Kao slipped a sheet of paper across the table.

Morarji Desai took one look at it and then rocked back in his chair. 'Are you serious?'

'Absolutely.'

Morarji Desai—who had been India's finance minister twice before he became prime minister—was no stranger to the vagaries of public accounting. 'It will be somewhat awkward to make people overlook such a large amount, Kao.'

Kao nodded. He had been prepared for just such a comment. Over the next thirty minutes, he outlined a comprehensive plan to secretly finance Beta Protocol. As Kao spoke, Morarji Desai began to smile. It was a brilliant, if devious plan. Instead of asking for a lump sum, Kao had come up with an idea that would ensure a steady stream of funding for the Beta Protocol project. The cash flow would run indefinitely into the future, thus ensuring that successive Protocol operatives would have the means to upgrade technology, equipment and the secure location itself without ever having to ask again for official approval.

'This is excellent, Kao. No wonder nobody in Delhi trusts you. Not even those who respect and admire you.'

'I will take that as a compliment, sir.'

'And what do I get in return for this, Kao?'

Kao nodded. He knew exactly what the new prime minister of India was getting at. 'In six months, you will have my resignation, sir. You are then free to appoint your own head of RAW and restructure the agency as you wish.'

Desai laughed. 'Very good. I like your plan. It saves both of us a lot of time and trouble.' Desai thought for a moment. 'So what happens when I approve?'

'As far as you are concerned, nothing happens. In fact, if all goes well, you will be the last prime minister of India to ever hear of Beta Protocol. I hope things will never reach such an impasse that it needs to be invoked.'

Morarji Desai flipped through the file one last time before handing it back to Kao. 'You have a deal.'

A few days later, Morarji Desai's government announced its intention to finance a number of indigenous consumer brands. These would replace foreign brands like Coca-Cola and IBM that had been forced to leave India in 1977 under new government regulations. In parliament, Desai's finance minister read out a long list of products the Indian government would now make that included mopeds, computers, spectacle frames, washing machines and even a soft drink named Double Seven.

There was one peculiar item on this list—a last-minute addition that had been included following an express request from the prime minister. His finance minister didn't understand why, but Desai suddenly insisted that India develop the capacity to make high precision quartz chronograph watches.

More than one person tried to talk the prime minister out of this absurd plan. Few people in India, at the time, could afford such luxuries or the batteries that these extravagant gadgets demanded—so, if quartz watches didn't have much demand, why even bother trying to make and sell them?

Then there was the problem of technology. The cheapest solution was to import parts from Japan and assemble the watches in India. But Desai was adamant. He wanted every single component to be made in India. Over and over, Desai was warned of the prohibitive costs involved. Engineers would have to be trained abroad; costly equipment would have to get imported; and lakhs of rupees would be spent on testing samples and prototypes. Nothing would sway Morarji Desai's steely resolve.

In late 1977, Desai went to Tumkur in Karnataka. He had been invited to preside over a ground-breaking ceremony for a new HMT Watches Ltd workshop. Desai delivered a rousing speech to a tiny audience. He promised that he would spare no expense in making this one of the world's great centres of watchmaking research and technology. The audience—that included Kao—applauded politely. Then, everyone got into their cars and drove away.

The ceremony was not reported in any of India's major national newspapers. Decades later, the public sector watch workshop that had racked up losses running into hundreds of crores was shut down. In 2012, the workshop and all its contents, along with the plot of land it sat on, were auctioned off to a privately held outsourcing company named Nuance 24/7.

# 31

**Justice Kashyap Commission of Inquiry**

*Reference: PS 4/PI 17/Maha/Session 4*
*File type: Raw transcript of interview, audio recording*
*Location: Provisional Lok Sabha Complex, Port Blair*
*Security clearance level: 2*
*Note: This recording features two voices*

JK: Have you read any of the articles on Bombay Fever by Janani Ganesh or Annalisa Salmone?

AV: Yes, of course. Every single one of them. Many times over.

JK: Is there any truth in what they say? In your opinion . . .

AV: Sir, both of them have written many things. They have made several allegations. Which ones are you referring to specifically?

JK: Don't play games with me, Mr Vajpeyi. You know what I am referring to. But, if you insist, I will enunciate these allegations. Ms Ganesh wrote, and I quote, 'Even after several hundred deaths and thousands of cases, the government had no idea that there was an outbreak of a killer disease in Mumbai. The disease tracking system in Mumbai, if there was one, failed miserably. If it were not for a television news report on the outbreak and the panic that followed, the state and central governments may have ignored the outbreak for days and even weeks. Many, many lives were saved by that news bulletin.' Is she right, Mr Vajpeyi?

AV: I think so.

JK: Oh? So in your opinion the government did waste time and put lives in jeopardy?

AV: Not exactly, sir. Janani is right in that the panic did force the government to respond with a great deal of urgency. She is also right in that the disease tracking programme in Mumbai did not detect the outbreak until the TV news story broke. I have no fundamental disagreements with these points.

JK: So—I repeat—you think the government did not act quickly enough?

AV: Yes. The government did not act fast enough. But I believe . . . I sincerely believe . . . that it would have been impossible for anyone to act with greater speed *under those circumstances*.

JK: I don't think I follow . . .

AV: Sir, in an ideal world, the government, and all of us, would have been able to detect a new outbreak immediately. As soon as ten or fifteen people reported to a hospital with an unknown illness, a disease detection system would have alerted the authorities. That is how things *should have* worked.

JK: And things never work that way in the real world?

AV: Never. And there are many reasons. First, how do you know that there is an outbreak? How can you tell if it is a new disease? What if the disease takes a few days to fully show all symptoms? Remember, many who died of Bombay Fever had nothing more than a bad cough for four or five days. And then, in a matter of hours . . . they were gone. So you need time to gather data, draw patterns, rule out false positives . . . you can't go around declaring an emergency each time ten people land up at a hospital at the same time.

JK: So what you mean . . .

AV: Just one more thing, sir . . .

JK: Go on.

AV: Sometimes, it is not actual patients or dead bodies that give an outbreak away. Do you know how they discovered that something was wrong in Surat during the plague?

JK: Please tell me.

AV: Medical officers in the city noticed two things. First, pharmacies began running out of tetracycline, the antibiotic. People in the city, especially doctors and medical staff . . . people who saw the first few plague cases . . . began to buy huge stocks of the antibiotic for themselves, their families and their friends. Boxes of the stuff. Surat began to run out of tetracycline. That was the first worrying sign the medical officers noticed.

JK: What was the second sign?

AV: Doctors began to leave Surat. They were piling into cars, planes, trains . . . anything . . . and running away. It took authorities a few days to put these things together and see the pattern.

JK: Did this happen during the Bombay Fever outbreak?

AV: Not in the same scale. There were some drug stock-outs—especially during the Legionnaires' rumour. However, the doctors didn't get a chance to flee Mumbai. The city closed down before they could react. Otherwise, we would have seen an exodus of doctors, 100 per cent. I am certain of it.

JK: What about Annalisa Salmone's argument? That the government delayed reacting to the outbreak so that VIPs would get a chance to leave Mumbai? Didn't the prime minister leave after the lockdown?

AV: I have no idea about that, sir . . .

## 32

## Outbreak + 6

Annalisa Salmone entered Bella, a restaurant in the
Prithvi Mahal Hotel in Delhi, at the stroke of noon.
It was her first visit to this particular hotel and she
was somewhat surprised to find it completely empty.
Eateries in and around Connaught Place usually filled
up at lunchtime with office-goers. It was hard to find
a table anywhere between noon and 2 pm.

*Maybe the food is dreadful. Or dreadfully
expensive.*

Annalisa picked a table by the window. She sat
down and moments later a waiter hurried out of
a pair of doors marked 'Staff Only' and placed a
menu in front of her. Belying all expectations set by
the unexceptional decor and tired cutlery, the menu
proved to be exciting. There were Italian dishes that
Annalisa had long given up hope of ever finding in
India. She was so engrossed in the menu that she
didn't notice the young man in the sleeveless silk
jacket, kurta and pyjama walk into the restaurant
and towards her table.

'Annalisa?'

She stood up, startled. 'Yes. Hello. It is good to meet you, minister.'

'I would prefer it if you called me Sumit,' he said, shaking her hand. 'Please sit down. Isn't it a great menu?'

'This is amazing. I had no idea this restaurant existed.'

'Few people know of it,' Sumit said, waving at the waiter. 'This hotel makes its money almost exclusively catering to airline crew on stopovers. It makes no effort to reach out to other customers.' He asked the waiter to bring him a diet cola with a lemon wedge. 'Don't judge it by the service or the decor though. Its focus is food.'

'Do you eat here often?'

'Oh, yes. It is my wife's favourite restaurant.'

'Do the waiters know who you are?'

Sumit Jaiswal, the minister of state for home affairs, shook his head from side to side. 'They don't have a clue. I have made no effort to tell them. The moment they know they'll tell the chef to make "VIP" food. Which usually ruins it.'

Annalisa smiled.

'Besides I am a minister of state. We are . . . nobodies.'

'Would you recommend anything?'

'The stuffed sardines for a start, with a glass of Vermentino. Followed by the porcini mushroom risotto and the panna cotta.'

'They make sarde a beccafico?'

'Very well.'

The waiter came with the drink, and left a few minutes later with their orders.

'Why did you want to meet me?' Annalisa asked.

'I would like to give you an exclusive story,' Sumit said.

Annalisa reached into her haversack and pulled out a battered old Filofax and a ballpoint pen. 'Do you mind if I take notes?'

'Do whatever you have to. All I want is the story out in the next twenty-four hours.'

'Is that why you called me? Because BuzzWire will publish anything?'

Sumit sipped his diet cola, and thought carefully before replying. He sensed a frisson of indignation in Annalisa Salmone's voice.

To an extent, Annalisa was right. Sumit had chosen to speak to BuzzWire because it was known to publish first and think later. It would pour all its resources into broadcasting his story, make sure it got picked up by every other website and wire agency on the planet, and only then pause to reconsider.

However, Sumit had also chosen BuzzWire because he liked Annalisa Salmone's work. She brought a talented, old-school journalist's sensibility and craft to BuzzWire's fast and furious business model. Some months ago, she had published a series of articles on health and safety conditions in factories in Gurgaon. The stories were so well researched and powerfully written that they became a topic of discussion in parliament. Ever since, Sumit had kept an eye on the Italian's work.

There was another, vastly more important reason why Sumit had called Annalisa and requested this meeting. 'I like your work. And I like your website's appetite for risk. But more than that . . . I don't think anybody else will carry my story. Nobody will want to make an enemy of the prime minister.'

Annalisa pursed her lips, trying to suppress her excitement.

Sumit paused while the waiter placed a bread basket in front of them.

'You know about this outbreak in Mumbai . . .'

'Of course. And the potential GCC travel advisory—those rumours. The news is everywhere. But the details have been very sketchy so far.'

Sumit sipped his drink again. He didn't like what he was going to do next. But now there was no turning back.

'Do you know why the government took so long to enforce a lockdown?'

'I am not sure I understand what you mean,' Annalisa said after swallowing a spoonful of the delicious stuffed sardines. 'I thought Nishtha Sharma announced the move as soon as the government realised the seriousness of the outbreak?'

'No. What if I told you that the government knew about the outbreak at least twenty-four hours prior to all announcements? That it intentionally delayed the shutdown, just so that a handful of VIPs could run away from Mumbai?'

Annalisa furrowed her brow.

'I want you to call up the Somerset Hotel,' Sumit said. 'Ask the manager when delegates for the India Summit started checking out. Then ask him where the prime minister is.'

'You mean to say they were warned of the outbreak before the public came to know of it?'

'I am saying that not only were they warned, but the shutdown itself was delayed so that a bunch of foreign delegates could leave Mumbai on time. I am also telling you that the prime minister, along with members of his staff, was allowed to violate the shutdown. They left Mumbai shortly after the chief minister's broadcast.'

'But that is . . . insane, minist . . . Sumit,' she said correcting herself just as the waiter approached with the sardines. 'That means they could have possibly allowed infected people to travel out of Mumbai just to let the VIPs out?'

'Exactly. This also means that while hundreds of healthy people now want to leave Mumbai, only the prime minister is allowed to run away to safety. That is what I want you to write about. That according to high level sources in this government, the prime minister ran away from Mumbai with his tail between his legs.'

Annalisa silently made notes. Then she looked at the minister. 'Sumit, I have a bunch of questions. First of all . . . why are you telling me all this?'

'Why does it matter? You have your story.'

'Well . . . pardon my French, but I don't want to get fucked over because of some petty rivalry within the coalition.'

Sumit ran his fingers through his hair and sighed. 'Look, my wife and children are in Mumbai. All of them are ill. They are in a hospital. I asked the PM to help me bring them here. The righteous bastard said no.'

'So you want me to destroy his reputation? As revenge?'

'Exactly.'

'I think that can be arranged,' Annalisa said, slipping half a porcini mushroom into her mouth. 'By the way . . . do you know where the PM is?' she asked after swallowing a mouthful.

'I have no idea,' replied Sumit. 'Nobody does.'

## Outbreak + 6

As Sumit Jaiswal and Annalisa Salmone conspired against the prime minister over lunch, hundreds of kilometres away Nitin was beginning to realise the full extent of the problem that confronted him.

The hourly updates from his health minister were appalling. So far, the NCDC had made little progress in identifying the illness, isolating the bug, or suggesting a response. And to make things worse, reports were now emerging of outbreaks in Pune, Nasik, Nagpur and, worst of all, New Delhi. Meanwhile, the home minister was still being held somewhere inside the high security zone in AIIMS. There was no confirmation regarding what exactly ailed the veteran politician.

Nitin Phadnavis sorely missed his home minister. The old man, with years of experience, brought a hard, steely perspective on administration that Nitin had learnt to admire over the years. And during a crisis like this, it was exactly the kind of perspective Nitin needed. Sumit was filling in for his boss as best as he could. Despite the awkward conversation earlier, Nitin appreciated the young man's ability to set aside his personal problems and focus on the job at hand—but there was no ignoring the fact that Sumit was relatively inexperienced.

And now, there was this. Nitin sat in front of a monitor that displayed the face of his external affairs minister.

'I can't hold them back any more,' said the exhausted man in Hindi. 'Now that it has spread to Delhi, they will no longer wait.'

Nitin Phadnavis spat out in anger: 'But we don't know if the outbreak in Delhi is related!'

'It doesn't matter any longer. They've already started cancelling Gulf Air, Etihad, Qatar and Emirates flights from India. The travel advisory will be out any moment now. You know what happens next.'

Nitin nodded grimly. There had been a narrow window of opportunity to deal with the outbreak in Mumbai before it became an international incident. That window had now closed. As soon as the Gulf Cooperation Council published a joint travel advisory, other international governments would announce their own notices. UN and World Health Organization protocols would kick in, governments would start evacuating embassy staff, and international media would send in their 'war zone' correspondents.

'What do we do now?' Nitin asked. 'What does the foreign secretary say?'

'He is waiting outside. Shall I call him in?'

'Please.'

The foreign secretary was a tall, thin, bald man who wore a purple sweater under a charcoal grey suit. 'I hope you are well?' he started to say.

'I am,' Nitin replied. 'What options do we have?'

'We have two standard options. We can dismiss these travel notices, deny that there is a major crisis, assure the world media that we are on top of things . . . the usual. Or we can admit there is a problem, tell them we are doing our best, and say that we are reaching out to the UN, World Health Organization and the Center for Disease Control in Atlanta.'

'So I suppose we go with the second option then?'

The foreign secretary glanced at the external affairs minister, and waited for a nod before replying. 'Sir, I would not recommend doing that.'

'Because it will make us look incompetent?'

'That it will. But that is not the only difficulty,' the foreign secretary said.

The moment India admitted it had a problem it couldn't deal with, he explained, the panic within the country would boil over. The scenes that were unfolding in Pune would repeat in every small and large city all over India. The public—convinced that the government was powerless to help them—would do whatever it took to save themselves and their families. Curfews would break down, government offices would get stormed, and the local government could and would collapse.

'So you want me to lie? And act as if nothing is happening? Do you have any idea how many people are dying in Mumbai right now? And we still have no idea what is killing them . . .'

The external affairs minister leaned towards the screen. 'Well, the foreign secretary has a plan. I think you should listen to him.'

'Go on.'

The plan was simple enough. The Indian

government would immediately release a press note saying that the outbreak in Mumbai was being managed and that a high power team of experts was already in the city. While isolated cases with similar symptoms were being investigated in other cities, at this point, there was no evidence of a national outbreak. The disease had been successfully contained within Mumbai. As things stood, India believed it had the capacity to deal with this outbreak quickly and comprehensively. With the exception of Mumbai, there was no reason to enforce travel restrictions to and from cities in India.

To Nitin this sounded suspiciously like a statement of denial. He began to speak. But the foreign secretary ignored the interjection and continued: 'While the official statement is being released, the health ministry and the NCDC will secretly get in touch with the World Health Organization, the UN and the Center for Disease Control in Atlanta. Even as India says that it has the capacity to deal with the outbreak, it will prepare for exactly the opposite scenario. This is how we avoid panic, while still getting the help we need.'

The foreign secretary waited for Nitin Phadnavis to respond.

'Can we pull this off? A secret confabulation?'

'It happens all the time. It is what we do. And we know how to deal with the UN and the World Health Organization discreetly. You can leave that to us.'

Nitin sat silently for a few moments, thinking. 'Fine. Draw up the press note. Do it as soon as possible. See if we can release it before those GCC guys announce a travel advisory.'

The foreign secretary got up to leave. Suddenly Nitin asked him to wait.

'What are the possible fuck-ups here?'

The foreign secretary, still standing, leaned towards the camera. 'Media, sir. If anything leaks out of the government . . . if anybody says anything that is in conflict with the official release . . .' He shrugged.

'Well, let us hope we all have better sense than that.'

## Outbreak + 6

Just as the prime minister's conversation ended, another chat in Delhi also drew to a close. Sumit Jaiswal paid for lunch and stood up. Annalisa Salmone remained seated, sipping her espresso and making notes in her Filofax.

'I want to see him suffer,' Sumit Jaiswal said before walking out of the restaurant.

Annalisa watched him leave. She then put down her Filofax, pulled out her laptop and placed it on the table. A few moments later, she had her headline: 'Thousands of poor Indians in Mumbai are dying from a mysterious disease. So why is Nitin Phadnavis running away?'

## 33

**Outbreak + 6**

By mid-morning, on the sixth day of the outbreak, the Srivatsa office at Opera House slowly began to empty out. A steady stream of men and women walked out of the complex carrying cardboard boxes, whiteboards, computers and telephones. One SMO tottered beneath a cardboard box filled to the brim with extension cords and mobile chargers. The boxes and hardware went into a hastily assembled fleet of mini-vans, cars and buses. Most of them had been hired for the journey, but some of the vehicles were marked with the name of the organisation they belonged to: The Haffkine Institute for Training, Research and Testing.

That morning, surrounded by dozens of exhausted, hollow-eyed, sleep-deprived SMOs, health workers, district medical officers and other staff, the NCDC team went over a set of grim statistics. As far as they knew there had now been 1,300 deaths within the urban agglomeration of Greater Mumbai alone. The death rate showed no sign of abating. Neither was there any indication of the number of cases tapering.

There wasn't a hospital, health centre or nursing home within the lockdown zone that wasn't bursting to the seams with patients. Most hospitals had long given up hope of managing the chaos. They could do little other than set up a row of tables, with doctors and nurses on one side, and a growing queue of patients walking past on the other.

As patients inched past doctors, they matched their symptoms against an ad hoc checklist put together by the NCDC command centre: stiffness in the finger joints, bloody or detached finger nails, blood-filled rashes under the skin, and bleeding from the nose, mouth, ears or rectum. Anyone displaying three or more of these symptoms was immediately pulled out of the queue, and admitted to a special isolation ward.

As patient numbers exploded, and hospitals began to run out of room, a simple solution was devised: entire hospitals were turned into isolation wards. Patients matching symptoms were let in, everyone suffering from anything else waited outside. If they were lucky, the ones outside eventually found a nurse or a doctor to look at their 'low priority' complaints.

There was just one problem. The hospitals-turned-into-isolation-wards were now slowly running out of room. This disease, whatever it was, was ravaging an entire population—invading bodies, blasting past immune systems, destroying respiratory and circulatory systems.

At first glance there seemed to be no pattern to this carnage. Hospitals were filled with rich, poor, old, young, thin, fat, male and female patients. The first few cases had erupted from Ward A. But then, the disease quickly scythed through the city, spreading from ward to ward, building to building, office to office.

'But there is always a pattern,' the NCDC official said that morning to the assembled staff at the command centre. 'And we have to find it. The longer we take, the worse this is going to get.'

He then announced that the ad hoc offices at Srivatsa had outlived their purpose. Following a call with the health minister, it was decided that the command centre would move to the Haffkine Institute in Parel. Along with the National Institute of Virology in Pune, the Haffkine Institute was the best equipped medical laboratory in Western India, with the finest facilities for studying microbes and analysing diseases. It had the infrastructure needed for the pitched battle that lay ahead.

There was another reason for the move. If the NCDC eventually had to call in teams from the World Health Organization and the Center for Disease Control, it didn't want to host them in a set of sweltering rooms inside a half-abandoned office block in Opera House. The Haffkine Institute would make for a much more serious first impression.

If the NCDC officer intentionally omitted this detail, it was because the entry of the Center for Disease Control and the World Health Organization confirmed that the Indian effort against the outbreak had failed. Nothing could be more demoralising.

## Outbreak + 6

By noon—even as boxes from the now-abandoned Srivatsa office got unpacked inside the Durbar Hall at the Haffkine Institute—Aayush Vajpeyi and Sati Rout stood by the wreck that had once been Ratnakar Joshi's car.

They had spent much of the previous night and the following morning organising and then leading a search party for the MultiSampler. Aayush, Sati, and a group of riot policemen had formed a line that stretched across the Mumbai-Pune Expressway, the divider, and extended 200 metres out on to the shoulder of the road on both sides. They had started two kilometres south of the point where the car had rammed into the divider. And then, they had slowly walked four kilometres north, combing every inch of land, and checking with every shop, hut and house by the side of the highway.

Hours later, they had nothing to show for the effort except for some mobile phone footage of the car losing control, likely captured by a bystander.

'Do you think the MultiSampler just melted in the heat?' Sati asked, exasperated.

'As if,' Aayush replied. 'Someone took it. Along with Ratnakar's phone. Just after the accident.'

'So, that person had to be standing close when it happened.'

'Yes. Which means the fucker was possibly involved with the rioting. Long gone by now.'

'Damn it,' Sati muttered.

'Sati . . . do you recall how much power the MultiSampler had left in it before the accident?'

She looked at Aayush. But her eyes were glazed. She was doing the math in her head. 'It must have been down to half its capacity. Nine hours. At best, under a day. Unless the idiot decided to plug it into a socket.'

'I very much doubt that happened.'

'So what do we do now?'

Aayush stood by the side of the highway and looked around. 'The rioters came from the north. So they must have run back in that direction. It has to be somewhere there,' he said, pointing up the road. Several kilometres up in the distance, the Mumbai-Pune Expressway swung past some hotels and restaurants and entered Pune.

'No way. The MultiSampler is heavy. You can't just pick it up and run,' Sati said, recalling how she helped Ratnakar load it into the car. The memory made her think about the poor virologist. And about how he had died. Sati shook her head quickly to clear her head of the image.

Aayush thought for a minute. And then came up with a plan. He asked Sati to talk to the riot policemen and see if any of them recalled any of the rioters having a scooter or a motorcycle or a car. Meanwhile Aayush would go through various mobile phone recordings to see if any of them had a clue.

'Nine hours only. *Nine*,' Sati said, as she turned around and walked away.

## 34

**Outbreak + 6**

It was 4 pm on the sixth day of the outbreak. The Matunga branch of Jai Lakshmi Bank was completely deserted, except for a solitary figure who sat inside a small glass cabin.

This cabin was located in a corner, away from the counters, tables, machines and writing desks that formed most of the branch's vast interior space. It was also furnished in a distinctive palette of colours that set it apart. This cabin was the branch's premium banking department, and the man inside was the designated premium client executive.

The man, dressed in a smart navy blue blazer and grey trousers, idly flipped through a product brochure. He was a meticulous employee and had long ago committed every single word and number in the brochure to memory. But he had nothing else to do—and he refused, as a matter of principle, to spend time in the office browsing the internet, reading a book or watching a film on his mobile phone like some of his office colleagues.

In fact, he hadn't attended to a single client over

the past two days. There had been a brief explosion of general 'non-premium' customers the day after the outbreak had been reported. But, since then, footfall had dropped precipitously; employees stopped coming as well. Some had fallen ill. And the rest were too scared of the disease to leave home. As with most other offices in the city, absenteeism at the branch had hit levels never seen before.

And now, on the sixth day of the outbreak, the client executive was the only employee to turn up for work, apart from the security guards.

As he reread the brochure titled 'International Investments and Risk Profiles', one of the security guards pushed the glass door open and leaned inside. The guard spoke in Marathi: 'Sir, nobody has come today, sir. Shall we go home?'

The client executive looked at his watch. It was much too early to lock up. But even he realised the futility of it all.

'Okay, fine. Give me ten minutes. You can start shutting down.' The guard left, beaming.

The client executive was just reaching for his computer mouse, when his mobile phone rang. He glanced at the screen. It was his mother. She had already started speaking by the time he hit the green button on the smartphone screen. 'Can you please bring tetracycline and gentamicin when you come? Buy as much as you can . . .'

'But what . . .'

'The children are also coughing now. Please just buy as much as you can.'

'Who told you . . . have you gone to a doctor?'

'There is no time, son. We went to the hospital and came back. They are not letting anybody inside. Please just bring the drugs when you come. Can you leave office immediately?'

Suddenly, he heard someone coughing in the background. And then the line went dead.

He instantly felt a wave of fear and nausea rise up within him. But he suppressed it by thinking about his mother's oddly specific request. She knew nothing about medicines or antibiotics. And yet she had asked for tetracycline and gentamicin. As he watched his computer shut down, the man frowned. He knew exactly why his mother wanted those drugs.

It was all because of those stupid WhatsApp messages.

Ever since the outbreak had been first reported in the media, his friends and relatives had started forwarding messages with 'secret' remedies for the illness. Most of these were obviously ludicrous—like the one that claimed that gargling with hot, salted water every three hours would kill bacteria, or that the disease only affected those who were non-vegetarians.

Other messages sounded dubiously scientific,

given the credentials of the senders. Earlier that day, an absent colleague had sent a message that recommended urgently stocking up tetracycline as this drug had helped cure the plague in Surat. Another message exhorted recipients to buy large quantities of gentamicin before 'doctors and politicians and businessmen stole it all'.

His mother was, doubtless, taking no chances. She was going to hoard both.

After double-checking the shutters once the guard locked up the bank, the client executive took a short walk to a pharmacy nearby. There was a crowd of roughly 200 people outside, all clamouring for drugs. He walked back to the bank, got into his car and decided to drive to another pharmacy two kilometres away—only to find another throng of people shouting for tetracycline and gentamicin.

An hour-and-a-half later, he finally spotted a pharmacy, near the Wadala flyover, that was besieged by a relatively small pack of about sixty people. He parked his car in the vicinity, jogged up to the crowd and plunged into the melee. As he pushed and shoved, his phone rang again.

'Did you get it? She is very ill, and now the boy is also coughing a little blood. Please bring it immediately. Please.'

'I am getting it now. Have you tried calling Dr Ambwani?' he asked nobody. She had already cut the call.

He slipped the device into his pocket, and shoved past the crowd. Eventually, he reached a counter were a man was handing out small plastic pouches of drugs, each for Rs 2,000.

'Tetracycline and genta . . .' the client executive began to say when the pharmacist interjected. 'It is already there inside the pouch. Only cash. Come now. Don't waste time.'

Just as the client executive reached for his wallet, there was some commotion inside the pharmacy, and a tall, stocky man walked in through a back door. The staff jumped off their chairs and cowered before him.

'Pack it all up and put it in my car,' the visitor said.

The crowd began to scream.

One of the pharmacists pulled down a creaking shutter. The client executive yanked back his arm just as the shutter slammed shut. He was so angry he could the feel the blood pounding through his ears.

As the crowd quickly dispersed, rushing to other pharmacies, the tall, stocky man walked out. A few minutes later, one of the pharmacists appeared with a large cardboard box, rushed towards an SUV parked on the road and shoved it on to the back seat. The client executive walked up to the SUV and knocked on the windowpane. It lowered and he looked into the face of the intruder who had driven him mad with rage.

'You cannot do this!' he said in Hindi. 'You can't

just take all the medicines. My wife and children are very ill.'

'Please go away. Fuck off,' the driver of the SUV said. The vehicle began to move. The client executive ran alongside. 'Please, just one packet. Please.'

The SUV stopped. The tall, stocky man got out. He had a revolver in his hand. 'Fucker, I will kill you here, and nobody will say a single thing. You were told to get lost, no?'

The client executive took a few steps back. The menacing man hopped back into the SUV. As it sped away, the client executive spotted a government-issued number plate. He ran back to his car, jumped in, swung it on to the road, and began to follow the SUV.

His phone rang again. He took the call, his eyes still glued to the SUV in front of him.

'Son, we're taking her to the hospital again. She is very serious. Can you at least bring some medicines for the children? Okay? I have to take her now.'

He placed the phone on his lap, and smashed his fist into the steering wheel.

The SUV swung through open gates and into a courtyard of a seven-storey apartment building. The client executive slowed down and parked his car just outside the gates. He then watched as the tall, stocky man got out of his SUV, picked up the box of drugs, checked his mailbox, and then sprinted to the lift.

A few minutes later the client executive got out

of his car and picked up something from the boot. He then walked through the gates, checked the flat number on the mailbox, and slipped into the lift himself.

He rang the doorbell and waited. The door opened, and the tall, stocky man now stood in front of him.

'Will you please give me at least one packet?'

'Fuck you. I am going to get my revolver if you don't leave now . . .' the man said as he turned around.

The client executive picked up the tyre iron that was resting on the wall next to the open door and swung it. It hit the man on the back of his head. He instantly fell to the ground.

The client executive walked into the house. A young boy stepped into the corridor, spotted the puddle of blood on the floor, started crying, and ran back into the house.

The client executive found the cardboard box on the dining table. He opened it, fished out a few packets, and placed them on the tabletop. Then he picked up the box.

He was walking out of the flat when the young boy returned. He had his father's revolver in his hand. He fired once. The bullet glanced off the client executive's shoulder, drawing blood. Shocked by the sound of the shot, the boy dropped the weapon.

The client executive briefly considered picking up the tyre iron. But then he heard several doors opening in the building. He fled.

When he reached his home forty minutes later, there was no sign of his wife or his mother. His son lay on a sofa in front of the TV, blood soaking into the upholstery. His daughter was in bed, coughing incessantly. She seemed delirious, flitting in and out of consciousness. The client executive slipped a tablet each of tetracycline and gentamicin into her mouth. He then called his mother's mobile phone. She didn't answer.

On the TV, in the living room, news was breaking about a deputy commissioner of police (DCP) who had been clubbed to death.

So far, the outbreak had seen little actual violence in the city of Mumbai. This attack would prove to be the inflection point.

At a pharmacy, two kilometres away, there were reports of a stampede. Two women had died, four men were severely wounded.

The client executive tried his mother's number every fifteen minutes. Then his wife's. No one would ever pick up. He would never see his mother or wife again.

# 35

**Outbreak + 6**

'How can you kill a DCP?' Nishtha Sharma asked as she glanced at the large flat-screen TV in her office. 'Are people mad? Is this related to the disease?'

The chief minister of Maharashtra stood before a number of men, most of them in the uniform of the Mumbai police. They had arranged themselves into a semi-circle, Nishtha facing them.

'Madam . . . the situation is very complex,' one of the men in khaki—a senior officer in the crime branch—said in Marathi.

'Very good. Very good observation. Very useful inputs. Have you been thinking about this for a long time?' Nishtha spat out in contempt.

The man winced. One of his superiors spoke next. 'What he means to say is that the DCP behaved . . . inappropriately. I am not saying anything justifies . . .'

'What do you mean *inappropriately*?'

The officer described the events leading up to the attack with the tyre iron.

'This is public knowledge?' Nishtha asked, dreading the inevitable fallout.

Just as she spoke, one of the talking heads on television said: '. . . this is not to justify what has happened . . . which is a tragedy for the officer and his family and for this already heartbroken city . . . but we are receiving reports that the police officer may have behaved inappropriately in the hour leading up to his attack . . .'

Nishtha mouthed an obscenity. She then walked to her swivel chair.

'What happens now?' she asked the men assembled before her, even as she pointed a remote control at the TV and turned down the volume. There was an awkward moment as the men looked at each other in silence.

And then, Nishtha's home secretary spoke. 'There will be more violence now, madam. Many people will feel that this type of behaviour is justified. That they can do anything to protect their families from this disease. And anybody who stands in the way is the enemy—be it the government, the police, doctors, or hospitals . . . *anybody*. We need to be prepared for mob fury. I think you should speak to the PM . . .'

Nishtha wasn't ready for this. Not now. Not when she hadn't been given a single opportunity to respond to the crisis herself.

'You are telling me that unrest or violence is inevitable?'

'I am afraid so . . .' said one of the policemen.

Nishtha vaguely recalled that he worked in the state intelligence department. 'We can try to control the panic . . . but unless the disease itself is brought under control . . .'

'Get me the NCDC team,' Nishtha yelled at her personal secretary.

A few moments later, over her speakerphone, Nishtha could hear cacophony at the Haffkine Institute. Shouting over the din, a policeman briefed the NCDC team about the DCP's murder. Then, Nishtha leaned over the speaker-phone. 'First of all . . . how close are we to a solution to this outbreak? Do we know what the disease is?' she asked.

One of the NCDC doctors told her that they would have some sort of update within the next six hours. He left out a tiny detail—that this update could be nothing more than confirmation that they were still clueless.

So far, the NCDC doctor explained, the team had drawn up a checklist of symptoms that was being used to isolate patients. They were still no closer to figuring out how to control the outbreak, or why the disease seemed to kill patients so randomly. And now, he said, his voice growing even grimmer, health workers were also reporting symptoms. At least half a dozen volunteers at the command centre had been moved into an isolation ward with coughs and bloody blisters. 'Madam, if I may be perfectly frank with you

. . . I think the World Health Organization and the Center for Disease Control are going to get involved very soon. We're doing our best. It won't look good, but if they come in, it can save lives and time.'

'I don't care how it looks to anybody. There is a death toll beyond which patriotism has zero value,' she said. 'Also, have you seen any of these messages that are going around on WhatsApp and social media? All these tetracycline and gentamicin messages?'

'Yes, we have. And there are many more. Salt water gargling, Vicks inhalation. Even garlic juice. All useless. In fact, self-medicating at this stage could possibly make things even worse.'

Nishtha nodded sharply. She'd attended enough seminars on drug-resistant microbes to understand the problem. 'Do you think I should release a press note? Or a TV broadcast? Clarify that these remedies don't work?'

There was a brief moment of silence. Nishtha could hear murmuring at the other end of the telephone line. And then the voice resumed. 'Madam, you could do this. But there is little point. In our experience, there's no use telling people not to try a remedy, unless we can actually recommend something that *will* work. And right now there is nothing we can recommend—except asking people to stay indoors and away from patients—which we are certain will prevent meltdowns. Also, there is a collapse of trust.

If you ask the public not to buy gentamicin, and someone important is seen purchasing it . . .'

Nishtha understood. But she decided she would reach out—if not to warn people against self-medicating, at the very least to petition for peace.

'Thank you for your time. Please . . . keep me informed. About any news. Good or bad. And one more thing . . . you called it . . . *meltdown*?'

'Yes. That is what we are calling the final phase of the disease . . .'

'Why?'

'Madam, perhaps we can send you a video of a patient. It is not easy viewing. But you will understand why the final phase comes with this name . . .'

'My secretary will call you in a moment to get this video.'

Nishtha then hung up and informed the assembled group of men that she was going to release a brief communique asking for calm. A one-line version would be sent out to every mobile phone in Mumbai. If violence was inevitable, she said, the city had to have men in uniform out in full force. They had to limit the damage as well as they could. Already the disease was killing people. Panic and violence could not claim more lives.

Every man in the room nodded.

After the group left, Nishtha summoned a cohort of bureaucrats who had been asked to prepare reports on civil and medical supplies, and government services.

Despite a high level of absenteeism, she was told, government services were still functioning. Waste disposal, sewage and sanitation departments were facing the most severe staff shortages. The situation with civil supplies was uncertain. Supermarkets and government ration shops were yet to see the chaos that had descended on pharmacies, and the warehouses of the Food Corporation of India were not seeing abnormal levels of offtake—at least for the moment.

It was the status of the city's medical supplies that was the most troublesome. Many government hospitals had not only run out of key medicines, but had also failed to manage inventory. With every available staff member being asked to handle patients, it was impossible to keep track of stocks. To address this impasse, the health minister had already spoken to the emergency medical relief department in Delhi for fresh stocks.

When the bureaucrats left, Nishtha sat back in her chair for a few moments to catch her breath and organise her thoughts.

This was an unprecedented crisis. Over a thousand people were dead, thousands more were dying. On the basis of everything she had heard so far on the sixth day of the outbreak, Nishtha's government had few options. All they could do was limit the damage, arrange for supplies, and keep the state machinery functioning—while hoping that the NCDC, the World Health Organization, the Center for Disease Control . . . *somebody* . . . would make sense of this bloody outbreak.

One of Nishtha's assistants knocked on her door twice and walked in with a tablet computer. On it was a video ready to be played. The assistant informed her that it had just been emailed from the Haffkine Institute; she left the room.

Nishtha hit play. As the scenes unspooled on the screen before her, Nishtha went pale in the face; she gasped and began to gently sob. It was the most horrible thing she had seen in her life.

First, the patient, a young woman of around thirty-five, lay on the hospital bed coughing up blood and phlegm. Her skin was covered with angry rashes. The camera moved towards her fingers, and Nishtha saw that the nails fell off the fingertips at the lightest touch.

Then, the coughing intensified. More blood.

Suddenly, the woman went silent. She arched her back a little, opened her mouth, and began to gargle out thick, brown-grey sludge streaked with blood.

Just when Nishtha thought it couldn't get any worse, the body heaved a final time, and collapsed on to the bed. Thick, congealed blood poured out of every orifice—so much fluid that it soaked through the mattress and began streaming on to the floor.

As the camera zoomed out, the chief minister noticed that the body of the woman seemed to have collapsed into itself. It was as though catastrophic blood loss had left behind an empty shell.

The woman had literally . . . melted.

## Outbreak + 6

'Sucks to be a Mumbaikar! Nobody wants us anymore! Somebody send some love to Saravli please!' read the tweet. The picture that accompanied it showed a large group of people—women, men, children—huddled on the platform of a small railway station on the Konkan line. Some sat on the floor, eating from plastic bags and drinking from plastic bottles. Others slept on blankets and bed sheets. Most seemed exhausted.

The tweet came from the account of a seventeen-year-old girl named Priya Kewalramani who lived in Kalina, in an apartment building that overlooked the University of Mumbai campus.

Two weeks previously, she had left with friends on a backpacking trip to Kerala—a trip that had culminated in some splendid DSLR photography at the Edakkal caves in Wayanad. Unfortunately for Priya and her friends, they boarded their train back to Mumbai merely hours before the lockdown was announced.

Much later, when she was interviewed in her hospital bed, Priya told video cameras that had she been aware of this lockdown, she would have never boarded the train at all. Instead, her friends and she would have extended the Kerala trip, or taken a bus to Mysore and found another way back home.

At first, when Priya was caught in the middle of the chief minister's announcement of a lockdown, it seemed like a bonus adventure to her. Her group welcomed the disruption, even as the train crawled to Bhatkal and onward to Ankola—stopping frequently and then starting again, as railway managers struggled to deal with sudden hold-ups and numerous cancellations.

The first night, girls slept inside the bogey and the boys took turns staying awake to keep an eye on them. In the morning, the news filtering in from Mumbai was confusing at best. There was some kind of coughing disease. Every once in a while, a passenger reported that someone back home in Mumbai was ill. Priya and her friends had no idea what was unfolding in their city's hospitals, nursing homes and clinics.

At Saravli station, the train finally came to a complete halt. Railway officials weren't sure if its onward passage had been cancelled. While some passengers left with their luggage in a bid to make their way back home, Priya, her friends and two dozen other Mumbaikars stayed on at the station.

At least, they thought to themselves, there were toilets here, and a restaurant. It was safer to wait on a platform than board a rickety bus from Saravli to Mumbai.

Besides, who knew if buses would be allowed into Mumbai?

Soon the mood of the whole group began to sour. They began to hear of entire families in Mumbai falling prey to the mysterious disease—calls coming through every other hour, then every other minute.

By the sixth day of the outbreak, nearly every single passenger on the platform knew somebody in Mumbai who had been rushed to a hospital.

Shortly afterwards, the food and drink at the station began to run out. Tempers began to flare when local traders agreed to supply bread, milk and biscuits at several times retail price. When stranded passengers complained to railway staff, the station manager told them that they were welcome to leave. He was under no obligation to clothe or feed them.

It was after yet another argument with a local trader that Priya Kewalramani posted the photo on her Twitter timeline. At the juncture, she had under 1,000 followers on the social media network, most of them bots. For hours, hardly anybody noticed the tweet, lost as it was in the barrage of increasingly horrifying updates from Mumbai.

And then it was spotted by Annalisa Salmone in New Delhi.

## 36

**Outbreak + 6**

As Dr Bansal flitted in and out of consciousness, he began to see a series of images that made little sense. This only added a feeling of helpless confusion to the cocktail of pain and nausea that coursed around his body.

He was sitting at his desk at Tripoli.

He was back in medical college, watching a group of naked freshers dance on a table.

He was using a tongue depressor on a patient, and the patient was coughing into his mouth.

He was on the phone with his brother, shouting.

He was looking into a swirl of red as he flushed the toilet.

He was screaming as a fingernail, caught in the fabric of his shirt, tore away.

He was begging his brother on the phone to help him. Something was wrong with him.

He was seated on his swivel chair in the consultation room, waiting for the next patient to come in.

He was on the floor, the cold tiles against his cheek; thick, bloody liquid pouring out of his mouth.

He was standing in front of a stack of cardboard boxes, crying, as his brother hugged him.

He tried coughing once or twice, but he couldn't. The fluid was pooling within his lungs, suffocating him.

He reached for his mobile phone one final time, trying to push the buttons with the bloody stubs that were his fingertips.

He fell backwards, and suddenly felt his body fill up. Then he vomited thick purple jets, the liquid staining the carpeted floor of his bedroom.

Suddenly, there was silence. Complete and utter silence. He couldn't even hear the sound of his breath. He felt every muscle in his body strain, his fingers turn stiff as steel, his back arch.

And then, as every muscle in his body relaxed and fluid began to drain out of each orifice, Dr Arvind Bansal died.

At that moment his mobile phone rang.

## Outbreak + 6

At Tripoli Hospital, Dr Anil Bansal no longer remembered when he had last had a break. Every square inch of space in his clinic had been taken up by patients and their families. Many had landed up at Tripoli after being turned away by other healthcare centres.

During the initial phase of the outbreak, when he

still had no idea what he was dealing with, Dr Anil Bansal had encouraged his patients to go home if they felt better. One old woman reluctantly returned to her residence after much coaxing by her son-in-law. An hour or so later, the man came running back with the rest of his family but not the old woman. She had crashed shortly after leaving the clinic. He then proceeded to describe her meltdown in graphic detail. Dr Anil had to ask him to stop scaring the other patients. But the damage was done. Not a single patient or paranoid relative left the clinic after that.

*Which is fair enough*, Anil thought. *No point in leaving before we get a sense of what this disease really is.*

While most of his patients were well beyond saving, somehow none of them had crashed at the clinic itself. Nor did they get substantially better. In some way, the doctor had been able to avert death within his clinic—the waiter being the sole exception.

Dr Anil Bansal had no idea what he was doing right. Was it the antibiotics he was pumping into his patients? Was it the fact that he insisted on constant hydration? Anil was mulling over this, and changing the bandages around a patient's bleeding fingertips, when he heard a boy running into the waiting room.

'Doctor, another gang is coming!'

'Roll down the shutters, go, go, go.'

The boy rushed to the entrance. Anil quickly went

around the clinic, switching off the lights, and calling for silence. A few moments later, there was the sound of the shutter outside being rolled down. The boy locked it from the inside, and then dashed back to the waiting room.

Everyone paused in the dark. There was absolute silence for a few minutes. And then the banging on the shutters started. Followed by a scream. 'If you don't open, we will burn this place!'

More voices. 'Chutiyas want to die. But won't give us medicines.'

'Boss! If you have some tetracycline or gentamicin . . . give it now. Or we will just . . .'

'Burn the lauda's car. Burn it.'

Dr Anil Bansal exhaled.

Fifteen minutes later, when he was certain the mob had left to wreak havoc on some other clinic, Anil slowly unlocked the shutter, and peeped underneath. Then he rolled it all the way up. He walked to his car and looked inside. The mob had done an inept job—the seats in the front were scorched and the glass was smashed, but everything else was intact. He tried starting the car. The engine whined to life. He turned it off.

He walked into the clinic and saw two dozen pairs of eyes observing him.

This was not going to be feasible. He may have been able to keep his patients alive so far. But this was of little use if they were all going to get burnt alive by some crazy drug-mob. He had to move them somewhere safe. But where . . .?

No, first, he had to figure out what was happening outside. Anil Bansal looked up and saw the television on the wall. It hadn't been switched on since Jacintha had gone home on—

Dr Bansal could no longer remember days or dates—they blurred into one another—but he knew for certain that Jacintha hadn't reported to work for a long time . . .

*Now, where is the remote . . .?*

Anil Bansal walked around the reception desk and began rummaging through some drawers. He found the remote control on top of a sheet of paper folded neatly in half. On the back of the paper, Jacintha had scrawled: 'For Dr Anil'.

Anil pointed the remote control at the TV, switched it on, and changed channels till he reached a news broadcast. That's when he remembered what the sheet of paper was for.

He pulled it out of the drawer, unfolded it, and placed it on the reception desk. As he smoothed the crease, he began to glance through a list of names, phone numbers, occupations and addresses.

It seemed like a lifetime ago, when the first set of patients had come to his clinic, and he had asked his nurse to draw up a list of those battling coughs, along with their details. At the time, Anil Bansal had wondered if there was a pattern to this sudden cough outbreak.

Now, of course, he knew that this was anything but a cough epidemic.

The list was intriguing. Anil Bansal read through it once, then twice. Then a third time.

## Outbreak + 6

'Are you a policewoman?' asked the man behind the counter.

'No. But I work for the health services. I am looking for something urgently,' Sati Rout said. She showed the man a picture of the MultiSampler on her cell phone. 'It is the size of . . .'—Sati looked around the restaurant—'. . . your television set. But much heavier.' Then, for what felt like the hundredth time that afternoon, Sati explained the circumstances under which the device had gone missing.

For the hundredth time that day, the man behind the counter shook his head in the negative. 'No idea, madam. As soon as the disturbance on the highway started, we pulled down the shutters and locked the doors.'

'And nobody got out?'

'Nobody.'

'Not even staff? You didn't go out to have a look?'

'Not a single person stepped outside,' lied Mohan Thomas.

'Okay. Thanks. If you hear anything useful please dial this helpline number,' Sati muttered, scribbling a number on to a piece of paper on the counter.

'Madam, what is that machine used for?'

'It may help us find a cure for this disease.'

Mohan Thomas looked towards his kitchen. 'I hope you find it,' he said, watching one of his chefs prepare a new batch of ECB Specials.

Sati turned around and almost reached the door when she suddenly decided to eat something. She was famished. She couldn't even remember her last proper meal. Had it been at the Srivatsa office? At the airport?

She walked back to one of the vacant tables inside Expressway Cool Bar and sat down. Instantly a waiter in uniform appeared and placed a laminated menu before her. Sati ordered an ECB Special and a Diet Coke. Just as the waiter turned away, Sati's phone began to ring. She answered.

'Where are you?' Aayush asked.

'Just getting a bite.'

'I saw some footage from a CCTV camera on the highway. It is not very good. But . . . I think I noticed two people in uniform near the car.'

'Uniform?' Sati asked as the waiter placed her food in front of her.

'Yes. Yellow polo shirts with red collars . . . maybe pink.'

Sari sat upright, the food and drink now forgotten.

Aayush went on: 'And on the back . . . I can't say for sure, but it looked like it read . . .'

'ECB?'

There was a moment of silence on the phone. 'How did you . . .'

At that very moment, one of the chefs dropped a fresh batch of ECB Specials into the fryer. The sound of sizzling oil filled the restaurant.

That was it. That was the sound Sati had heard on Ratnakar's phone when she had got through the last time. The sound of crackling plastic sheets.

'Let me call you back,' Sati said and hung up without waiting for Aayush to respond.

She then dialled Ratnakar Joshi's number.

A moment later, she heard the first faint notes of Eric Bibb's 'Kokomo' from somewhere inside Expressway Cool Bar's kitchen.

She cut the call and dialled Aayush's number again.

'I need you to come to Expressway Cool Bar immediately. And bring some riot police with you.'

Sati then read the restaurant's address off the paper napkin on the table in front of her. When the waiter returned, she asked for another ECB Special. For once, she was in no hurry to go anywhere.

# 37

**Outbreak + 6**

Inside her small, cluttered flat in Delhi, Annalisa Salmone read through her 1,123-word piece for the final time. It was unusually long by BuzzWire standards—the website rarely published anything longer than 400 words. But, then, BuzzWire correspondents rarely got access to ministers of state leaking information on a terrible outbreak—information that the government was desperately trying to downplay. It hadn't taken Annalisa more than one email to convince her editor in New York.

For all its explosive potential, two things about the story bothered Annalisa. First, it was entirely based on a single source—Sumit Jaiswal. Annalisa had been tempted to reach out to other people in the government, especially health workers in Mumbai. This had always been a part of her journalistic process—finding a second source to corroborate her first one, and giving the other side a chance to respond. But Sumit had warned her against doing anything of that sort. The moment the government got wind of her story—he had warned her in the

Italian restaurant—it would try to stall it, delay it or, if nothing else worked, block its publication. On the other hand, once word got out that the government had intentionally withheld information on the outbreak in order to evacuate VIPs—in other words, once Annalisa's story took on a life of its own—the government would be powerless to kill it. It would go viral.

Second, Annalisa was worried about what her story would do to the situation in Mumbai. What if it made things worse? Already, in addition to relentless pressure on healthcare systems, the city was having to deal with an 'antibiotic panic'. The crazy, baseless demand for tetracycline and gentamycin had led to the murder of a senior police officer and, now, several pharmacies were being ransacked by 'antibiotic mobs'.

*How much fuel will my story pour over this fire?* Annalisa wondered, as her mouse arrow hovered over the 'publish' button.

She paused, moved the arrow to another button, and clicked. A laser printer on her desk came to life and produced a copy. Annalisa read it one last time. Just to be sure.

Her headline was okay. Ruthless but factually accurate.

She had used two photos, both from Twitter. One showed a large crowd pushing and shoving outside a health centre in Kurla. The other displayed a group of wretched rail passengers on a platform at Saravli station. Annalisa had left two tweets for the girl who posted the photo online. The girl had not yet responded.

Annalisa double-checked every instance where she had anonymously quoted Sumit Jaiswal. Could anything be used to identify her source? No.

And, finally, was her conclusion strong enough? Yes, it was.

Her only regret was that she had coined a rather boring name for the illness: *Bombay Fever*. But now it was too late to change that.

Annalisa clicked 'publish' and checked the BuzzWire homepage. There it was, right on top. Immediately, she shut her laptop, emailed her editor, and curled into bed. She fell asleep, exhausted by all the nervous energy. A little later, Annalisa Salmone was woken up by a knock on the door. She opened it to find three men in uniform.

## Outbreak + 6

They found the MultiSampler in the storeroom of Expressway Cool Bar. It had been hidden there, behind several sacks of potatoes, under a wooden shelf heaving with bags of buns.

The search had been frantic. In one corner of the dining hall, Mohan Thomas and his staff squatted on the floor, on their haunches, watched over by a riot policeman with a gun.

Once Mohan Thomas admitted to putting up the barricades that killed Ratnakar Joshi, Aayush was filled with white-hot rage. He took it out on Expressway Cool Bar's furniture.

Soon, the main dining hall looked like a storm had blown through it. Tables and chairs lay scattered. Even the ice cream freezer was upended. It stood upside down in a puddle of melted ice.

Mohan Thomas watched blankly as a few policemen carefully walked out of the storeroom with the MultiSampler. They carried it across the wrecked dining area, carefully stepping around the furniture and menus strewn on the floor. They then hoisted it outside and into the boot of a waiting car. Aayush rushed towards the vehicle and, after saying something to one of the police officers, took charge, sped up the road, back into Mumbai. Sati accompanied him.

The police officer walked back to the restaurant and spoke to his boss. 'Sir, what do we with them now? Should I call the control room for a van?'

'Not yet,' said the armed boss looking around the restaurant. 'Doctor sir has asked us to continue searching here for some more time.'

Mohan Thomas gritted his teeth as he saw the police officer walk away into the storeroom. He heard something crash to the floor. They were ripping his restaurant to shreds.

## Outbreak + 6

It was the fastest Aayush had ever driven a car.

When Sati and he arrived outside the Durbar Hall at the Haffkine Institute, a group of anxious men and women were already waiting for them. There were some familiar NCDC officials. But there were new faces as well.

So many hands came forward to carry the MultiSampler that one of the senior NCDC officials had to intervene. Eventually, the machine was carried through the Durbar Hall, down the length of the auditorium, and into a room towards the back. It was immediately connected to a wall socket. Then, one of Ratnakar Joshi's assistants plugged a laptop into the MultiSampler.

'Okay, can we give the technicians some peace and quiet please?' shouted Sati Rout, as she ushered everyone out of the room. 'Can we all just let them work on it?' Some of the senior officials were startled by her insistence.

'It has completely run out of power,' said one of the technicians standing in front of the open laptop. 'All the samples have deteriorated.'

'Fuck!' shouted more than one person.

'So, we'll have to go through the data dump,' one

of the female technicians said, looking at the laptop screen.

'How long will that take?' Aayush asked.

'Who knows? We've only done this while being trained.' With that, one of the technicians walked up to the double door and shut it.

Sati approached Aayush. 'Do you smoke?'

'Sometimes.'

'Give me company?'

Both stood outside the Durbar Hall, puffing on cigarettes they had borrowed from someone working inside.

'What a fuck up, no?' Aayush muttered.

'Hm. I don't know what to think any more. Eight or nine days ago, I was getting bored of this SMO gig. I was thinking of quitting, you know?'

'Really. Why?'

'I didn't see the point. People are stupid, Aayush. You tell them not to self-medicate. They don't listen. No matter what you say.'

## Outbreak + 7

In the early hours of the seventh day of the outbreak, there was a huge ruckus inside the Durbar Hall.

'We can't be 100 per cent certain,' one of the MultiSampler technicians muttered.

'Just fucking tell us!' Aayush said.

'Legionnaires"

'What?'

'Legionnaires' disease,' the man repeated, shrugging.

'That is what it is?'

'Apparently.'

'But can Legionnaires' kill like this?'

## 38

**Legionnaires' Disease**

On 21 July 1976 around 2,000 members of the American Legion—an influential organisation of US war veterans—assembled at the Bellevue-Stratford Hotel in Philadelphia, Pennsylvania. They spent the next three days in meetings and, also, merry-making. On the evening of the 24th, one of the legionnaires, a sixty-one-year-old retired air force captain named Ray Brennan, left early, citing exhaustion. Three days later, Brennan died of what seemed to be a heart attack.

Soon after, seven more legionnaires who had attended the convention passed away. Within a week of the convention ending, 130 attendees ended up in hospital with pneumonia and fever as high as 107 degrees. Twenty-five were declared dead by then—a toll that spiralled to thirty-four as the days crept by.

What had killed these legionnaires?

An investigation, unprecedented in scale, followed. The Communicable Disease Center (now the Center for Disease Control) in Atlanta sent a team of twenty epidemiologists to study the outbreak—a number unmatched in the agency's history.

Yet, weeks later, the investigators were no closer to figuring out the mystery illness. There was intense media speculation, and public panic, that the disease was swine flu. This proved to be an unfounded fear.

Influenza was ruled out completely.

Tests also dismissed poisoning from seventeen different metals.

Exasperated officials, now confronting building media pressure and ridicule, kept going back to toxins and poison gases.

By the close of 1976, researchers had all but given up. It was definitely not a bacterium, many authorities said. Beyond that, they had no clue what had attacked the legionnaires at the hotel in Philadelphia.

The mystery of the outbreak may never have been solved if it wasn't for a Christmas party in 1976 attended by Dr Joseph McDade, a scientist at the Center for Disease Control. Or, to be more precise, if it wasn't for the humiliation McDade suffered at the party—when revellers laughed at his agency's inability to identify the enigmatic disease. As Lawrence K. Altman later wrote in *The New York Times*: '[. . .] the doubters overlooked the importance that human factors like compulsiveness, embarrassment and public pressure can play in solving scientific riddles and making discoveries.'

Incensed, McDade went right back to his lab at the Center for Disease Control to look at the legionnaires' samples again. By January 1977, McDade had cracked the puzzle. Only to create a new one. The disease had, in fact, been caused by a type of bacteria—and it wasn't strange or mysterious at all. In fact, the bacteria that caused the outbreak had been identified as disease-causing at least as far back as 1947. But it had been catalogued as a bug that only affected animals.

Yet here it was, now named *Legionella pneumophila*, killing human beings by the dozens. What had happened? What had the researchers missed over previous encounters with the microorganism?

Legionella proved to be something of a prima donna among bacteria. First of all, it was very picky about the environment it grew in. Scientists found it exceedingly hard to cultivate colonies of Legionella in their laboratories for further studies. Later, they realised that Legionella had a particular fondness for modern technology—air conditioning systems, cooling towers, room coolers, spas and misting machines. This is where the bug tended to multiply in clusters, before being thrown into the air by fans and blowers, to form an infectious aerosol. Indeed, subsequent research revealed that Legionella had thrived in the air conditioning vents of the Bellevue-Stratford Hotel and had—on being pumped out during the convention—been inhaled by the attendees.

Then, scientists discovered that the Legionnaire

bacterium could manifest itself in two forms of illness—the first, the one that hit Philadelphia, now called Legionnaires' disease, produced pneumonia and systemic ailments; the other, Pontiac fever, only caused mild illness. Why the same bug causes two discrete patterns of sickness has not been understood.

In the decades following the convention at the Bellevue-Stratford Hotel, pinning down Legionnaires' continues to be a problem. There are numerous reasons for this. First, patients suffering from it can present a very wide range of warning signs from fever, aches, pains and bloody coughs to dysentery, vomiting and neurological symptoms. Several seem to be down with the flu or pneumonia and, even more deceptively, temporarily respond to normal flu treatment. This means that many doctors, even in countries with excellent healthcare, can misdiagnose an attack of Legionnaires'.

In the decades since the outbreak and McDade's discovery, medical professionals have developed sophisticated methods of responding to Legionnaires'—assuming they identify it. Antibiotics, especially when administered early, are fairly successful. However, fatality rates remain variable. Anywhere between 5 to 30 per cent of patients can die in an outbreak, and the numbers can go up to 50 per cent if the patients are especially susceptible.

Due to its scandalous past, Legionnaires' continues to enjoy media attention when outbreaks occur. And they occur often. In 2015, there was an outbreak in a prison in California, and three in New York. In 2014, a Legionnaires' epidemic in Portugal led to 302 hospitalisations and seven deaths. Authorities were mystified about the source of the illness, though there is speculation that the infection erupted from the cooling towers of a fertiliser factory around the outskirts of Lisbon.

One of the deadliest of all outbreaks was in March 1999 at the Westfriese Flora show in Bovenkarspel, the Netherlands. Around 188 visitors fell ill and at least seventeen died—with a case fatality rate of roughly 10 per cent. Two whirlpool spas and a sprinkler at the flower exhibition tested positive for *Legionella pneumophila.*

Bovenkarspel, however, was not the *largest* outbreak. That dubious title goes to a 2001 epidemic in Murcia, Spain, where more than 800 suspected cases were reported, of which 449 were confirmed. Later investigations implicated the cooling towers at a city hospital.

There is little data on Legionnaires' outbreaks in tropical countries and in developing nations. They happen, no doubt, but they may often be misreported as the flu or pneumonia. Besides, in poorer countries, the disease rarely sets alarm bells ringing. This is, perhaps, because Legionella does not spread from victim to victim.

But what if it did?

## 39

**Outbreak + 7**

Aayush Vajpeyi was puzzled by the MultiSampler results. He began to piece together everything he knew about the outbreak, and then compare that to his sketchy recollections of Legionella from medical school.

Legionnaires' normally broke out at one location. Bombay Fever was clearly erupting all over. Also, unlike Legionnaires', Bombay Fever appeared to be spreading from victim to victim. But how? Touch? Fluids? Mucus?

Aayush kept going back to the visions of meltdowns he had witnessed. Legionella simply did not destroy a human body like that.

Yet the machine said—

'Aayush . . .' Sati cried out in alarm.

Aayush looked at his colleague who pointed at an approaching cavalcade of cars. Moments later, Nishtha Sharma jumped out of a vehicle and rushed into the Durbar Hall, her staff trailing behind her.

As soon as she was out of earshot, Sati spoke: 'Finally someone who can take charge of things. Eh?'

'I hope so,' Aayush muttered. 'At least let's hope she doesn't make things worse.'

## Outbreak + 7

At around 7 am—on the morning of the seventh day of the outbreak—Rachel Soanes sat up in her hotel bed in New Delhi. She yawned loudly, gently turned her head from side to side, stretched her neck, and said to herself: 'Oh . . . I feel much better . . .'

She still had that niggling irritation in her throat that made her want to cough a little. And there was that odd little purple sore—flat and soft and squishy—underneath her left arm. Otherwise, she seemed perfectly fine. Her fever had subsided, her limbs no longer ached, and that dreadful headache had disappeared.

The TV journalist swung her legs out of bed, smiling with relief, and reached for the phone on the nightstand. There were a number of messages from her family in London. And they all sounded very concerned. What was this disease in Mumbai? Was she still coughing? Could she fly back home as soon as possible? Was she safe? Had the disease reached Delhi?

Rachel placed the phone back on the nightstand.

'How did I get here?' she thought to herself. How did she go from being one of the BBC's most respected employees to an out of work, unwanted, desperate hack-for-hire, running around India trying not to get killed by a mystery bug?

She could go back home right away. Even if a travel advisory were to be issued, Rachel knew enough people at the BBC's office in Delhi to pull strings with the high commission and get on to the next British Airways or Virgin flight out of Delhi. Preferably to London but anywhere far enough from this plague business.

However, Rachel Soanes also knew that the Secretariat TV deal was the last throw of the dice as far as her career was concerned. She was tired, and frustrated, and disillusioned. She had spent her entire life working in the space of public policy broadcasting. She was good at it, yes. But she also believed in it. Rachel Soanes didn't just enjoy producing programming about parliaments and cabinets and policies and bills and acts . . . she actually had faith in the virtue of it. She had complete conviction that such television was instrumental in making a democracy a success.

Or did she? Did she really believe that these days? Rachel wondered sometimes. Especially of late, when her work had completely dried up.

India hadn't been first in her list of potential clients when Rachel had started looking for work. She didn't know a whole lot about the country. One of her ancestors had briefly worked in India during the Raj, at Tranquebar on the southeastern coast. But, then, he had quickly sailed back. There were allegations of smuggling . . . or was it a local girl? Or both? Nobody really knew. James Cicero Soanes, suffice to say, did not bring back treasures from the colonies.

But when Nitin Phadnavis won the Lok Sabha elections, Rachel Soanes sensed a glimmer of hope. Here was the youngest prime minister India had ever seen. 'The most exciting thing to happen in Indian politics since Independence', was what *The Economist* had said. Phadnavis was well-educated; had an impeccable track record as a state and then a national lawmaker; spoke several languages, including Japanese; and had done wonders as finance minister in the previous government. Besides, he had achieved all this despite coming from a family with no political credentials. Most of all, Phadnavis enjoyed tremendous cross-sectional appeal across India. He had been elected by a landslide. More than one columnist observed that Nitin Phadnavis' rise seemed almost too good to be true.

A few days after the swearing-in of the Phadnavis government, Rachel Soanes sent an email to the editor of Secretariat TV. Ranveer Singhvi responded immediately and with enthusiasm. Of course he'd like to talk to her. Yes, they were looking to modernise the channel. And yes, they were very keen to do business with Rachel Soanes.

'I should have flown to Delhi directly,' Rachel thought for the thousandth time as she walked towards the sink and grabbed her toothbrush. The idea had preoccupied her ever since news of the outbreak first broke on TV.

While Ranveer's office was in Delhi, Rachel had an old friend who worked at an international school in Mumbai. She had decided to spend a weekend with her before flying to Delhi by the cheapest possible connection.

It had been a bad idea. The traffic in Mumbai was terrible thanks to the Summit at the Somerset, and Rachel spent most of the time indoors with her friend. They ate out once or twice. And then she started coughing.

At around 9 am—seven days into the outbreak—Rachel found herself once again inside the central hall of the Lok Sabha building with Ranveer for company.

'So, I was thinking,' Ranveer said, 'why don't we try something next week during the next session of parliament?'

Rachel beamed. 'Of course. What did you have in mind?'

'Let's do the whole thing. You can direct the session recording, plan follow-up stories, commission them, and then edit the tapes and prepare everything for broadcast. A complete trial run of your . . . skill sets.'

Rachel struggled to suppress a grin. But then she remembered something. 'Ranveer, how long do you think that will take? I am scheduled to fly back . . .'

'Oh, don't worry about that. I'll arrange for your accommodation and transport and all that . . .'

'I am grateful. But it isn't that. You've heard of this outbreak . . .'

'Yes, yes. We had a show on it today—a few ministers commented. I don't think you should worry at all.'

'I am not worried, Ranveer. But my family back home is really freaking out. They want me to go back home as soon as possible.'

'Do you want to?'

'Of course not. I want to work. Right now. Right away.'

'Then, don't worry. Look, Rachel, these things keep happening all the time,' Ranveer said as he walked over to one of the chairs pooled together in the central well of the Lok Sabha hall. 'Do you know how many people die of tuberculosis in India?'

'I have no idea.'

'At least 4,80,000 deaths a year. That amounts to, on an average, over 1,300 people dying of TB every day. You need to take outbreaks with a pinch of salt in this nation.'

Rachel frowned. She suddenly didn't like this man at all. Ranveer saw the sour look on her face.

'Sorry. That came out all wrong. What I mean to say is that you need to be careful about overreacting. This outbreak sounds terrible. I've seen some videos. Terrible. But we still don't know what it is. It could be a bacteria. Or some kind of poison. Or maybe the Pakistanis have launched a chemical attack—Mumbai first, and then maybe Delhi.'

*Well, that would be great, fuck you very much,* Rachel thought.

'The media will always panic. That is what they do. Panic is the lifeblood of the fourth estate.'

Rachel smiled. Ranveer went on, even as he pulled out his mobile phone and began to scroll through updates: 'The public will, in turn, worry because it has no idea what is going on. Because there is no information. But things tend to sort themselves out. As soon as it is clear what this outbreak is and how to treat it, all the nervous energy will dissipate. And don't worry about travel advisories. The government is working on this as we speak.'

'So you think it is safe for me extend my trip? And, if all goes well, stay on?'

'Absolutely. 100 per cent. And the moment you think you're falling ill, I'll get you to the best doctor in Delhi.' Ranveer paused, then said, 'Also, just so you're clear, I'll pay you for your time and trouble.'

Rachel was both relieved and delighted. Finally. A project. Some money. She didn't know how much.

But at least this was work she actually wanted to do. She would have to have a long chat with her family. They would hate her for staying back with this disease looming. But maybe, like Ranveer said, the government would figure it out . . .

Ranveer's voice interrupted her thoughts. 'See, Rachel! I told you. Look at this . . .'

He handed his phone to her. She read a message from one of his reporters: 'Maha CM on TV in 30 minutes. They've figured it out. Something called Legionnaires'. Treatment plans and emergency drug supplies being arranged by NCDC. Top story today.'

'This is such a relief, Ranveer!'

The editor smiled broadly as he took his phone back. 'What did I tell you? Everything is going to be fine.'

Rachel nodded. It was time to get back to work. 'So, where does the prime minister sit during sessions . . .'

# 40

**Outbreak + 5**

The prime minister sat in a small but comfortable armchair and looked around him. The room, like the chair, was tiny but cosy. However—with the exception of one object—everything about it seemed curiously outdated. At first glance, Nitin Phadnavis thought, it looked like the set for a 1980s Hindi film.

Everything was beige—from the switches, to the lampshades, to the intercom on the wall next to his chair. The carpet was a deep burgundy and the wallpaper was a hideous pattern of rectangles and triangles. There was a poster that was definitely Russian—or was it?—with letters in a script that was either Cyrillic or gibberish.

The two most striking features of the room were the very low ceiling and the absence of even a single window.

There was a knock on the door, before it slid open to one side and a man in a suit entered.

Phadnavis pointed to a small stool nearby. 'I am sorry about the uncomfortable seating,' he said. 'As you can see, the furnishings here are somewhat humble.'

The man merely nodded and sat down.

'So this . . . Beta Protocol. How long have you known?' Phadnavis asked.

Prakash Rao said nothing.

'How does this work? Is there a training programme?'

'Sir, everything you need to know about Beta Protocol is in that folder on the desk.' Prakash pointed to a tiny Formica-topped writing desk in the corner. 'I cannot add anything more to that. I am afraid that is the . . .'

'Protocol?' Phadnavis said, smiling broadly. A hint of a smile flashed across Prakash's face.

Phadnavis got up carefully and walked around the room. 'So, how does a secret department of the government—one that even the government is unaware of—steal a submarine from the Indian navy?'

'I am not privy to that, sir.'

'Hmm . . .' Nitin Phadnavis said, walking back to his chair and sitting down.

'Can I at least ask you where we are in the ocean? Somewhere along the east coast, I suppose? Away from Pakistan?'

'I am not aware of that, sir.'

Phadnavis smiled. But his composure was getting ruffled. Nothing in his political or professional life had prepared him for recent events.

Mere hours ago, he recalled, his security team had

secretly whisked him away from the Somerset Hotel in a pair of unmarked cars. They had told him that, flouting all terror alert protocols, they were taking him to Juhu airport. Phadnavis had found it strange that he was accompanied only by the head of the SPG, Prakash Rao, while the rest of the team was in the other vehicle. It had seemed like a security risk. At some point, the two cars split up. One drove to the Juhu airstrip. Phadnavis' vehicle seemed to take a detour and then headed towards the Force One base near the Taj Mahal Hotel. Force One, established in 2016, was Maharashtra's elite terror response unit.

Phadnavis was hurried from the car to a waiting helicopter. 'Why are we here?' he asked Prakash Rao, who politely but firmly asked him to board the chopper. For the briefest of moments Phadnavis felt that he was the victim of a conspiracy—perhaps, after a biological attack on Mumbai, he was being kidnapped.

That feeling of terror only intensified when, a few minutes after taking off, Prakash handed the prime minister a sealed envelope. Phadnavis' eyes widened. 'What is this? A message from some high-tech terror outfit?' he wondered.

He carefully broke the wax seal, and pulled out a sheet of paper with the stamp of the Government of India. His eyes darted past the text to the name and signature at the bottom.

*Atal Bihari Vajpayee.*

'What the . . .'

'Please read it fully, sir. You will receive more information when we land.'

Phadnavis read the letter in astonished silence.

*Dear Prime Minister,*

*If you are reading this letter, it unfortunately means that Beta Protocol has been activated. This implies that the nation, including the government and you, are facing imminent danger from known or unknown sources. Beta Protocol is a mechanism to safeguard the government in times of great crisis. There is, without a doubt, much for you to do at this stage. So, I will be brief while explaining what happens next . . .*

Seventy minutes later, Nitin Phadnavis and Prakash Rao were lowered from the chopper on to the deck of a surfaced submarine. They were received by a single crew member in unmarked uniform, who then escorted both of them into the vessel. Phadnavis, struck dumb, quietly did as he was told. He was led into a room—sparsely furnished but with a state-of-the-art satellite videoconferencing workstation.

Within minutes, Prakash set up a videoconference link with New Delhi for an urgent meeting. It was after this that Phadnavis had his uncomfortable exchange with Sumit Jaiswal.

Then, after a brief break to wash up, the prime minister was handed the folder that now sat on his desk. It was a longer, more elaborate explanation of Beta Protocol than Vajpayee's letter had been. When he was done reading this, Phadnavis had a vague notion of what had transpired.

As soon as news of a potential disease outbreak had broken within SMO circles, Prakash Rao had initiated the first step in Beta Protocol. The submarine, with what he assumed was a skeleton crew, was placed on high alert, along with transport and communication networks. The tipping point came when—soon after the crash at the airport—the outbreak spiralled out of control. At that stage, someone or something—the prime minister wondered if there was some sort of computer-aided decision-making at work here—took a call to push Beta Protocol into full activation mode. Making the prime minister of India vanish was merely how it began.

'What are your assumptions?' Phadnavis asked Prakash Rao.

'Excuse me, sir?'

'What is your worst case scenario? Surely you assume some kind of crisis is unravelling? You are not doing this because of a disease . . .'

'No, sir. Our worst case scenario is that this is some kind of biochemical attack . . .'

It was a reasonable assumption to make,

Phadnavis thought. That had been his precise fear, too, when he had been bundled on to the helicopter.

What was it? A virus? A bacteria? A poison of some sort? Had one of the delegates at the Summit brought it from abroad? What the hell was going on in Mumbai and the rest of India?

'Prakash, can you set up an hourly update system for me? Talk to the NCDC perhaps? I want to know what is happening.'

'No problem, sir. Our communication works best when we are close to the surface. And our plan is to dive only if we have to. So, right now we can do whatever you want us to.'

'Can I get a cup of good coffee?'

'I will try, sir. But I think you should get some sleep while you still can. You are going to have some difficult days ahead.'

Phadnavis nodded. 'Before you go, Prakash . . .'

'Yes?'

'Has this ever happened before?'

'Sir . . .?'

'Beta Protocol. Has it ever been invoked before?'

'I am not aware of that, sir.'

'Of course not,' Nitin Phadnavis said before dropping into the armchair inside his underwater office.

Phadnavis waited for Prakash Rao to return with a cup of milky coffee and a small plate of biscuits.

The prime minister hadn't realised how hungry he was and ate with enthusiasm.

Afterwards, Nitin got up and went to the communications terminal. He spoke to his wife and daughter briefly, without divulging the details of his unusual location. They were both worried but the call calmed them considerably. They had already been transferred to a holding facility within AIIMS with a dedicated team that kept them under constant medical surveillance. So far, they exhibited no symptoms.

Phadnavis wondered if this, too, was part of Beta Protocol. Where did it begin and where did it end?

After the call, he took a shower in a tiny cubicle and then went to bed. He fell asleep almost immediately.

## 41

## The Submarine

The submarine that held Nitin Phadnavis and a skeleton crew of around a dozen hand-picked personnel did not officially exist. Nothing on the outside or the inside of the vessel could help in its identification. Expert defence analysts would have been able to identify it up to a point, and no further. From its shape and the three-screw propulsion system, they'd know it was a Foxtrot-class submarine designed and manufactured in the erstwhile Soviet Union. And that was about as far as they'd get.

Foxtrots played an important role in the early years of the Cold War. And four such submarines were involved in the Cuban Missile Crisis. The average Foxtrot had twenty-two torpedoes that could be fired from ten tubes. It could carry a full crew of seventy-eight sailors. It held an unusually heavy load of batteries that slowed it down and ate into crew space—but these also gave it up to ten days of underwater endurance.

By the early 1980s, Foxtrot-class submarines became altogether obsolete, getting superseded by more modern Soviet submarine classes.

Between 1957 and 1983, though, the Foxtrot was recognised as a state-of-the-art piece of equipment that, despite some shortcomings, was capable of standing up to most rival Western ships. Of the seventy-four Foxtrot-class boats—several of them manufactured at the Admiralty Shipyard in St Petersburg—fifty-eight were used by the Soviet navy. Sixteen were manufactured for other countries. The Indian navy inducted four of them between 1967 and 1969, and called them 'Kalvari-class'—after the lead vessel, the *INS Kalvari*. The other submarines were *INS Khanderi*, *INS Karanj* and *INS Kursura*.

After roughly three decades of service, the Kalvari-class vessels were all decommissioned. Of these, one—the *INS Kursura*—ended her service in somewhat unusual fashion. Shortly after being decommissioned in 2001, the submarine was towed to the Ramakrishna Mission Beach in Visakhapatnam and inaugurated, in August 2002, as India's first submarine museum.

Or that, in any case, is the official version of events.

The truth is somewhat more complicated.

The vessel that is currently displayed in Visakhapatnam is, in fact, not *INS Kursura*. Most of its chassis belong to *INS Karanj*.

The real *INS Kursura* became the victim of a peculiar seafaring blunder in 1969 that did not involve the *INS Kursura* itself. During a training exercise off the coast of Mumbai, her sister submarine *INS Karanj* collided with the destroyer *INS Ranjit*. No lives were lost, but *INS Karanj*'s superstructure was severely damaged. The accident became an embarrassment for the navy and the government.

The navy promised to quickly repair *INS Karanj*. But, then, the Russians seemed reluctant to share drawings and specifications—an all too common problem with such purchases. Running out of time, the navy decided to use *INS Kursura* as a template. Both vessels were docked side by side at Bombay Dockyard and work commenced on *INS Karanj*. Technicians and engineers shuttled from vessel to vessel, copying specifications and carrying out repairs. Some months later, a gleaming and fully operational *INS Karanj* was paraded in front of relieved military and political leadership, and the foreign press.

Or so the records state.

The truth is far more complicated. Despite the presence of the perfectly functional *INS Kursura* next door, technicians found repairing *INS Karanj* extremely challenging. Without help from the Russians, even basic structural work took months where the navy had budgeted for weeks. It quickly became clear to the naval leadership that *INS Karanj* would simply not be ready to sail again for at least eighteen months. This not only would be an unacceptable loss of face, but would also, if disclosed, embolden India's strategic rivals.

Something had to be done.

And something was: the submarines swapped names. It was an elegant but risky idea. A functional *INS Kursura* was unveiled before the world as *INS Karanj*. As for the real *INS Karanj*—the navy claimed that it was *INS Kursura*—a perfectly functional vessel that had now been assigned for special training and research duties in port. It was quietly docked away— unbeknownst to most, it was crippled and essentially useless.

It had been a shrewd sleight of hand on the part of the Indian navy. But it had underestimated RAW and Rameshwar Nath Kao. Kao made a detailed dossier on the navy's subterfuge and locked it up in his archives. Who knew when such information would come handy . . .

And then, the moment arrived. Shortly after his meeting with Morarji Desai in 1977, Kao went to the chiefs of the Indian navy. He took the dossier with him. His plan did not need much convincing. After all, Kao assured the chiefs that it was all a matter of national security.

It had been eight years since the accident that had crippled *INS Karanj*. Since then, however, the Indian navy had figured out every single nut, bolt and rivet on the Kalvari-class submarine. Repairing the old vessel was no longer a problem.

A year after he had shown them his dossier, the navy handed over to Rameshwar Nath Kao his very own submarine. In a moment of whimsy he named the submarine *Shark*. The name stuck.

Kao's engineers spent a month sweeping *Shark* for bugs before turning it into a floating command centre. It was then put into cold storage at a small base in the Lakshadweep islands that the navy generously allowed Kao to borrow. *Shark* was equipped with a skeleton crew of special RAW operatives trained by the navy. And there it would wait, day and night, day after day, for a phone call.

Meanwhile, in 2002, the navy decided to set aside one of its obsolete submarines for a museum in Visakhapatnam. That submarine would be what the world knew as the *INS Kursura*. The remaining Kalvari-class boats, the navy announced, had been scrapped.

As far as the world is concerned, there is only one Kalvari-class submarine left in India—the one called *INS Kursura*, a splendid museum vessel.

# 42

**Outbreak + 7**

On the real *INS Kursura*, Nitin Phadnavis was startled by Prakash Rao.

'Sir . . . sir . . .'

'Yes, I can hear you. This room is the size of a suitcase . . .'

'Sir, we've received a message that the terror alert in Mumbai has been lifted. Rahul Bhandari was one of those felled by the disease outbreak.'

'Ah!'

'Also, news just in from the NCDC—they believe it is Legionnaires' disease.'

The prime minister sat up. 'Legionnaires' disease? What is it?'

'I am putting together a file for you right away.'

'Thanks. Give me ten minutes to get ready. I want to speak to my cabinet and then Maharashtra's chief minister . . .'

'Sir, that is the other thing. She is about to make an announcement right now . . .'

'Get me a copy immediately,' Nitin Phadnavis said, jumping to his feet. He winced as his head hit an exposed pipe that ran along the length of his cubicle.

Phadnavis was annoyed by Nishtha's impetuousness. Still, he thought, what was the worst that could happen?

It was not like a press conference could make the outbreak even deadlier.

## Outbreak + 7

It was a decision that Nishtha Sharma would revisit over and over again in the weeks and months that followed the outbreak. Should she have waited a little longer for an announcement? Would that have made any difference? Had she jeopardised thousands of lives?

In the early hours of the seventh day of the outbreak, Nishtha barged into the Durbar Hall at the Haffkine Institute, her staff behind her, demanding to hear more about the MultiSampler results.

'Is this the machine?' she asked, jerking her chin at the squat, black object that hummed gently.

'Yes, madam,' one of the NCDC experts responded deferentially. Nitin Phadnavis' presence evoked respect and admiration. Nishtha Sharma, on the contrary, wore a steel armour of intimidation.

'Can we trust these results? Is it really . . .' she glanced at the sheet of paper in her hand, 'Legionnaires' disease?'

The team of NCDC experts packed into the tight little chamber glanced at each other furtively. The technician working on the MultiSampler looked away, trying to make no eye contact whatsoever with the Maharashtra chief minister.

Nishtha Sharma seethed: 'Speak! Somebody!'

'Madam . . . we cannot say with 100 per cent certainty that it is Legionnaires', and if it is . . . what type of Legionella it is,' an NCDC staff member—a short, stocky woman in a faded pink sari—mumbled.

'Why not?'

'There are a few reasons,' the woman in the sari continued. 'First of all, this machine itself is an experimental device. It is not designed to give results in a few days or even a few weeks. All we can say at this point is that the bacterium shows several similarities to certain known varieties of Legionella.'

'I still don't follow why we can't just start reacting to the assumption that it is Legionnaires'. Can you prescribe drugs?'

The researcher swallowed before speaking, beads of sweat forming on her forehead. 'Madam . . . some of us feel that it is premature to announce anything right now. Even if it is Legionella . . .'—she looked at her colleagues for some support, but everyone looked away— 'even if it is Legionella . . . madam, this is not how Legionella presents itself . . .'

'The symptoms, you mean?'

'Yes. People with Legionella just don't die like this. I have never seen anything like this. None of us has.'

'So, you are telling me to announce that we have some information finally, but it cannot be shared at this moment? And that our experts need more time?'

'Ideally, madam . . . you need not make any announcement right now. All of us are working very hard to figure this out. Dr Joshi's accident was a tragedy but we're getting more help. Now, at least, the bacter . . .'

Nishtha did not wait for the women to finish. 'Tell me Ms . . .?'

'Selvi . . .'

'Tell me, Ms Selvi, how many people do you have in this location right now?'

'You mean, health workers and NCDC staff and . . .'

'Grand total. Everyone. Don't waste my time. How many people are here in this building right now . . . working on the outbreak?'

'I am not sure. Somewhere between 200 and 300.'

'And how many of them know that this could be some form of Legionella?'

'I think all of them know by now . . .'

'How long do you think it will take a TV channel somewhere to get in touch with somebody here . . . maybe even a peon or a sweeper . . . and leak such news?'

The woman said nothing.

'This news . . . this Legionella . . .' the chief

minister slashed the air with the sheet of paper in her hand as she spoke, 'is going to hit headlines in one hour. Maybe even in thirty minutes.'

Her priority now, Nishtha explained, was to prevent any more panic, rumours or violence. She had riot police on the streets in Mumbai and Pune, hundreds of policemen guarding government buildings and some hospitals, and battalions of CRPF constables barricading roads and overseeing the airport.

'I have asked for army support,' she admitted, 'because I have no other response. I cannot . . . we don't know what to do if this gets worse . . .'

She paused for a moment to catch her breath. Then, she spoke in a calmer voice. 'So, I am going to draw up a statement. Ms Selvi, come with me. The rest of you, do your job. Figure this out. Please. How many dead so far?'

'Around 1,600,' Aayush Vajpeyi said.

Nishtha walked out of the room shaking her head, followed by her retinue, and a petrified NCDC staffer.

Around 9.30 am on the seventh day of the outbreak, Nishtha Sharma was outside the Durbar Hall, in front of a lectern. She struggled to see past the camera lights that shone in her face, even as two hundred reporters, cameramen and photographers waited to hear from her. Many of them wore face masks and clutched on to little bottles of hand sanitiser.

Nishtha spoke first in Marathi, much to the consternation of the English language press, and then delivered a near-verbatim English translation. In both cases, she conveyed her message without greetings.

'In the last hour or so, members of the team from the National Centre for Disease Control have informed me that they have made a preliminary breakthrough in the effort to identify the disease that has already affected thousands of Mumbaikars and killed hundreds.'

This was an intentional understatement.

'I want to stress again that these results are yet to be confirmed and studied in detail. But the NCDC experts tell me that this disease . . . it may be caused by a bacterium belonging to the Legionella family. As you can imagine, I am not an expert on Legionella and cannot elaborate any further. But if this is confirmed, there is very little need for panic. I have been assured by the dozens of experts working in this building that Legionnaires' is a disease with a known cure and a low fatality rate.'

This was also an intentional understatement.

'At the moment, I ask everyone—citizens, media and health workers—to maintain calm. We have already seen stray incidents of violence in Mumbai and Pune. Such mayhem achieves nothing but only hampers relief efforts and makes it even harder for the government to help. Please, please don't panic. Please cooperate with the authorities and health workers. Inside the Durbar Hall and all over Mumbai, dozens of government servants and health workers are risking life and limb to help the public. Please support them.'

*So far, so good,* Nishtha thought.

'Finally, I have asked the NCDC and state health department staffers here to provide you with updates every three hours. My colleague from the health department will give you a detailed overview regarding what is happening in the city and what steps are being taken. I assure you on behalf of the Maharashtra government and the prime minister that everything possible is being done to fight this disease.'

Nishtha walked away from the lectern to a barrage of questions from the assembled press.

'Madam, do you know how many people have died so far?'

'Madam, what is the medicine for Legionella?'

'Madam, do you know where the prime minster is? Are the rumours true?'

Nishtha walked back into the Durbar Hall and stood next to a bank of telephones manned by startled SMOs.

'What rumours?' she asked her secretary.

'A news website—BuzzWire—has a story that the government covered up news of the outbreak for twenty-four hours.'

'Why would we do that?'

'To allow the prime minister and other VIPs to evacuate.'

'But I am here, no? What nonsense . . .'

'But that is what they are saying. They've even quoted an anonymous source in the government.'

Nishtha chaffed. 'Where is Nitin? We are in touch, but I have no idea where he is . . .'

'We don't know either.'

'Did he really run away?'

'I have no idea.'

'This is ridiculous.'

'There's another thing—BuzzWire has referred to the outbreak as Bombay Fever. It has gone viral.'

Twenty minutes later, Nishtha Sharma was in her car, driving back to Mantralaya at top speed, as policemen held the roads open for her.

'What the hell is going on?' she thought to herself. She had a city under siege thanks to a killer outbreak. And now she also had to deal with these ridiculous rumours of a cover-up. Where was the most powerful man in the country during this moment of crisis?

*Coward*, Nishtha thought to herself. He was just a coward like all the others. A coward with a smile, a coffee fetish, a posh suit and a fancy degree.

Two phones vibrated in her car at the same time. One was her secretary's device, confirming the receipt of a new message. The other was Nishtha's own phone. She picked it up.

'Hello?'

'Nishtha, this is Nitin Phadnavis.'

Next to her, the secretary read a WhatsApp message and frowned. This was precisely the kind of baseless rumour-mongering they were trying to avoid. 'SWITCH OFF ALL AIR CONDITIONERS RIGHT NOW TO STOP SPREAD OF LEGIONELLA . . .' started the message on a family WhatsApp group.

Somebody has been reading about Legionnaires' disease online, the secretary thought.

## 43

**Outbreak + 7**

At Tripoli Hospital, Dr Anil Bansal was so absorbed
by the temporary residents in his clinic and Jacintha's
patient list that the preceding night slipped into day.

As he sat hunched over the list, patients and their
families sat huddled on chairs or on the floor. At that
point, there were twenty-three of them, including
the doctor. Eight of these were patients with rasping
coughs and flu-like symptoms ranging from the mild
to the severe. The rest were family members, and one
petrified boy who worked in the general store next
door—he had begged to be let in after his shop was
ransacked by a gentamycin mob.

Eventually the groups had arranged themselves
around a large surge protector that sat in the middle
of the floor. Several wires snaked away from it to
mobile phones.

'Thank god they've stopped bickering over power
points,' Anil thought.

As the hours passed, his visitors learnt to get along
and use the toilets, water purifier and power points
responsibly. Food was still a problem. The previous

night, Anil rolled up the steel shutter outside just long enough for the boy to transfer several days' worth of food and water from the gutted shop next door.

Anil Bansal went through every name on Jacintha's patient list, calling up phone numbers when available, and drawing up small patient profiles. Not all his calls were answered. And when he did get through, he usually ended up speaking to a dead patient's parent or spouse. It was harrowing work. But Bansal went about it meticulously.

'Do you know where he worked?'

'When did she first start coughing?'

'Where do you live?'

'Has anybody else at home fallen ill?'

He even managed to speak to a couple of patients who had got better and seemed to stay that way, except for a fever and a mild cough. He spent as much time as possible with these exceptional cases.

At some point, Anil Bansal went to a room towards the back, cracked open a window, and smoked a cigarette. Suddenly he smiled. What the hell was he doing—amateur epidemiology? Using a phone, a notebook and a ballpoint pen? There was very little chance that anything he was working on would be useful. Epidemiology was hard work. And these days researchers went around with mathematical models and geoinformatics systems and all kinds of gadgets.

What did he have?

Still. It was better than sitting at home doing nothing like his brother or Jacintha. Anil had tried reaching out to both of them and had failed. Where were they? A thought kept coming into his head but he pushed it out.

'Sir! Sir!'

Bansal turned around. It was the boy from the shop. 'What is the problem now?' he asked.

'Sir, where is the switch for the AC?'

'What?'

'We have to switch off the AC immediately. The disease is coming from the AC.'

'Who told you?'

The boy grabbed him by the arm and dragged him into the waiting area. A news bulletin was playing on loop on the TV screen at high volume. Bansal watched it quietly for a few minutes.

'Sir, please switch off the AC, no?' the boy pleaded with him. And then some of the others joined him.

'I just got it on WhatsApp,' one of the men next to the surge protector said. 'Look . . .' he handed his phone to Anil Bansal.

It was a message, phrased and formatted with the paranoid urgency of all WhatsApp forwards.

'SWITCH OFF YOUR AC RIGHT NOW TO STOP BOMBAY FEVER. GOVERNMENT HAS ANNOUNCED THIS JUST NOW. THE DISEASE IS COMING FROM YOUR AIR CONDITIONER.

SAVE LIVES. ACT NOW. FORWARD THIS TO EVERYBODY RIGHT NOW.'

Others showed Anil Bansal similar messages on their phones. All these forwards emphasised one single thing—switching off the air conditioner.

But that was ridiculous, Anil thought. He jogged his memory, trying to remember the Legionella case study from medical school.

Sure, the bacterium liked to live inside ACs and cooling towers. But switching off ACs was hardly a scientific solution—the move would only make overloaded hospitals and filthy wards even less tolerable. And even if it were Legionella . . . the bug didn't spread from air conditioner to air conditioner.

What a ludicrous rumour, Anil thought.

'Sir, please sir, please.' The requests were beginning to get louder and more fervent.

'Fine,' Anil said. He walked over to the reception desk, fished out a remote control from inside the drawer, and switched off the air conditioner. Within thirty minutes, the room began to feel stuffy.

Anil Bansal walked away and began to go through his medicine stock for drugs to treat Legionella—just in case there was truth to the report. Did he have anything? Would strong doses of flu drugs work? He wished he had his brother with him right now.

Of the two brothers, Arvind was, by any measure, the better doctor. Anil was good with people and had endless patience, but the elder Bansal had the gift of healing. He also had a prodigious memory. Anil knew that if his brother were around right now, he'd already be suggesting treatment schemes for Legionella from memory.

'Where is he?' Anil wondered, not for the first time.

He picked up a few bottles of drugs and went back to the waiting area.

Soon, it was nearly noon. Anil Bansal was exhausted. After administering a fresh dose of drugs to his patients, some of whom seemed to be squirming in the suffocating heat, he went back to his little epidemiology project.

He wasn't convinced it was Legionnaires' disease—but who was he to dispute an official announcement?

Still—maybe he could investigate.

The hours progressed. Anil decided to call it a night.

He wished his patients and walked down the corridor. He stopped at his brother's consulting room with the corpse in it. The air conditioner was still running.

Dr Anil Bansal proceeded to his own room—it was cool, the AC blasting air. Too exhausted to think, he climbed into the examination bed and immediately fell asleep.

## Outbreak + 8

Dr Anil Bansal was woken up by incessant knocking on the door.

It was that wretched boy again.

'What do you want? You want to switch on the AC again?'

'No, no, doctor. The disease is getting much worse now. Please do something.'

'What?'

'The disease—'

Bansal ran into the lobby. A patient, an eleven-year old boy, was shivering violently. But what caught Anil Bansal's attention was the state of his skin. It was beginning to break out into flat, purple blisters. This was bizarre. Anil remembered seeing the boy playing with a tablet computer as he went to bed.

He looked at his watch. It was 5 am. He had to do something about the boy. Otherwise he knew exactly what would happen next.

'Bring him to my room!' Anil said, rushing to his consulting room.

Three men brought the boy in and placed him on the examination bed.

'Okay, now go away and leave us alone.'

Anil closed the door behind him and looked at the boy who writhed in agony. He picked up the boy's right hand. His fingers were beginning to stiffen, blood welling up under the fingernails.

'I don't know what to do,' screamed Anil Bansal. 'What do I do for you!'

The doctor fell to his knees and started sobbing.

And then, ever so slowly, the boy stopped squirming.

## 44

**Outbreak + 7**

'Honestly, how many times will you look at it?' Sati Rout asked.

'Sati, any news from the airport?' Aayush answered, ignoring his colleague's question, his eyes fixed on the MultiSampler printouts.

'Some patients are still in quarantine. No news otherwise.'

Aayush was surprised. 'Nothing? No news at all? No recent deaths or anything?'

'There are a few cases of persistent bad coughs. But as far as I know, no one has crashed in the airport since I left.'

'*Thoda strange hai, na?*' Aayush commented. 'Isn't it bizarre?'

'Hmm . . . given the fatality rates we are seeing elsewhere . . . the airport is an outlier,' Sati said. 'By the way, I managed to get a copy of the on-board video camera from the jeep that crashed. Do you want to see it with me?'

'Send it to my phone, no? I am still troubled by this Legionnaires' thing, Sati . . .'

'Don't be. They're loading up the MultiSampler with another set of samples. And they're flying down more MultiSamplers today from Singapore. We'll figure it out sooner or later. At least, now, we have some kind of idea. Things are getting better, don't you see?'

The two SMOs were standing outside the Durbar Hall at the Haffkine Institute waiting for the NCDC team to issue fresh orders. The last few hours had seen a semblance of calm within the command centre. Doctors and medical staff were being flown in from Delhi and emergency medical supplies were already being distributed across hospitals in Mumbai.

The lockdown also seemed to be working well. Besides a few cases of severe coughing in Pune, there were no further reports of patients going into meltdown anywhere outside India's business capital. The death toll in Mumbai, too, now appeared to stabilise at a fatality rate of 37 per cent. This was still abnormally high, especially given the number of patients afflicted. But, at least, things weren't getting worse.

Aayush, Sati and everyone else at the centre, especially the experts from NCDC, knew that besides isolating and identifying the exact bacterium, the next big step was figuring out a way of recognising patients suffering from Bombay Fever—and early. Distinguishing between relatively harmless flus and coughs and Bombay Fever was paramount. That was the only way to contain the disease, then treat it.

But Aayush reckoned they were still several days away from that stage.

'It is a relief to step outside,' Sati said, inhaling deeply.

Inside the Durbar Hall, the air was stifling. Someone had switched off all the air conditioning, and despite windows and doors being opened, the men and women inside were beginning to shimmer with sweat.

Aayush found the WhatsApp forwards currently surging across mobile phones all over India amusing. It made absolutely no sense to switch off air conditioners or room coolers. But people everywhere—not just in Mumbai but all over the country—were falling over each other to switch off cooling devices and, in some cases, even refrigerators.

Suddenly, a man came jogging from inside the Durbar Hall. 'Are you Aayush Vajpeyi?'

'Yup.'

'Okay, so they're running some models right now. They want you to go to Ward A and double-check the numbers. The details are on this sheet.'

'Can do. No problem.'

'Also, can you specifically go back to Cusrow Baug to assess the situation . . .'

'Of course.'

The man paused, then spoke again. 'You are not afraid, sir?'

'Of what?'

'Bombay Fever?'

Aayush grinned. 'If I had to get Bombay Fever, I would have got it by now. So, maybe I am resistant somehow. What about you, Sati? Coming?'

'No. You go ahead. I'll probably get my own orders shortly. I want to check out the scene at the airport. You're right. It is strange. The fatality rate there is something like . . . 2 per cent.'

Aayush shrugged his shoulders and jumped on to a motorbike parked outside. He decided to get to Cusrow Baug first and then work his way northwards through the hospitals and clinics mentioned on the data sheets.

There were policemen everywhere—especially outside hospitals, where they tried to maintain some form of crowd control. He drove past the shells that were once pharmacies and general stores— some ransacked, some still smouldering, but none presently under attack. Public transport was running again, although the buses were empty. Even more surprisingly, Aayush saw a few restaurants open. A handful even had customers grabbing a meal.

Things had quietened down a bit, the SMO noted with some satisfaction.

But only just.

In isolated pockets of the city, there were patients clamouring to get into hospitals, sheathed bodies in parking lots, and occasional bouts of violent shouting and pushing and shoving.

'Mumbai is weird,' Aayush thought as he swung his bike off the main road and through a narrow lane lined by slums. It took a few moments for him to realise something. Aayush slowed down his bike, then parked it by the side of the road, right outside the doorway of a small hut with a blue tarpaulin sheet for a roof.

'What do you want?' asked a woman walking out.

'Has anybody fallen ill here?'

'Ill? You mean of that plague? Bombay Fever?'

'Yes. Anybody with coughs? In this area?'

She looked at him silently.

'I am not a policeman. I am a doctor. I work for the government. Please tell me.'

She told him, after a brief moment of silent appraisal, that nobody in that neighbourhood had fallen ill. Everyone was okay—except for some of the little kids who always had runny noses anyway.

Aayush was taken aback by this. So far, at least going by the reports received at the command centre, the disease seemed to be attacking the city with brutal consistency, sparing no locality.

'Not a single person along this stretch is ill?' he asked again, pointing to the shanty rows on both sides of the road.

'Not that I know of. There is one fellow who lives further down the road . . . hasn't come back from office for two or three days and his wife is very upset. But that beggar is generally drunk. So nobody is surprised by his absence.'

Aayush thanked her and walked towards his bike. As he swung his leg over the seat, he shouted a final question. 'Miss . . . do you know where he went to work . . . the missing drunkard?'

'Let me think . . . Somerset Hotel. He is a cleaner or sweeper or something there.'

Aayush started his bike and drove towards Cusrow Baug. When he hopped off, he walked straight into pandemonium.

The residents of Cusrow Baug were crashing by the minute. The only person still on her feet appeared to be the Patels' neighbour.

'Oh my god! What happened?'

'I have no idea, my son. Everyone seemed to be getting better. Even last night everything was fine . . . but today . . . oh lord . . .' She was trying to help a man doubled over near the stairs, vomiting blood.

'They got better and then they got worse?'

'Yes . . . I think so . . .'

The man struggled for air. Aayush knew what was coming.

'Move him to his apartment. Quickly, quickly . . .'

'But I was trying to . . .'

'Just listen to me, Diane . . .'

Aayush stumbled backwards through a wide open door, the patient slumped in his arms. He placed him on the floor gently and turned to leave with Diane— when the patient called after them.

'Please help me. Please help me. I am dying. Please . . .'

Aayush and Diane paused by the door. Aayush turned to her. 'Look . . . go to your room and wait for me.'

'But what about Mr Zenulbhai . . .'

'GO.'

Diane staggered away. Aayush knelt on the floor next to the dying man and slowly lifted his palm, careful not to touch the bleeding fingernails.

'Can you save me?' he asked

'I will try, sir. But for now, I want you to relax. I am a doctor and medicines are coming. Just relax, sir.'

The man nodded, his head barely moving. 'I did everything they told me. I had my medicines and switched off all the air conditioners. Every single one.'

'Good, sir. Then you will be okay very soon. Don't worry. Just relax.'

'Thank you. I am an old man. I live alone, you see. It is difficult . . .'

The man suddenly arched his back. His eyes bulged. Aayush braced himself for what would follow.

In an instant, Mr Zenulbhai's body disintegrated. Aayush leapt backwards, avoiding the stream of blood.

Minutes later, he walked to the kitchen. He took a bar of soap and washed his hands and his face. Then, he vomited into the sink.

He wept.

In a bit, Aayush left Mr Zenulbhai's house and closed the door behind him. He pulled his phone out of his pocket and called the NCDC office. The line was busy. He tried again. Then again. No luck.

This was because calls were pouring into the command centre. For some reason, all over Mumbai, hundreds of patients who looked like they were recovering had suddenly begun to crash.

## 45

**Justice Kashyap Commission of Inquiry**

*Reference: PS 4/PI 17/Maha/Session 4*
*File type: Raw transcript of interview, audio recording*
*Location: Provisional Lok Sabha Complex, Port Blair*
*Security clearance level: 2*
*Note: This recording features two voices*

JK: Mr Vajpeyi, what was your initial reaction to these rumours about the air conditioners?

AV: I thought it was bullshit.

JK: Why so? Please elaborate but without resorting to profanities, please.

AV: Sorry. I thought that it was typical—ill-informed pubic response to a piece of news. Surely you have seen this for yourself?

JK: Of course. To this day, I get messages from family members suggesting that Bombay Fever was a secret government experiment that turned south. There are many such rumours.

AV: Yes, I have seen them.

JK: So, you did not think the 'magic cure' was worthy

of a response? Did nobody think it made sense to put out a press release or a clarification?

AV: Not to my knowledge. I don't think most of those who were a part of the medical response teams had the time to check their WhatsApp messages or figure out the relevance of air conditioning.

JK: Why did you ignore these things?

AV: We didn't pay attention because we had other things to worry about. Consider the situation we were in. On the one hand, fatality rates had stabilised but were still very high. People were dying every few minutes in Mumbai and we had no idea how to help them.

*The recording has registered silence for twenty seconds.*

JK: Mr Vajpeyi, are you okay?

AV: Sorry. Yes, I am fine.

JK: Do you want to take a break?

AV: No. Thank you, sir. As I was saying . . . on the one hand, we had no idea how to help people. On the other, we had a vague sense of what the bacterium was . . . but nothing more. We had no clue what medication to prescribe. Instead we were carrying out epidemiological and biological studies at the same time.

JK: Could you explain that please? Those two types of studies . . .

AV: So, two things were happening. Epidemiologists were trying to track the disease, build models and estimate the pattern of propagation and expected future patterns of disease outbreak.

JK: So, in a sense, they were not finding a cure but trying to map out the spread of the bacteria?

AV: Exactly. Another team was looking at samples and trying to identify the bug itself. And figure out how to stop its onslaught. All this requires time, manpower and tremendous effort. There was simply no time to waste on stupid rumours circulating on social media and messaging applications.

JK: But . . .

AV: Also, at the time, it just seemed to be hearsay. You want to switch off a room cooler? Go ahead. There was nothing in our database to suggest that this would make things better or worse. Yes, there is a connection between Legionella and air conditioning systems. But switching them off would have done nothing to help patients who were already infected. As far as we were concerned, switching ACs off at the time made as much sense as throwing away knives to help a stab victim.

JK: And yet if you could turn back time . . .

AV: If I could turn back time, I would have reacted differently. I would have done something . . . anything to counter that rumour. I would have also tried to stall the press conference by the then chief minister. It should have never happened. That was a big mistake. We did not know it at the time.

JK: Do you think the politicians responded badly? Do you think we needed better leadership?

AV: You are asking me if the CM could have saved lives had she reacted differently?

JK: Could she have?

AV: Sir . . . the CM had to release some sort of information. She had no idea . . . none of us did . . . that this is how the public would react.

JK: So you are blaming the public for what happened?

AV: No, sir. We can't blame people for panicking.

JK: Hm. What do you think of the prime minister's leadership during that period?

AV: I have no views regarding this, sir.

JK: You don't think he placed his safety first before that of other citizens?

AV: Yes, I do. But I don't see how his continued presence in Mumbai could have saved lives.

JK: Okay. So now—to Dr Anil Bansal.

AV: Yes. If there is a hero in this story . . . Dr Bansal is the man.

JK: Of course. He is a national hero. An international hero.

AV: He saved many lives. So, yes.

JK: Why was he the first to connect the dots?

AV: Partly it was luck. And partly it was his intelligence. He was lucky because his nurse made a patient list with contact details. He was intelligent because, unlike the rest of us, he didn't panic. He looked for patterns and he found them. The experts from NCDC would have eventually seen those patterns, too. But Bansal saw them first.

JK: Tell me about these patterns. What exactly did Dr Bansal see that everyone else with equipment worth millions didn't?

# 46

## Outbreak + 8

'So, who sits here?' asked Rachel as she stood in the Lok Sabha hall, before coughing into her handkerchief. Rachel drew the piece of cloth away from her mouth and slid it into a pocket in her suit jacket. She didn't notice tiny flecks of blood on the fabric.

'Let me see,' said a Secretariat TV employee flipping through a clipboard. 'Arvind Kejriwal.'

'I read he's important . . .'

The young man chuckled. 'If you want good television, he is the guy . . .'

'So, one camera to focus on this area?' she asked, waving her hand in the general direction of Kejriwal's seat.

'100 per cent.'

'Kamal, you do realise that we are trying to do serious journalism here?' Rachel said, smiling. She then walked over to a small bottle of water on the table and drank from it. Rachel was trying not to worry about her health. But she was definitely under the weather. Her cough was back and so was her fever. Her back ached.

And there was the heat. The air conditioning in her hotel room had been switched off the previous night. Rachel had tried throwing open the windows. But the hot, dusty air just made things worse. Eventually, she demanded a pedestal fan from the housekeeping manager.

The Lok Sabha hall was only marginally better. There was some kind of central air conditioning, but it barely kept the room cool enough to be comfortable. Rachel Soanes was getting by thanks to several cups of coffee and a dose of painkillers—but, all told, she was miserable.

'Okay, so that means we have a location for all six cameras. What next, Rachel ma'am?'

'I was wondering,' Rachel said, 'if we could have some graphics on the screen. You know, so when an MP is talking about . . . I don't know . . . the economy . . . we could have a little box on the screen with data and graphs . . .'

'I don't quite see what you mean . . .'

'Okay, give me a sheet of paper and a pencil.' Rachel sketched a TV screen, complete with a stick man in front of a microphone and a little box with a pie chart and some dollar symbols.

'Ah, I see. Great idea. I think we can do that, Rachel ma'am. Especially if we know what they are going to talk about in advance.'

'Do we know the agenda?'

'The original agenda was the new dual-citizenship proposal. But I think they are going to talk about the epidemic in Mumbai.'

Rachel instantly felt like coughing again. She pulled out her handkerchief. This time she saw the blood spots. She coughed twice and put the fabric away again.

'Okay, let's break for lunch, Kamal. We can spend the post-lunch session discussing some ideas I have for integrating social media reactions into our coverage.'

'No problem. We can take as much time as we want. Ranveer sir has got us access till 8 pm.'

They went to the canteen for a quick meal. Afterwards, Rachel and Kamal asked an officer to show them around the parliament building. There was some hesitation—especially given that Rachel was a foreigner—but a few phone calls to Ranveer Singhvi's office sorted things out.

It was 4 pm by the time Rachel and Kamal made their way back to the empty Lok Sabha hall.

'I think we should have a special feature on this building itself. Did you know any of that stuff we just saw?'

Kamal shrugged.

'Did you know there was a museum inside the parliament building?'

'Ma'am, everything we saw was new to me. I think your idea is very good.'

Rachel nodded. Her knees hurt and she felt a strange tingling towards the tips of her fingers. She tried to shake it off a few times. And then, she decided to focus on her work.

'Okay, so tell me what we do on social media right now.'

Kamal was enthusiastic. But at around 6 pm, Rachel realised that his eagerness was beginning to ebb.

*That is another thing I can help them with. These kids need to realise that broadcasting is a twenty-four-hour job.*

'Okay, Kamal,' Rachel said, 'we can do the rest tomorrow. 9 am sharp.'

Kamal beamed.

'Shall we leave together? You look very tired— also, you have a very bad cough. Is it Bombay Fever?' Kamal asked, chuckling at his macabre joke.

Rachel felt the hair stand on the back of her neck. 'No, you go ahead,' she muttered. 'I am going to spend a little more time getting a sense of this space.'

Kamal vanished in moments.

Rachel sat down in one of the clerk's chairs in the centre of the room. She had never felt this tired in her life.

'Come on, Rachel. Get up. Get up,' she told herself, popping a couple of painkillers. She picked up her notebook and began to walk all over the hall, visualising a raucous session of parliament.

A little after 7 pm, one of the housekeepers popped into the room. 'Madam, you are still here?'

'I will be out by 8 pm.'

'No problem. We are shutting down the central air conditioning. Just wanted to inform you.'

*Oh, for fuck's sake,* thought Rachel.

'No problem, thank you very much,' she screamed across the empty hall.

The housekeeper left and then came back sharp at 8 pm to switch off the lights. He looked around and was somewhat surprised to find the space empty, except for Rachel's mobile phone on one of the clerk's tables. Perhaps, she had forgotten it while leaving, he thought. He picked it up, locked up the hall and then deposited the phone with the security officer in the lobby.

## Outbreak + 9

On the ninth day of the outbreak, another housekeeper from the morning shift opened doors to the Lok Sabha hall and switched on some of the lights.

Kamal arrived at 9 am, as he had promised Rachel, deposited his bags on the clerk's desk and waited for her. Twenty minutes later, he gave her a call and was surprised to find himself speaking to one of the parliament security officers.

Where in the world was Rachel Soanes?

At 10 am, Kamal decided to start work anyway.

He wanted to double-check his camera placements. Rachel had insisted on making sure that none of the cameras fell into each other's fields of vision.

Kamal walked up to the last row of seats towards the left. The stench hit him instantly, almost knocking him out. He looked around. Within moments, he found Rachel on the floor, wedged between a seat and a table. It was the most horrible thing he had ever seen.

Rachel Soanes' body had disintegrated.

It took Kamal a few moments to realise what had happened. He picked up his bags and ran out, screaming for help.

Security guards reacted instantly. Kamal was placed in a quarantine room in the Lok Sabha complex, and then moved to AIIMS. Biochemical specialists in hazmat suits entered the hall and gently transferred what was left of Rachel Soanes into a body bag. This bag was then rushed to the NCDC.

Specialists debated whether to decontaminate the area immediately. But then, following advice from NCDC officials in Mumbai and Delhi, they decided to seal off the hall and close down the parliamentary building.

By the evening, a vast medical team had descended upon the Lok Sabha complex. They took samples of virtually everything they could—the air, blood and fluid, and even Rachel's mobile phone. They tested

dozens of employees for symptoms and several were
sent into quarantine.

It would take days to arrive at meaningful results.

But one thing became clear immediately. Nobody
was going to use India's parliament hall for a long
time.

## 47

**Outbreak + 8**

Anil Bansal couldn't believe what was happening. Within less than an hour of being transferred to his consultation room, the eleven-year-old boy was beginning to get better. While the boy was still coughing very badly, his writhing had stopped and his fever had dropped. He was also recovering lucidity.

All Anil had done was fall to his knees and weep in frustration.

What was happening? It just didn't make any sense.

Anil asked the boy to keep lying down; he opened the door. The boy's parents were waiting outside, eyes red and voices hoarse.

They were drenched in sweat.

Dr Anil Bansal froze mid-stride. Wait. What if?

He ran to the waiting area. Just as he had expected. Several other patients were now beginning to show elevated symptoms of Bombay Fever. A couple begged him to do something.

Anil Bansal walked to the reception desk, pulled open a drawer, and reached inside. He switched on the air conditioner and chose the coldest possible setting.

'Doctor but . . .'

'Shut up!'

The air conditioner roared to life like an engine but all Anil Bansal could hear was the blood pumping into his ears.

'Quiet!' he told another man who had started protesting.

While he waited to see if his hunch was correct, Anil Bansal went back to Jacintha's notes. He scanned through the sheet. It seemed like a crazy idea—but he had to know for sure if there was a pattern here that was linked to the air conditioning.

'Sir, my wife is better!' somebody said within an hour-and-a-half.

A murmur of approval went through the room.

Anil Bansal smiled. So, there it was—turning on the air conditioning, and the rapidly dropping temperature, helped make these patients feel better.

It was still a puzzle though—why did this help? Did it have to do with body temperature? Air content? Dust?

Dr Bansal went back to his notes and Jacintha's list. There had to be a clue there . . .

What did all these people do for a living? The dead boy in his brother's room had been a waiter at a five-star hotel. What about the others who had come in that morning? He read Jacintha's tight but legible handwriting: accountant, banker, clerk, HR assistant, store manager, salesgirl . . .

'Do you have an AC in your house?' he suddenly asked the parents of the eleven-year-old boy.

'No, doctor,' the mother said.

*Yes!*

'Does your son go to an air conditioned school?'

'No, doctor.'

*Fuck.*

'Is his school bus air conditioned?'

'Sir, we are poor people. Where would we have ACs?'

*Fuck. Fuck.*

'What happened, doctor?'

'Nothing. I was wondering if your son had spent any time in the last few days in an air conditioned environment . . .'

'Well, sir, actually yes,' the father said.

'What?'

'Yes. The day before we brought him here he had gone on a school trip to the museum.'

'How much time did he spend there?'

'The whole day. He went in the morning and came back at 5 or 6 pm. He fell ill the next day.'

'Did any of his other schoolmates fall ill?'

'Yes. Several of them,' the mother said.

Anil Bansal told himself to be calm. He went from

patient to patient in the waiting area, asking them the same questions.

Did they have an AC at home?

Had they been anywhere near an air conditioner shortly before they fell ill?

Did they feel better when he made the room cooler?

An hour later, Anil Bansal had formulated an unlikely theory to explain the outbreak. He still couldn't make complete sense of it. But he felt he'd worked out a pattern of propagation.

Anil walked up to the TV and waited for the NCDC command centre telephone number to flash again. He punched it into his mobile phone. The line was busy.

He tried over and over again for the next hour. Nothing was working. He dialled every phone number he could think of: the NCDC head office in Delhi, the state health department, even the local police station. The networks were swamped.

While Anil Bansal may have figured out a crucial piece of the jigsaw puzzle to help fight the outbreak, he now had no way of getting this information out to the people that mattered.

He picked up his mobile phone again and, for the umpteenth time, dialled the NCDC helpline. This time he didn't get a busy tone. In fact, there was no tone at all. His phone line was dead.

And so were phone lines over all of Mumbai.

Anil Bansal told his patients to stay inside, and crawled out through the semi-open shutter. He then jumped into his vandalised car.

Dr Anil Bansal bounced past the footpath and exploded down the road. His destination was the Durbar Hall at the Haffkine Institute.

# 48

**Outbreak + 8**

The early hours of the eighth day of the outbreak were the worst. Everywhere there were scenes of unrelenting human suffering. The NCDC command centre was inundated with so many phone calls that all communication systems broke down.

Eventually, many months later, experts would calculate that the fatality rate of Bombay Fever went from 37 per cent—on the day of Nishtha Sharma's press conference—to 58 per cent soon after. As hospitals, nursing homes and offices began switching off the air conditioning, Bombay Fever went out of control. Hundreds of lives were lost.

These numbers were never made public.

By noon, on the eighth day, hospitals began to run out of space in their mortuaries. Bodies, sometimes of entire families, were stacked over blocks of ice. Death was everywhere.

As pictures of these scenes began to find their way to the internet, Nishtha Sharma reacted immediately. First, she ordered an internet 'brownout' all over the state of Maharashtra. This slowed down the internet to make it almost useless. The Maharashtra government later vehemently denied that it had done any such thing. It blamed excessive internet usage and panic for the drop in bandwidth.

Then, when the BBC broadcast a telephone interview with a dying patient at a hospital, Nishtha Sharma asked for a telephone blackout. This was the same blackout that had forced Anil Bansal to take off in his car. As with the internet, the collapse of phone lines, too, was attributed to some kind of infrastructure breakdown and not government orders.

As the death toll rose, Nishtha Sharma made numerous appearances on television. She assured the public—with remarkable sincerity—that everything was being done to bring Bombay Fever under control.

More than what she communicated, however, it was where and how she spoke that would always be remembered afterwards. Nishtha held press conferences outdoors, away from the safety of her office. In addition to making appearances at the Haffkine Institute, she visited several hospitals and, on more than one occasion, was spotted speaking to patients fighting an advanced stage of the disease. She did this without wearing as much as a face mask.

Much later, many would allege that this was blatant political opportunism. Nishtha Sharma, they said, was trying to upstage an absentee prime minister.

Nothing, in fact, could be farther from the truth.

Her very public role during the Bombay Fever crisis was one she discussed frequently with Nitin Phadnavis. She was frightened each time she visited a hospital and thoroughly disinfected every inch of her body afterwards. A personal physician constantly kept an eye on her. If she persisted with her work outdoors, it was because Phadnavis had asked her to become the face of the fight against Bombay Fever. The city needed a leader, the prime minister told her, and at that moment, she was the only option.

If Bombay Fever was finally contained it was thanks to two factors.

The first was the nature of Bombay Fever itself. A good contagion must infect slowly and kill with patience. In other words, it must linger within the host—give him or her enough time to go to work or school for several days, and spread microbes during every trip. If it kills too soon—if the bug doesn't get enough time to infect several new hosts before the existing one is destroyed—an outbreak runs out of steam. Thanks, in part, to the air conditioning rumour, the Bombay Fever bacteria killed with ferocious speed. Even as researchers from the NCDC and the Center for Disease Control figured out how to slow down the bacterium's onslaught and isolate patients, Bombay Fever began to run out of hosts. The killing stopped.

The second more immediate factor was Dr Anil Bansal.

## 49

**Outbreak + 8**

Dr Anil Bansal drove his car faster than ever before. The wind, blowing in through the broken windshield, whipped the insides of the vehicle. Anil's eyes watered. As he approached the main gate of the Haffkine Institute, he noticed a security cordon around the building. He parked nearby and ran up to a policeman.

'I need to speak to someone from the NCDC right now. I am a doctor and I may have something that can help them.'

'Oh? What?'

'The air conditioning . . .'

The policeman did not let him finish.

'Sir, please go. We are aware of the AC rumour. Those inside also know. Please don't create trouble.'

'No, please. They should switch on the ACs. Not switch them off.'

'What? Please leave. We're fed up of this AC business. You people are mad. The officers have other things to do inside.'

Anil was exasperated. He persisted anyway,

attempting to reach out to several policemen. Nothing worked.

That is when he spotted two people driving towards the Haffkine Institute on a motorcycle. He recognised the man in the front.

'Aayush?'

Aayush Vajpeyi and Sati Rout turned to him. Anil ran towards them.

'Anil Bansal?' Aayush recognised him immediately. Aayush has visited his clinic once during his SMO rounds. He was well aware of the clinic's illegal status. 'This is not a good time to talk about your . . .'

'Fuck that. I think I can help you with this madness.'

'How?'

Anil explained his theory and then pulled out Jacintha's list from his pocket. Sati and Aayush listened intently but both seemed sceptical.

When Anil finished he begged them to let him speak to one of the NCDC personnel.

Moments later, Aayush and Sati barged into the anteroom that had the MultiSampler and shoved their way towards a desk. Anil Bansal found himself speaking to a woman in a faded pink sari who looked utterly exhausted.

'Selvi ma'am, this is Dr Anil Bansal. We think you should listen to him.'

Selvi looked at him warily. 'What is it? Please don't waste my time.'

'No, ma'am. Give me five minutes.'

Anil Bansal then spoke slowly but firmly for exactly four-and-a-half minutes.

'What if,' he asked, 'Legionella has mutated and assumed a deadlier form? So, it kills like nothing else, but it still grows and propagates a little bit like Legionella.

'Now we all know that the Legionella bacterium tends to grow in very specific conditions. Cooling towers and all that. We are aware. But what if this mutant variant is much more sensitive to temperature ranges than most Legionella,' Anil continued as more and more heads began to turn toward him.

'What if this bacteria loves cool weather? It grows but remains dormant while the conditions are mild. As soon as the temperature begins to rise, however, it begins to react in some way.'

'In what way?' someone asked.

'I am not sure. Perhaps it gets more aggressive, maybe it disintegrates into something else, maybe it unleashes some sort of destructive DNA. I don't know. I don't have the equipment to figure that out. But maybe the reason why mortality rates have gone up is because people are turning off their air conditioning—because a higher body temperature activates the bacterium.'

'I still don't completely get it,' said Selvi, 'but tell us how you worked this out.'

'Look at this list,' said Anil, placing the crumpled sheets on the table. 'Here is a catalogue of my first forty or fifty patients. I've marked out the ones with early symptoms of this . . . Bombay Fever.'

Several heads craned to look at the sheet.

'Do you see? They all work or have spent long periods in air conditioned offices. This is when they may have inhaled the bacterium somehow.' Heads nodded.

'Now look at where they live.'

The addresses all belonged to downmarket neighbourhoods—to shanties located near Tripoli Hospital.

'None of them had air conditioning at home,' Aayush commented. 'Temperatures rose as soon as they left office.'

'Precisely! And that is when the bacterium began to . . .' Anil Bansal shrugged his shoulders.

Selvi stood up and looked around. She took a deep breath. 'Okay, I want you to come with me. We need to speak to my team in Delhi . . .'

'Ma'am,' Sati interrupted. 'I have another idea.'

She outlined her plan. It was taken to Nishtha Sharma who approved without even waiting to run it by the prime minister or the minister for civil aviation.

Within hours, army trucks, BEST buses and all available vehicles were being used to evacuate patients to the airport complex. A call from the chief minister of Maharashtra—followed by one from the prime minister—ensured that the air conditioning in the airport was set at its lowest possible temperature. All over the vast airport building blowers roared to life.

## Outbreak + 12

On board an unmarked submarine somewhere off India's coast, Nitin Phadnavis recorded a video message for the nation. In it, he expressed his deepest condolences for the tragedy that had unfolded in Mumbai. It was a week, he said, in which the city had been stretched to breaking point. At least 40,000 citizens had been infected—of which at least 6,000 had died. It was the worst such epidemic, he said, in the history of Independent India. The good news was that the NCDC in Delhi was coming ever closer to finding a cure. Meanwhile, infection levels in Mumbai were well under control and fatality rates were plummeting.

'While the Maharashtra government has shown exemplary courage in responding to the crisis, my job now is to make sure that this never happens again. I have already spoken to the United States government and the World Health Organization, who will send expert teams to India. The international community has been generous in its offer of help, and we accept it gratefully. We will seek whatever assistance we can get to ensure that nothing like this repeats itself.'

This part of the speech had been the hardest for Nitin Phadnavis to write. Less than two weeks after telling the whole world that India no longer needed aid, here he was once again asking for help from the Americans and the United Nations. That combined with the allegation that he had been the first to flee Mumbai meant that his political future was no longer gilt-edged. Nitin Phadnavis was no more the first of a new generation of politicians. He would now become merely a footnote in history.

'You realise that Beta Protocol is something of a poisoned chalice?' Nitin told Prakash Rao sometime later.

'Sir?'

'I mean, you may have saved my life and safeguarded the present government. But you also made me look like a coward.'

'I am sorry, sir.'

'Oh, please don't be,' said Nitin Phadnavis, smiling. 'At least I got to travel in a submarine for a while. When do I get to go back home?'

'A helicopter will come to pick you up in two hours. You will go to Delhi first. And then you will be transferred to a provisional Lok Sabha Centre in Port Blair.'

'Do you know how long it will take to decontaminate parliament?'

'I am not sure, sir. But we have been told to assume

that the government will function out of a secure location in Port Blair for at least three months.'

'Very good. Thank you, Prakash Rao. You may have ruined my career, but you did it for the nation.'

'Sir, there is one more thing you have to do.'

'Oh yes. I remember. It will be done.'

After Prakash left the cabin, Nitin walked over to the small Formica desk and drew out a chair. There was a neatly typed sheet of paper on the table and a fine fountain pen.

Nitin Phadnavis took the pen, paused for a moment, and then signed at the bottom of the sheet just above his name.

The typewritten letter started with the words:

*Dear Prime Minister,*

*If you are reading this letter, it unfortunately means that Beta Protocol has been activated. This implies that the nation, including the government and you, are facing imminent danger . . .*

# 50

**Justice Kashyap Commission of Inquiry**

*Reference: PS 4/PI 17/Maha/Session 4*
*File type: Raw transcript of interview, audio recording*
*Location: Provisional Lok Sabha Complex, Port Blair*
*Security clearance level: 2*
*Note: This recording features two voices*

JK: Mr Vajpeyi, what exactly do we know about this Bombay Fever so far?

AV: In the sense?

JK: What is it? What does it do to us? How does it do it?

AV: Sir, some of the details are quite technical . . .

JK: Either skip those parts or explain it in common English. You are a civil servant, Mr Vajpeyi. Surely you have been trained to communicate complex ideas simply?

AV: I will try, sir.

JK: Good. I know this has been exhausting. But we are almost done.

AV: Yes, sir.

JK: So . . .

AV: Bombay Fever, we now know, is caused by a mutation of the bacterium that causes Legionnaire's disease.

JK: What caused this mutation?

AV: It is difficult to say. A lot of research is still being done to make sense of the nature of the bacterium. I think we will have a lot of new information in a few months.

JK: Do you still keep track of the research?

AV: Of course. That bacterium will never leave me.

JK: Anyway, you were saying . . .

AV: Yes. So we are not sure how this mutation, or these mutations, took place. Or even how many have occurred. But we do know that around three months before the outbreak, Hormazd Patel brought the bacterium to India . . .

JK: From Switzerland?

AV: Yes. Geneva.

JK: What happened in Geneva? Where did he get it from?

AV: We believe he may have caught the bacterium from a Sri Lankan. Recently, the NCDC tracked down some of the people who were with him in Switzerland when the Sri Lankan fell ill. Hormazd had tried to help her. But she died. He came to India the next day.

JK: But you are saying all this happened three months before the outbreak?

AV: More or less.

JK: Why did it take so long? The outbreak should have happened immediately . . .

AV: Maybe. Maybe not. We are not sure. In fact, an outbreak need not have happened at all. We were just very, very unlucky . . .

JK: Explain yourself.

AV: Sir, this is all speculation right now. We believe Hormazd did fall ill, but then he self-medicated. He took strong antibiotics.

JK: How do we . . .

AV: We found several bottles of strong drugs in his house. No prescriptions. We then checked with neighbourhood pharmacies. We collected enough evidence to suggest that the entire family regularly self-medicated.

JK: Okay . . . go on . . .

AV: These drugs almost definitely healed Hormazd's illness temporarily. But they also left behind a variant of the bacterium that was drug-resistant.

JK: So you are saying that he brought a dangerous bacterium from Switzerland and then made it even worse by self-medicating?

AV: Absolutely. That was the moment when this disease turned into a disaster. Hormazd had been infected with a slow-acting, if devastating, bug. His medication amped it up. If . . . if he had seen a doctor instead of drugging himself . . .

JK: All this could have been avoided?

AV: Sir, like I said before, we can only speculate . . .

JK: Please speculate . . .

AV: If Hormazd had seen a good doctor, perhaps things would have turned out differently. Perhaps we could have stopped this from becoming Bombay Fever. But you need luck, sir. And we didn't have any. And then, there is the weather factor.

JK: The heat in Bombay?

AV: Yes. The unique thing about this bacterium is its relationship with weather and temperature. I don't think we've ever seen a disease that is so tightly dependent on ambient temperature. It doesn't help that the bacterium seems to propagate through the air. If someone with Bombay Fever coughs in your face, you are going to fucking get it.

JK: Excuse me?

AV: Sorry, sir. But here's what we believe—if the temperature rises over 25 degrees, the bacterium seems to immediately disintegrate in some way. We are not sure how.

JK: So, switching air conditioners off should have prevented the disease from spreading . . .

AV: Yes. In fact, it probably did. But . . .

JK: I was waiting for that *but* . . .

AV: But switching off air conditioning was terrible for patients already infected. We now believe that once a patient is infected, it is vital for him or her to inhabit a space that is as cool as possible. The moment the patient's temperature rises, he or she starts to transition into meltdown.

JK: Do we understand why this happens?

AV: Not completely. But the guys at the NCDC think this has something to do with the bacterium disintegrating inside the body. At higher temperatures the bacterium appears to fall apart, and releases a stream of toxins and cell fragments into the body. What researchers are now trying to figure out is how these remnants affect one so badly . . .

JK: So, let me try to summarise this. You are telling me that Bombay Fever spreads from person to person only at low temperatures, but starts killing at high temperatures?

AV: Exactly. We don't know why it does that . . . but that is what it does.

JK: And you have been able to identify this pattern in the patients?

AV: Eventually, we were able to. But Dr Bansal saw it first. Take the case of Rahul Bhandari.

JK: One second . . . this is the man who crashed the jeep at the airport?

AV: Yes. We now believe that he caught the bacterium from one of the patients in the airport. He showed some mild symptoms but they went away when he was administered drugs.

JK: However, then he drove one of those patrol jeeps . . .

AV: And the transformation was . . . horrible. On the video, you can see him crashing as soon as the temperature inside the jeep starts to rise . . .

JK: The jeep is not air conditioned?

AV: No. It is an open jeep, so security personnel can quickly jump out in case of an emergency . . .

JK: So, Rahul crashed . . .

AV: Remarkably quickly. The average crash time seems to be around two hours. In his case, it was . . . quite bad . . . forty minutes or so. And you could see that in the surveillance video procured afterwards. You could see Rahul getting disoriented, bleeding, and then dropping off, unconscious . . .

JK: Unbelievable. So, essentially, this is a disease that targets people who alternate between hot and cold environments?

AV: Yes. Which is why, in Mumbai especially, it particularly targeted low-level office employees who worked in air conditioned offices but went back to poorly ventilated homes. People like them suffered disproportionately. Terribly.

JK: Hotel employees, airport employees . . .

AV: Yes. Waiters. Cleaners. Nurses.

JK: Do you think people will learn any lessons from this outbreak?

AV: What lessons?

JK: Self-medication, panic, crisis management?

AV: I hope so. I hope people realise that they have a part to play. But, sir, that is the thing with outbreaks. Each one is different. The next time something like this happens . . . who knows what we'll have to deal with.

## 51

## Sri Lanka

Shortly after the civil war in Sri Lanka ended, the Sri Lankan government signed a trade deal with the Chinese government. Besides a cricket stadium, several ports, and hundreds of kilometres of roads, the deal also included a new fertiliser factory on the outskirts of Jaffna.

It was a symbolic moment for the Sri Lankan government. The fertiliser factory would create hundreds of jobs for local Tamil youth and help rejuvenate a local economy that had been devastated by years of war.

Construction started in early 2016 and proceeded with great speed. Residents were initially sceptical about the whole project. But soon, as the factory started hiring and training locals, enthusiasm picked up. The factory also drastically changed what had been a drab, war-scarred terrain. In a moment of extreme cultural sensitivity, the Chinese also painted the two huge cooling towers with a variety of shapes, designs and letters that were significant to the indigenous population. People were thrilled. Employment numbers jumped.

In a house less than 400 metres away from the factory, an old Tamil couple proudly pointed out the towers to their visiting granddaughter. It belched great white clouds of water vapour all day, all night. The girl was suitably impressed. *Why don't you stay with us*, the couple asked. *You could easily find a job in the factory with your talent.*

The granddaughter thought about it a lot. But then, decided against it.

Before flying back to Geneva, she bought her grandparents two large air conditioners for their three-room house. It did little to assuage their sorrow at her departure. But they were grateful for the gesture and used the ACs as often as they could.

Slowly, the old man and woman began to notice something. If they switched off the air conditioner for a bit, they began to get bad coughs and mild fever. It was a strange situation, they thought. But life could be a lot worse.

So, they used the air conditioner all the time. Sometimes they felt cold. But, at least, they didn't cough or get a fever.

# Epilogue

Faced with relentless criticism, domestically and internationally, for his cowardly, inadequate leadership during the Bombay Fever crisis, Nitin Phadnavis was forced to step down from office shortly after the outbreak was brought under control. Phadnavis, who also resigned from his seat in Indian parliament, continues to maintain that his actions were entirely in line with established security protocols. The government has been unwilling to reveal what these protocols are.

Nishtha Sharma succeeded Phadnavis as prime minister. Her brave leadership during the outbreak makes her arguably India's most popular politician today.

BuzzWire journalist Annalisa Salmone was released from police custody after a brief period of detention. Her work visa was cancelled and she was deported to the United States. She is now collaborating with Janani Ganesh on a book about the outbreak. Ganesh continues to work for *The Indian Opinion*.

Dr Anil Bansal's Tripoli Hospital was sealed by

local authorities and eventually shut down after a brief investigation found several licensing violations. After fighting depression for months—depression fuelled by his brother's demise—Dr Bansal joined the Srivatsa programme as a consultant. He continues to work closely with the researchers investigating the bacterium.

Sati Rout was recently appointed national director of the Srivatsa programme. Like Dr Bansal, she collaborates with the NCDC and the National Institute of Virology on Bombay Fever and other research projects.

While Aayush Vajpeyi now works as an attaché at the Indian high commission in New Zealand, in charge of science, technology and medicine, recent rumours suggest that he will soon be transferred back to New Delhi where he will join Nishtha Sharma's PMO. It is not clear at this moment what his responsibilities will be.

# Acknowledgements

First of all, I would like to thank Dharini Bhaskar, Sayantan Ghosh and the entire team at Simon and Schuster. You guys have been patient and accommodating and meticulous. Now market the ass off this book!

I am grateful to the Gladstone Library in Hawarden and The Buttery Hotel in Oxford for providing much needed isolation and hospitality.

I would like to thank everybody at *Mint* for their endless patience as I shamelessly missed deadlines and filed reprehensible copy. I am particularly grateful to R. Sukumar for my continued employment. I am most of all thankful to Arun Janardhan and Pranav Srivilasan for running *Mint on Sunday* in the face of my endless slacking.

I must acknowledge the British Library, the London Library, and the library at Birkbeck College for helping me with all the research that may or may not be apparent in this book. Libraries are wonderful!

I would like to thank all my teachers and mentors at the Department of History, Classics and Archaeology at Birkbeck College, especially Carmen Mangion, Chandak Sengoopta and Rebecca Darley, for helping me think of history and many other things with new eyes and from fresh perspectives.

I am eternally grateful to the Lok Sabha elections of 2014 for ruining Twitter so that I no longer spend as much time on it as I used to, and worked on this book instead.

I am endlessly thankful to the Kapoors and Vadukuts for always, always believing in me.

But most of all, I must thank Ruchika Kapoor, my wife, and Saira Vadukut, my daughter. The authorly pursuit is particularly hard on your loved ones. My debt is infinite and eternal.

Finally, as always, I am grateful to everyone on the internet who has been reading my work since I first started blogging in the summer of 2004. I will never forget. Group hug.

# Exclusive Simon & Schuster Q&A with the author, Sidin Vadukut

Q: **First things first, after three humour novels and a book on Indian history, you've now written a medical thriller set in Mumbai . . . why? Authors don't usually shift so much from genre to genre.**

A: This is true. First of all, I must be frank. I shift genres because I can. I've had just about enough success in the past to convince publishers to work with me. But I've not been *so successful* that I am stuck with one major genre. This gives me the freedom to dabble a bit. And I enjoy it. I have a 'you have one life, make the most of it' approach to what I do. Be it books, studies or jobs . . . of course, I am grateful that publishers indulge me.

Q: **So did you always know that your next book was going to be something like *Bombay Fever*?**

A: Not at all. In fact, this book is the coming together of three different projects that I was very keen on—a history of Mumbai, a crime novel, and a story with an element of modern Indian history in it. Between 2012 and 2015, after I had wrapped up *The Sceptical Patriot*, I worked on all these ideas intermittently.

I would outline the history of public transport in Mumbai for a few months. And stop. Then outline a crime novel. And stop. Then outline some kind of historical manuscript. Stop. Then, I'd go back to the Mumbai book . . . over and over again.

I think I was well aware throughout this period that I might end up writing something entirely different. But that is how I like approaching books. My computers are full of first chapters. Most of them are just horrible, horrible stuff. But I love the process.

Books are such wonderful things when you set out to write them. The possibilities are limitless. You can create people, places, things . . . I still have an utterly childish enthusiasm for this.

**Q: When did you hit upon the idea for this particular book?**

A: You know what? I can't pick a decisive hour. But the closest I came to a 'moment of epiphany', I think, was when I wrote a column on the Spanish Flu for *Mint*. Almost nobody in India remembers this any more. It is subsumed by other history from this period. But during the global Spanish Flu outbreak in 1918, millions upon millions of people in India died. Experts still don't agree on the numbers.

I usually end up accumulating far more research for my columns than I end up using. And one of my sources was a report on life in Mumbai as the flu reached the city and began to wreak havoc. This is a remarkable document by a British administrator. It shows you how cities can be resilient but also lose their minds during an outbreak. I learnt that, when the Spanish Flu broke out in Mumbai, nobody took things seriously until absenteeism exploded in offices.

So, I began to think . . . how would Mumbai react if a new outbreak hit it today? Or in the near future?

**Q: The book has a massive universe populated with people and history. Some of it is made up but a lot of it is real and researched. It must have been very hard work.**

A: Yes and no. Research is one of those things that is physically exhausting but mentally exhilarating. My professors keep telling me that I need to calm down when I work instead of finding every single little thing exciting.

While writing this book, I first spent a few months trying to understand how epidemics work in theory and in real life. Especially when they hit cities. I tried to keep an eye on not just what happened at the cellular level inside the human body, but what happened at the level of individuals and groups.

I looked at the plague outbreak in Surat, cholera epidemics in Italy, the Spanish Flu in India . . .

Once I had a rough idea of the outbreak, I began to create a Mumbai that would fall victim to it. Many questions followed. Where would the disease hit? Who would be the lead characters? Were there good and bad guys? What made them good and bad? How political would the politicians get?

Along the way, I invented Beta Protocol and the MultiSampler. Both do different things to the story.

Q: Such as?

A: What I wanted across the book was plausibility. I wanted readers to think: *This could happen, and it could happen like this.* Beta Protocol—an entirely plausible historical sideshow—is the subplot that knits together some major events. I remember, when we were editing the manuscript, the editor kept asking me: *Is this real? Did this happen?* And I was so happy. Because that is what I want readers to think.

The MultiSampler is also an invention that is slightly plausible—it gives the plot a moment of genuine shock.

I was very clear that for all the research, this was not a textbook on epidemiology. This is supposed to be an action-packed thriller. Fingers crossed.

Q: You set this book in the future. Though you don't say that explicitly . . .

A: Yes. The main reason for this is simple: I can ignore contemporary politics while writing the book. I don't want to give away spoilers, but the central and state governments form a major part of the narrative. Setting the book slightly in the future helps me invent an entirely fictional government machinery populated by make-believe characters. In a book like this, I think it is important that the politics is handled with a little bit of detachment. At no point do you want people thinking: *Is this guy right wing or left wing or chicken wing . . .?*

Q: There are a lot of characters in *Bombay Fever . . .*

A: So many. At one point, I remember sitting down and thinking: *I have to make a choice here. I have to choose between plot progression and character development.* There was no way I could do both without writing a 1,000-page book. And then, I decided the plot was important. Also, because that is how outbreaks work.

When epidemics unleash their fury, there are seldom good or bad guys, and there are at least dozens of heroes. I wanted to give a sense of the unfocused frenzy that accompanies an outbreak.

But it is also a pain in the neck to do this. So far, I have never had to invent more than half a dozen characters for any of my novels. In this there are ... *so many.*

Q: What next? Will there be a sequel? Or several sequels?

A: I want to sleep for a few months. Which I can't do because I have a Master's dissertation due in September. And then a PhD starting in October. But I suspect I will want to take some time off in late October or early November. This has been exhausting. I don't think I have ever spent so much time post-producing a book, so to speak. Edits, fact checks, rewrites. Phew.

Could there be a sequel? I am completely in love with the idea of Beta Protocol. And the world of the Srivatsa programme. I have the faint outlines of a crime novel forming in my head that is set in this universe. And if I do write it, I think it will be the exact opposite of *Bombay Fever*—small in scope, few characters, intensely personal problems, and a Manichaean sense of right and wrong.

Q: *Bombay Fever* could be the first real medical thriller set in India and written for an Indian audience . . .

A: Is it? I am not entirely sure. But I have always felt that India could use many more popular genres of fiction—crime, thriller, police procedurals, science fiction, and so on. And I think readers are more receptive than we think. Before the first *Dork* came out, I remember so many people saying that a comic novel set in a management consulting firm would be very niche—I don't know how many editions *Dork* has gone through now. Seven? Eight? People are cool. They will read stuff.

**Q: Final question. What are you hoping will happen to *Bombay Fever*?**

A: I hope lots and lots of people read it. I hope many of them find it as thrilling as my wife and editor and I have found it. I hope it will transport them to this crazy, complex place full of heroic people and hard choices. I hope they will enjoy the research that has gone into it. I hope somebody will make a Netflix series out of it. I hope the series will have Raveena Tandon in it.